MW01126648

KEY WEST

AND

CUBA

1955

ADVENTURES OF A WOMAN TRAVELING ALONE

PATRICIA JOHNSON

iUniverse®

KEY WEST AND CUBA 1955
ADVENTURES OF A WOMAN TRAVELING ALONE

Certain characters in this work are historical figures, and certain events portrayed did take place. However, this is a work of fiction. All of the other characters, names, and events as well as all places, incidents, organizations, and dialogue in this novel are either the products of the author's imagination or are used fictitiously.

iUniverse books may be ordered through booksellers or by contacting:

iUniverse
1663 Liberty Drive
Bloomington, IN 47403
www.iuniverse.com
844-349-9409

ISBN: 978-1-6632-3064-5 (sc)
ISBN: 978-1-6632-3065-2 (e)

Library of Congress Control Number: 2021921448

Print information available on the last page.

iUniverse rev. date: 10/18/2021

1 PREFACE

Genealogists search old legal records attempting to find information about someone looking as far back as those records were kept, but who knows the personal stories not revealed there? Sometimes we can hear tales never told if we simply talk with the oldest person in the family.

Oral history was the first way of keeping stories remembered. At night in an Indian's teepee it was grandmother who told about when the white man came. Those strange men shot buffaloes not for food or animal skins. They killed multiple buffaloes, as many in one episode as they could, leaving the carcasses, riding away and laughing. Very crazy people.

In an African village one old woman told about the time a man offered the village chief money for a strong young man. At first the chief was offended but every place has one trouble-maker, like Bolu, a constant upsetting influence. The man lured Bolu to his boat with a tale about going to work on a rich man's plantation in America.

Norwegian *bestemor* would tell tales about red-haired Viking men and women who chose to leave the safety of home for the adventure of sailing into the unknown. Chinese *lao lao* knew about when, long ago, young girls suffered having their feet bound so they might be chosen as having the most exquisite tiny feet.

American pioneer women sat at the bedside of their children with stories about their choice of leaving towns on the East coast to brave the trek in a covered wooden wagon toward the unknown West.

This story is told by a woman born almost 100 years ago, about the time when she was a brazen young woman who, back in 1955, had the urge to travel, alone and fearless.

Her first trip was from Newark, New Jersey to San Francisco, California. Next were British Columbia, Canada and New York City. Then, on to Mystic, Connecticut and Key West, Florida, plus the tropical island of Cuba (only 90 miles from Key West).

Grandma told stories about those trips, but that pioneer did not travel in a slow and dusty wagon train. She traveled via airplane and an old DeSoto automobile.

KEY WEST AND CUBA IN 1955

2 "TELL ME A STORY"

Old Lady Steele lived in the second house from the corner on Bunker Street. She was also called Grouchy Old Lady Steele, but she had her reasons. People said she was a witch, a thief and just generally hateful. For one thing, it was her last name. Rumor was she had stolen money but that just shows you how people hear a word and make up a story from that. And it's true, she really did look a lot like the Wicked Witch in the movie *The Wizard of Oz.* Plus the fact she liked to take naps so anyone making noise outside her house would see her appear on her porch, shaking her fist and shouting "Go away!"

The house next door had been a ramshackle mess. The wood had not been painted in any time within memory. Rusted gutters dangled down from the roof, the wind causing them to sway against the side of the house. Some windows had been broken when neighborhood boys threw rocks, trying to rouse up the ghost or hermit who supposedly inhabited the place. The yard was a jumble of weeds. The remnants of a picket fence leaned against overgrown bushes.

Oh, someone lived there, all right. It was Willie Forbes. The house had come down to him through inheritance, him being the last of the original line of a once-upon-a-time wealthy family who had lived in it generations ago. The home had been a showplace, a site of many extravagant parties, with women in pearls and lace ball-gowns, men dressed in formal finery, too.

Willie inhabited the top floor. Years ago he had befriended a simple soul, known as Higgy, and had made an arrangement for Higgy to bring him food each day. Higgy would stop by twice: in the morning he'd bring the local newspaper, a cup of coffee and a grilled cheese sandwich. In the late afternoon Higgy would deliver another cup of coffee, a cheeseburger and a bottle of whiskey.

He would walk up the path of broken bricks up the rotting wooden stairs to the porch, then ring the brass bell that hung outside the front door. Although Higgy's routine was set in the same time daily, it was important to ring the bell because Willie had a shotgun.

Then Higgy would open the door, which was unlocked, and call out, "It's me." Willie would lower a reed basket on a long rope, down the stairwell from the top floor to the foyer. In it were some rumpled dollar bills. Higgy would place the prescribed items in the basket, then turn and leave.

Willie had that gun because several times the local boys would try to sneak into the house, certain that Willie had money stashed throughout the house. They soon learned Willie would use that gun. Those who had been able to view anything on that first floor said it was a mess of old newspapers and empty bottles.

One morning when Higgy called out "It's me" no basket was lowered. Higgy couldn't figure that out, so left the food on the bottom step of the staircase. That afternoon he came again, but when Willie didn't answer he got scared. He went back to the coffee shop and told them about that strange break in the routine. Someone called the police. Sure enough, Willie was dead. Old age, malnutrition and alcohol did him in.

The place was empty a long time. The County wanted that property, but Willie had kept up on that one bill, his real estate taxes. Then some lawyer did a little genealogy search and found a niece. Arrangements were finalized and she moved in with her husband and her 7-year-old daughter, Shirley.

Nellanore Steele was seventy-two years old with a full head of white hair, so lush it looked like a huge cotton-ball as if she might have slipped it over her head like a cap. Like many older persons she didn't sleep much. She woke up early and was out in front of her home, sweeping the sidewalk. Tall and thin, she stood stooped over, leaning against the broom. She stayed up late, reading *Good Housekeeping* or *Saturday Evening Post* or *Collier's Magazine.* Those hours that she did sleep in the nighttime were restless. But she did enjoy her afternoon nap.

It had been difficult when Willie Forbes' old house was being refurbished, what with the workmen sawing wood and hammering away. Thank goodness that was finished and over with. Inheriting that old house had been a gift from God for the young couple, because the company owning the factory where her husband had been working announced they were closing it down entirely. Luckily, he got a job in the local hardware store.

They had torn down the rickety old picket fence, saying there should be no fences between neighbors, but they really hadn't seen much of the old lady next door. When the weather was nice and the windows were open they could hear her sweeping the sidewalk early in the morning. Sometimes in the late afternoons she would be sitting in the rocking chair on her front porch. She never seemed to look over their way.

Seven-year-old little Shirley lived next door. She had big blue eyes and curly brown hair and when she smiled she looked like the movie star Shirley Temple. What this little girl liked to do was roller-skate. There was a new cement driveway adjacent to their house but it had a rough finish that made skating kind of a jiggly affair, and she couldn't slide very far. It was like skating on sandpaper. However, the sidewalk leading up to the porch stairs of Nellanore Steele's house was made of slabs of very smooth slate. Wonderful skating surface.

At first Shirley was afraid to venture there, but it was so tempting. She couldn't imagine how it could hurt anything for her to skate there. She timidly tried it a couple of times when the lady didn't seem to be around and nothing happened, so she would skate from in front of her own house, past the neighbor's house, then all the way to the end of their block. Next she would skate back and sort of reward herself, as a grand finale. She would dart up the slate sidewalk to the neighbor's steps, turn around and skate back to the front sidewalk and home again. It was such great fun. It certainly made Shirley smile.

Until one day, when the old woman slammed open the front screen door, timing it to when she knew Shirley would turn onto the slate. She yelled, "Go away. I'm trying to take a nap!" Then she went right back inside, slamming the door again.

Shirley was so startled! She wondered what she had done that was so bad. No one had ever yelled at her before, because she was one of those quiet children who almost always did what they were told. The most her mother did was raise her eyebrow and point one index finger up, as a warning. That would suffice to make Shirley behave.

The little girl hastily skated home and by the time she got inside to tell her mother, she was crying. Her mother soothed her, and when Shirley calmed down her mother explained, "I just think that lady is lonesome, living all alone." Next, her mother suggested "Let's you and me make some peanut-butter cookies." The part Shirley liked best was pressing a fork in the top of each cookie, one way and then the other making a nice pattern.

When the cookies were cooling Shirley's mother was going to take a plateful of them to her neighbor, but she thought that wouldn't help her daughter learn not to be afraid of the old lady. Believing that everyone is basically good, she felt the lady was not doubt sorry she had been so hard with a child. Shirley's mother gave the little girl the hard chore of taking the plate of cookies next door by herself.

Shirley had her mother's positive outlook. She bravely marched up to the door and knocked. It's true, Nelllanore Steele did feel a bit ashamed. Seeing Shirley at the door she didn't know what to expect. She opened the door and quietly asked, "yes?"

The little girl held out the plate of cookies. "My mother sent these to you."

In response the woman asked Shirley if she would like to come inside and share the cookies, but the little girl told her "No, thank you, I'm not allowed to go inside anyone's house."

"Well, how about we sit on the porch and have some milk with your cookies?"

That sounded fine to Shirley. She sat in one of the rockers and looked toward her house, wondering if her mother was outside watching, but could see no one. Her mother was, of course, standing behind the opaque curtains, making certain her daughter's gesture to the neighbor was well received.

Two glasses of milk were placed on the small wicker table between the rocking chairs. One might think they wouldn't have much to talk about but Nellanore Steele had raised enough children to ask a few questions like "What's your name?" and "How do you like your new house?" and Do you have any brothers or sisters?"

It was Shirley who kept up the conversation, being a chatterbox. When the cookies and milk were gone, the woman stood up. "Ask your mother if you can come back on Saturday. I'll bake us some sugar cookies."

Thus started the melting of the old lady's heart. She didn't have to be in the role of moral-guidance counselor. That was a parent's role. She didn't have to do anything except enjoy the company of a little girl.

Saturday Nellanore Steele had set up a lace-covered table and two chairs under the large oak tree in the back yard. It was a setting for an artist to capture: the woman bending over and talking with the child. She asked Shirley where her grandmothers lived. The answer was one had died and one lived 'far away'. Continuing that subject the old woman asked, "Of course I am not your real grandmother, but would you like to call me Grandma?" Shirley thought she'd better ask her mother first, but she could feel the answer the old woman wanted. She answered, "Okay."

Next was a tour of the flower garden, looking at the peonies, hollyhocks, snapdragons and pansies. Shirley was a little leery of squeezing the snapdragon flowers to make them 'bite' and she said the pansies were her favorite. Truth was Grandma Steele was especially fond of her prize peonies but she said to Shirley "Pansies are my favorite, too."

One day Grandma Steele showed Shirley how to press flowers between wax paper to dry and preserve them. Shirley made one to give to her mother and Grandma Steele said she would give hers to her granddaughter Liz, who was expected to arrive soon from San Francisco.

3 HOMEWARD FOUND

On the long cross-country airplane flight from San Francisco back to the East Coast Elizabeth Steele rested her head back in her seat, remembering when she had first arrived in California. Looking for somewhere other than Newark (derogatorily called "Nerk") she chose San Francisco as her ideal of sophistication.

Leaving New England in March three years ago, she arrived in San Francisco carrying her old black winter coat, fleece-lined snow boots and wool scarves. She checked into the Fairmont Hotel in Union Square. When she awoke the first morning she eagerly wanted to walk in that golden sunshine, needing only a light weight jacket. From a sidewalk flower vender she purchased some violets for her lapel and continued on to a coffee shop for breakfast. She overheard an a woman order a Snail. When the waitress delivered a swirled pastry bun Liz could not stifle a laugh. The woman glanced at Liz and immediately Liz explained her expectation. The two women shared the laughter.

As the plane had continued its long cross-country flight Elizabeth Steele allowed memories of her life during the past several years wash over her: the newly learned delight of prawn-filled avocado, dinner at Sutter Lodge, after-work Rob Roy cocktails. She was hired at KPIX-TV in the Publicity Department, writing articles for TV/Radio magazines promoting the television programs. And she found an apartment across the Golden Gate bridge in Sausalito.

There were plays and programs and lectures to attend. A fellow-worker at KPIX invited her to hear a talk at the USF French Club meeting. A young Chinese man would be speaking in French. He would talk about his childhood in Hong Kong during the time it was occupied by the Japanese. Although her school-talk French was limited she was entranced by the speaker: It was there Cupid struck. Liz and the young man from Hong Kong had a whirlwind romance but months later the winds of Fate moved on. He returned overseas to his parents. When Liz recovered her mental stability she wisely chose a similar path: she was flying home to be with the woman who had raised her, Grandmother Nellanore Steele.

Elizabeth Steele had been eager to move away from her hometown when she was 20 but now Liz was eager to be back to the slower pace of home. The long taxi-ride from airport to her grandmother's house gave her time to relax, breath more slowly, and dream about returning to the old familiar setting. Sure enough, there was Grandma, sitting in a rocker on the front porch.

"Grandma!", Liz called out. She left her suitcases on the sidewalk and ran up the porch stairs. The older woman was still attempting to raise up from her seat before Liz reached her arms around her grandmother and lifted her with a hug. "I'm home." As they stood there, arms wrapped around each other, Liz realized she was getting a strong hug right back. They exchanged several sentences, social chatter that meant little. Both understood what each meant was "I love you" and "I missed you."

Suitcases retrieved, they entered the living room. Liz set down the suitcases without venturing any farther. She remembered when she was eighteen. She had thought she was the most grown-up person there ever was. When she was twenty-one she had looked back on herself at age eighteen and thought about how sophomoric she had been at that time. Now at the advanced age of twenty-five she felt like she was 14 again. She gazed around the familiar room, almost breathing in the memories.

That old brown mohair sofa she had once hated as being prickly she now looked upon with affection. The afghan that was draped on the arm of the overstuffed chair, ready to be pulled over Grand's knees if she got a chill, was made out of the end of many different colored skeins of yarn. Liz remembered holding out her arms with the yarn slipped over them while her grandmother had rolled the strands into a ball so there would be no tangling which she was crocheting.

The rug, now threadbare from so much vacuuming, was edged in a fringe. Liz remembered learning how to braid by taking three strands at a time. She had braided two feet long section of fringe before her grandmother had noticed. It was more difficult to unbraid it than braid it.

She looked with fondness at the old brown-leather hassock. That footstool was lopsided, tilted toward the chair where grandma sat with her feet up, causing the lean. Liz even remembered how it sounded: as if it was filled with straw whenever you sat on it, making a funny scrunchy sound.

Grandma broke her reverie by verbally nudging Liz to take her things upstairs to her room. As it had been when she had left the bedroom was sparsely furnished with one twin bed, an inexpensive chest and a mirrored vanity-table. She had slept in that single bed since she was four years old. The chest was bought unpainted. Grandma had set it on newspapers and painted it white. For her twelfth birthday present Grandma had bought another unpainted piece, the vanity. She painted it and thumbtacked a flounce of white dotted Swiss material to skirt it. Following her grandma's example but without asking permission Liz bought a small can of paint at the dime store and had painted the knobs on the chest drawers a bright pink color. Grandma wasn't happy about that, but she got over it.

Liz sat down on the chenille-covered bed and continued to absorb the Back Home feeling until she heard her Grandma call her name. She went downstairs to see the kitchen table set for supper. Ah yes, she remembered that tablecloth. And the dishes were the pink glassware that people got when they went to the Wednesday night double-feature movie. You had to go every week or you would miss something like the salt and pepper or a cup or saucer.

It was her favorite: salmon loaf and creamed peas with mashed potatoes. Dessert was gingerbread with applesauce on top. Like the old days, her Grandmother served her milk, as usual, in the pink glass tumbler.

"Grandma, while I'm home I don't want you waiting on me. I'll do the cooking and the dishes" Liz told her with a smile.

That didn't go over too well. "I'm not old and I'm not feeble. I have been doing all right by myself and I don't need you to cluck over me. Just eat your supper. After you say the blessing," Grandma added gruffly.

The next morning Liz awakened to a strange chipping sound, a rhythmic beat coming from downstairs. She hastily dressed, brushed her teeth and ran a comb through her hair, then plodded downstairs in her old house-slippers she had found in the closet. There was Grandma, defrosting the refrigerator, which she still called by the old name "Iceless."

"Grandma, you'll puncture the coils if you keep stabbing at the frost with that icepick!"

"Don't preach at me, Miss; I've been doing this for years with no mishap."

It was true that Liz found comfort in seeing the old furniture and accessories, but she was not nostalgic about appliances that made housework hard when improved items were available. It wasn't the right time just yet, but she resolved to buy a new refrigerator for her grandmother. This one had only room for two metal ice-trays. The small compartment was not separate, but within the refrigerated section Usually Grandma kept one tray for cubes and the other space she had room for one package of frozen vegetables, which was usually Birdseye peas.

One of the things that kept Grandma healthy was the necessity to walk to the grocery store almost every day, certainly every other day, although much of her diet was canned foods like tunafish. She ate macaroni and cheese, baked beans, sardines on crackers. But sometimes she made a meatloaf from ground chuck or bought a chicken to make soup. The refrigerator was small so she shopped frequently.

She still bought her chicken from the shop where you walked into the outside pen and pointed to a hen you might think was the most lively or plump. The worker would catch your selection and take it to the back room. You weren't supposed to watch when they slit the throat of the chicken and hung her upside down by her feet to facilitate drainage. They would collect the blood, which was a big seller for making homemade Blood Soup. For an extra charge they would de-feather the bird for you.

Liz continued to think about memories of life with grandma but it was startled from her daydreaming when she heard her grandmother.

"Lizzie, I've got your oatmeal ready,"

"What about you, Grandma? Some oatmeal?"

"I've already had my breakfast. I'll join you. Another cup of tea for me."

After doing the dishes together and making sure the kitchen was immaculate, Liz said, "let's go sit on the front porch for a while and talk"

It was still a bit chilly. The morning sun hadn't yet warmed up the day, but the two women sat on the rocking chairs. Neither said anything. Each sat rocking back-and-forth and looking out at the maple tree in the front yard. Grandma wasn't going to ask Liz any questions. She waited for Liz to reveal whatever was on her mind.

"Thank you for letting me come and stay with you for a while, Grandma."

Nellanore Steele reached to Liz's hand that rested on the arm of her granddaughter's rocker and said, "That's what family is for, darling. I love you."

"That's what I want to ask you, Grandma. I was so little and everything happened so fast: my mama and daddy dying and my brothers going away. It was just you and me from then on. I was confused and couldn't understand. Why haven't any of them tried to contact me? The same goes for me but I don't really remember them. I've been self-focusing for too long. I want to find them. Please tell me, Grandma, the story about what happened and where are they now?

4

OLD STORIES - SOMETIMES TOLD, SOMETIMES NOT

Times were hard everywhere. Populations throughout Europe were overcrowded, money was scarce. Farmland soils were depleted, fleas on rats were disseminating diseases rapidly, starvation was rampant. Nellanore Elizabeth Doherty and many others wished to emigrate to America but the $30 charge for one-way ticket to be crammed in steerage for two months was an unreachable goal. Thirty dollars!

It was 'luck of the Irish' that she won approval when she applied for a position with the rich American Steele family. Her overseas fare was paid for by the family. Her duties were to assist the other Steele family servants while accompanying the family on their trans-oceanic return trip to America. They would never have brought her along if they had seen the future — that one of their sons would marry Nell Doherty in less than a year.

Caleb Steele had six sons, big and strong. Also Caleb had sired his six daughters, whom he would declare were the most beautiful in the world. Perhaps he was getting tired of all those children clambering about. No doubt so was his wife. When she told him his 13th chid was to be expected soon, he seemed deflated, or so the maids commented to each other during an occasional gossip chat.

Clarence, the seventh son, was the butt of jokes while a baby, and the attitude of ridicule continued to follow him throughout his childhood and teenage years. Neither family nor friends saw the pain he endured...except the maid Nellanore Doherty. It was she who would give him a comforting word if no one would see or hear her comment.

One day, when Clarence was twenty, he felt unable to tolerate the jeering statements from his father. He ran out of the room. Like the rest of his family he did not usually notice the "invisible" servants. Nell was polishing the bannisters; he tripped over her and when he saw who it was he blurted out to her that he was going to run away. Would she go with him? She shook her head No.

Desperate, his response to that was to shout, "Marry me!"

Lucky or not, as one learns later, that moment was heard by his father, who had followed his son. How dare his son leave the room when he had been talking to him? Hearing the two words and without asking any questions of course, Caleb Steele told his son and Nellanore, "Get out! Both of you! I hereby disown you, Clarence Steele!"

Like many newly-weds, Clarence and Nellanore soon discovered that their life was not what they may have dreamed of when they were young. Nell was expected to take on the role of all the servants that Clarence was used to having care for his needs. And Clarence learned that money, as the saying goes, does not grow on trees.

He had not been trained to work for a living. When bare shelves and hunger brought him the realization that he must try something, he finally found that he could earn a little money by keeping the books for merchants, a role he felt was belittling to his station in life. His wife was thrifty, an art he had never been taught, so much of his earnings were spent in the bars before he returned to his home.

Nell soon became pregnant but she worked hard at bringing in some money for food. She did some sewing for neighbors and sold some home-baked goods. It wasn't enough. Finally she took in a couple of boarders, much to the dismay and embarrassment of her husband. He felt that belittled his ability to care for her, but he could not argue the point and the need for the income.

Baby Boy Charles was born and not long after that Clarence was elated when Nell became pregnant again. However, she lost that pregnancy and the next one, too, which Clarence took as his personal failure as a man. He began to 'prove himself' with the local Ladies of the Night. All he gained for himself was a whopping case of Syphilis.

Antibiotics had not yet been developed and the 'cures' available at that time were ineffective. Within three years his disease had progressed from faulty judgment, to impaired memory, depression and facial tics. Tongue tremors made his speech slurred and difficult to comprehend. Finally he progressed to full-blown insanity, paralysis, convulsion and the inevitable death from Syphilis.

Nell had cared for her husband throughout health and sickness but now she had lost her ability to feel joy, life-juices squeezed dry, left with a heart that seemed shriveled. There was no delight in her heart. It was only baby Charles that brought sunshine to her soul. By 1921 Charles Steele was twenty and a grown man. He found himself a wife, Agness O'Day.

That was the story of Charles and Agness that Nellanore told her granddaughter Elizabeth Steele.

5 CALEB'S GREAT-GRANDCHILDREN

Nellanore Doherty Steele continued to slowly rock back and forth in her rocking-chair. Her granddaughter had stopped rocking. She sat on the edge of her chair, looking at Nell, awaiting an answer. What was the story about her mother and father and brothers?

Grandma spoke. "Sometimes people don't want to remember sad things. Push them to the back of their brain and try to erase the thoughts. My husband's family had made things hard for us and then he became sick.

"When your mother and father married they rented a little cottage and asked me to move in with them, as was the custom of the time. A year later Matthew was born. Agness was a wonderful mother and had the gift of happiness that she spread, no matter what she was doing. In another two years it was Mark, then Luke. And you, Liz, my precious angel, were Number Four baby.

"It was a happy routine all of us. But your mother became ill with tuberculosis, so prevalent at that time. You use to love watching her brush her long golden-red hair. She would hand you a small brush so you could brush it a little bit, too. When she had to be put in an oxygen tent your father would take the five of you children to get a glimpse of her, just to reassure you she was still there for you. But then those visits stopped.

"After the funeral your father tried to make life as normal as possible. The three boys continued to attend school, Charles went to work, and you, little Liz, stayed home with me. I cleaned the house, washed and ironed the clothes, cooked the meals. You thought it was a fun game to try to help with whatever I was doing. When your father started having a cough and fever we thought it was just bad cold or flu. However, it was tuberculosis, too. There were no medicines, no cure. You either got better or not."

Grandma stopped talking. Liz had been sitting motionless, absorbed with the story being told. She had been gazing attentively at Nellanore and reached over to place her hand over her grandmother's fingers, clutched over the end of the rocker's wooden arm.

Liz spoke. "That's when my father died?" she asked.

Nellanore turned and placed her other hand on top of Liz's hand. She looked at her granddaughter and nodded a Yes.

Liz stood up. She leaned over and kissed her grandmother on her forehead.

"Do you want some water? May I get you something?"

Before there was a response both women heard the sound of roller skates, metal wheels pressing down onto rough cement. There was Shirley, her mass of blonde curly hair jiggling in response to the vibrations from skates tromping down onto the sidewalk. Grandma called Shirley up to the porch and made introductions, Liz to Shirley. Grandma told Shirley there would be three for the tea party next Saturday and Liz quickly offered to make chocolate-chip cookies. Shirley ran home to tell her mother the good news.

The unexpected visit from Shirley was the break the two women had needed. But now Liz urged her grandmother to continue telling her about her family.

"Your father's funeral was quick and simple. I tried to get you four children back into some sort of a routine, but it was difficult, particularly because there was no longer any money coming in to buy food and pay the bills and monthly rent. I didn't have to ask. Your mother's father, Sean O'Day, saw disasters often because of his job as a fireman. He knew we were destitute and our supplies would soon be gone. He had his own family, but out of the kindness of his heart your maternal grandfather pledged to me he would pay our rent and send money for food for our table."

"Oh," said Liz. "Was it that old man with the long beard that used to come by for a visit once in a while? He would kiss each of us, then leave. That was my grandfather?"

"Yes, your mother's father. He had a big family of his own but he also had a big heart, sharing for his grandkids." Nellanore chuckled. "He really wasn't old, you were just very young."

Grandma continued. "I don't know how he found out about us, weeks had gone by, but one day two men in business suits came to the door. They said they represented my father-in-law, Caleb Steele, your paternal great-grandfather."

Nellanore Steele looked up and out into the distance. She sighed, the weight of memories heavy in her heart. She looked back at Liz.

"I love you, Lizzie", then she continued with the story.

"They handed me a letter that was signed by Caleb Steele. In it he wrote that his son Charles Steele had sired three males, Matthew, Mark and Luke, hence in the Caleb Steele blood-line. Therefore he was having the three boys transferred from their current meager existence to be housed in the family estate mansion in Connecticut. There they would be tutored and in time sent to appropriate universities. The letter further stated there being another child, a mere female, she would have no need for higher education since she would marry young and begin child-bearing duties.

"It finished with the line 'As the grandmother of four children I understand losing them might make you lonely so I am leaving the female child with you to keep you company. If you need anything, come to the mansion and just ask. I am sending my car to get the boys on Saturday. Please have them ready.'

Nell turned to her granddaughter and said, "This is why I never told you. 'Come to the mansion and ask'. He knew I wouldn't and couldn't. That man was so cruel."

Both women were feeling emotions so intense that neither of them could move. Liz was first. She wiped her tear-dampened eyelashes with the backs of her hands. She stood, then moved in front of her grandmother, extending both hands out, encouraging the older woman to stand. Next move was a hug, the two of them wrapped together in the embrace until Liz leaned back and whispered, "Let's go in the kitchen and have some tea."

Liz remembered a phrase her grandmother had used occasionally when she was a child. Something about 'that sets my nerves on edge'. She could feel the story grandmother had been telling still had the two women too tense to get back just yet on that subject. Instead, she asked her grandmother about Shirley.

"Who is that little girl on the skates? She's a cutie pie. Live nearby?"

Nellanore smiled. "She and her parents live in the old Willie Forbes' house next door." She told Liz the story about their mutual love of cookies and tea parties.

"Reminds me of when you were a little girl." She continued, "I am so happy you chose to return home for a little while. I hope it will be a long while. Had you given any thoughts about what you would like to do?"

"Nope. No plans. Just coming home to your loving arms, Grandma. Maybe find a part time job. You know, something to do until I find a path I wish to follow."

After supper that evening, dishes were washed, dried and put away. The two women sat at the kitchen table, talking. Liz moved her hand over the cotton tablecloth, caressing it. "I love this old tablecloth. It has witnessed many days and evenings in our lives, Grandma. Maybe we could find your old Monopoly game and perhaps play a few hands of Rummy," she suggested.

Nellanore replied, "Now may be a good time to tell you about your brothers. You know, most men are not eager to write letters, least of all boys. But over the years I have heard about each of them from old friends of mine.

"Matthew went to Yale University, married but she divorced him and married a Count or some Prince. He met a girl from Mystic, Connecticut and they have been married for maybe ten years. He's a fisherman.

"Mark dropped out of Yale, became a Pacifist and moved to Canada where he works for an aluminum company.

"Meanwhile your great-grandfather Caleb Steele died. He did leave a Trust Estate so there was money for Luke to go to Yale. But he's a red-head, you know:

wants to do it his way. He got into Harvard and is enjoying his job in banking in New York City. That's sparse info, but really all I know.

The three seem happy is what I hear, which is all I care about, you know, Liz. I want each of you to be happy. That's a grandma's wish."

Wistfully, Liz said, "I wonder why they never tried to reach me. You have their addresses? I want to write to each of them. I want to meet them. That's what I'll do!"

6 DEAR BROTHER: I CARE

Writing to her siblings with whom she'd had no contact for 20 years did not come easily. Liz wrote and re-wrote. Whose fault was it? Theirs? Hers? She decided it didn't matter. There could be no further delay. She simply wrote she had moved from San Francisco and had returned to the home of their grandmother Nellanore Steele. Her mission was to meet each of her brothers.

There was nothing more she could do about that except to wait for any possible responses. To augment her meager savings account Liz decided to look for a parttime job in town. Grandma Steele said she had heard when she had been in the grocery store that they might hire someone to cover the cashier position when she and her family went on a two-week camping trip. The timing was perfect. Liz loved see old school friends and neighbors. It kept her mind off wondering what the postman might bring each day.

Mark's answer arrived first. He wrote that he had imagined the family considered him an old reprobate, morally depraved because he had refused to become a soldier and kill people. He said he would be happy to have Liz come and visit at any time convenient for her and he hoped she would stay in his home.

The letter from Luke was much shorter and more businesslike. He told her he had a very busy schedule but, of course, he could find time to spend an evening or two with her. He included his telephone number at work and at his apartment. Although Liz could not feel any warmth in the response from Luke, she remained undaunted in her goal to meet each of her brothers.

Thus far she had heard nothing from Matthew.

7 WHERE IS LUKE?

Liz discussed her trip with her grandmother and decided two days with Luke in New York and three days with Mark in Canada would be the best length of time. Visits longer than that, breaking into the host's routine, sometimes wore out the welcome of the visitor.

It took courage to make that first contact, but one evening Liz phoned Luke's apartment. A woman answered the phone. She said she was Luke's fiancee, Judy Pritchard, and that Luke had mentioned Liz to her.

Judy explained that Luke was working late, as he often did, and she asked when Liz planned to visit New York (Liz wanted to say she was not visiting New York, she would be visiting Luke, but refrained from the correction). A date was set and Judy told Liz hotel reservations were difficult to get, but Luke had some connections and they would take care of everything, if she would just let them know the arrival time of her Greyhound bus.

Liz completed her two weeks at the grocery store, made her bus and airline reservations, and notified her two brothers of the plan. She gave her grandmother a hug, promising to come home the next week with stories to tell.

The day she left New Jersey was sunny, but upon arrival in New York City, the weather which dismal, cold and raining. Judy Prichard met her.

She told Liz that Luke was on a job and she would explain everything when she was settled in her hotel. When the taxi stopped in front of the Grand Hotel just across from Central Park, Liz was intimidated by the posh look. Judy caught the look of dismay and smile to herself. Yes, she had sized the girl as a visiting hayseed. She and Luke purposely chose that hotel as a test, to see if Liz was as cosmopolitan as they prided of themselves to be. Judy thought, 'Let's see if she'll beg,' and was gratified when Liz turned her and said, "I don't think I can afford this place. Isn't there a more reasonable hotel, Judy?"

It was only then Judy allowed herself to disclose that Luke's firm kept an apartment within the hotel. Since no 'visiting firemen' were in town the place was free, literally, for the two days Liz would be in New York. It was then she explained that Luke's company had suddenly sent him out of town on assignment, and when he mentioned it was the time his sister was coming to visit him, use of the hotel was offered. The news Luke was out of town deflated Liz, but she said nothing hoping Judy meant it was only a short day trip.

They completed the check-in and went up to the apartment. It was quite handsome. There was silk damask lining the wall, silk brocade upholstery on the Louis Quinze sofas, carved golden framed mirrors, but the only feature that delighted Liz was the fact that the apartment overlooked Central Park.

Judy sat on one of the sofas and watched Liz with a bored expression. Quickly absolving herself of any responsibility to entertain Liz the next day, she said that she was so very sorry that she could not get away from her office tomorrow or even tomorrow night. The hotel had a transport service that would take Liz to the airport the following day for her flight to Canada.

"Because it is raining so heavily, Judy suggested," It would be best for the two of us to eat in the hotel dining room." (She didn't mention it would be written off to the room, at no expense to Luke or Judy.) Liz asked about how Judy and Luke had met. It was at the bank where Luke was Junior Officer in the real estate department. That was where his interests were at this moment. The bank had heard of a sudden release of prime government land up for auction in Key West, Florida. They had sent Luke there to bid on the 103 waterfront acres of the tropical island. Judy didn't know how long it would be before Luke could return to New York. Liz was very disappointed that she would not get to meet Luke this trip.

"Do you have a photo of Luke? I don't even know what my brother looks like."

Judy answered, "I don't carry pictures in my wallet. However, I will make sure Luke does send one to you in New Jersey."

Liz continued to ask a lot of questions about Luke but from Judy's answers she wasn't able to get a clear picture of just what her brother was like.

Judy drank several cocktails before dinner and several glasses of wine with her meal. She became more free-tongued by the end of the evening and told Liz why Luke had never bothered to visit his grandmother. The Steele family had raised him. They told him Nellanore Steele was an evil woman.

"Everyone knew she had killed her husband Clarence; she poisoned him. Ask Luke's brother Mark when you see him."

Continuing her role as hostess Judy asked Liz if there was anything in particular she might like to do next.

Spending the evening with Judy Pritchard instead of her brother Luke was not what Liz wanted, but she was determined not to let her visit to New York be entirely wasted. "Yes," she said. "I would love to be able to hear Dave Brubeck and Charlie Parker play jazz at Birdland."

Judy grudgingly complied, spending the night planning on how she might get payback revenge from Luke for making her entertain his long-lost sister from New Jersey while he, Luke Steele, was at this time partying at Sloppy Joe's bar in Key West.

The next morning cold rain was still pouring down from the New York sky with such force the drops look like millions of steel needles driving down onto the treetops in the park. It made Liz think of the old Saturday matinee scary movies where the iron spikes were closing in on the good guys, but don't worry, superman always rescues them.

She was determined not to let the dreary day depress her. With one day free to do as she wished, her destination was the Cloisters Museum in upper Manhattan. She asked the desk clerk who directed her to the concierge who directed her to the activities desk for instructions on how to get there via public transportation. All advised her to take a taxi cab but this thrifty New Englander persevered, insisting it was more of an adventure to see if she could do it via subway and buses. And, of course she did.

The rain was now a mere drizzle but she was scarcely aware of the weather as she approached the museum, absorbed in admiring the architecture. Devoted to medieval art, there were parts of five French cloisters, the covered passageways with one side open, allowing the view of extensive gardens. In addition to paintings, statues and tapestries Liz gazed at remarkable stained-glass windows. It was a perfect day to enjoy the Cloisters, because the inclement weather had kept potential visitors away.

Liz decided to pamper herself and splurge on a taxi back to the hotel. After a hot shower and change into dry clothes, she took off again, this time to window shop on Fifth Avenue the rain has finally stopped, but the streets and sidewalks were still wet.

As she ambled along the sidewalks, she compared the buildings to those she had become familiar with in San Francisco. There seem to be so many more here, compacted together, continuous and reaching so high that the sun could only shine down at high noon. True, New York did not have the fear of earthquakes that were not uncommon on the West Coast. Even so, it appeared as if the streets had already suffered a massive quake and she was now walking on the bottom of a chasm when the earth's surface has suffered a deep crevasse.

Her musings had distracted her from her intent to window shop, but she began to gaze at displays of finery like a child with a nose pressed of the window pane of the sweet shop. Her impression of New Yorkers this day was it they felt superior to persons who did not know the rules that a few of them had just made up yesterday, and those rules would change tomorrow, whether it be regarding fashion or rules of conduct. New Yorkers all seem so smug and belittling, she generalized to herself, moody because of her disappointment and not being able to meet with her brother Luke. She wondered what tomorrow's flight to Western Canada would bring.

8 RAVEN, FISH AND FROG

How strange to be traveling west again. Five years ago she left home in New Jersey to live in San Francisco, then her trip back east. Now she had flown west again, this time to British Columbia, Canada. She wondered if she should equate herself to those young people who go to India seeking to find themselves. Or perhaps religious pilgrims traveling to Mecca. There had been some ups and downs, but that's how life is.

Her time in San Francisco had been happy. Re-establishing a relationship with her grandmother, who had raised her, had been a great pleasure. The trip to New York and a failure to meet with her brother Luke was a disappointment, but she hoped for another try another time. And now to meet Mark.

As Liz disembarked from the plane in Vancouver and entered the terminal, a big burly man grabbed her and gave her a bear hug while saying, "Liz! I'm your brother Mark!" It all happened so fast that Liz had to quickly adjust from fear of the 'unknown attacker' to enjoying the warm reception from this brother.

He smiled and said, "Sorry I shouldn't have been so eager to say hello, Liz" as he pulled away from her but still held her at arms length.

Tears came to her eyes. She had braced herself to a possible cool reception, but Mark was exhibiting more warmth than she had anticipated.

He took her small carry-on and led her toward the baggage claim section of the airport, asking how her flight was and making other small talk, all the while keeping his head turned toward her, trying to adjust to the fact that here was his little sister.

He escorted her to his Ford station wagon. As they started to drive away, he told her his ranch was about one hour away. She finally got a word in and asked him about his life in Canada.

He said he was 31, had been in Canada 13 years, and worked for the Mudwin Aluminum Company. He said he loved his work and he loved his life in Canada.

Liz asked about his childhood.

Mark told about his youth on the Caleb Steele estate. A special memory he had was a field trip to the Smoky Mountains. One of his teachers, together with his young son Woody had arranged for the three of them to spend a week in a cabin in western North Carolina. That was where Mark had learned his love of minerals. The teacher taught the two boys how to search for gemstones.

There was an old man near their cabin named Mr. Perry. He had a place that he had leased to the jeweler Tiffany long ago. After the main vein of quality gemstones had been depleted, Tiffany gave up the lease and Mr. Perry was making his living by renting out shovels and buckets to visitors. They could shovel into his hillside and pan their dirt in a stream that ran through Mr. Perry's land. Mark and Woody learned to identify the gray hexagon tubes that were sapphires in the rough.

In another area close by, garnets could be found, washed down the hill and underneath a waterfall. The garnets look like dried currents.

Mr. Perry showed the boys a map of the world. He said it was his belief gemstones lay in a clear path from Canada to South America, which he outlined for them. It was as if a pirate had shown them a treasure map, but it revealed not just one chest of coins but an entire area of jewels. He told them, "you just have to dig deep enough in the right location, that's all."

The old man spurred their interest into studying Planet Earth.

"You dig through rocks then solid rock. The next layer, wrapped around the earth and about 3 miles thick, is a very hard rock called basalt. If you were to dig to the center of earth, you would come to a layer so hot it melts the underside of the basalt!

"Sometimes earth has to 'blow its stack' and the safety valve that would release pressure are vents called volcanoes, blasting the melted basalt magna up and out."

Meeting Mr. Perry so impressed the boys they both decided to become geologists.

SEARCHING: THE MEANING OF LIFE

Mark continued his story. He was sent to Yale, but soon dropped out. He started traveling "to find the meaning of life, like so many kids that age." He had become a pacifist and moved to Canada to avoid being drafted into the army where, he said, young men learn to kill other young men.

He glanced at Liz to see her reaction to that statement. Seeing no change in her expression, he continued, saying Woody went into the Air Force but he was shot down and died, which reaffirmed his feelings about valuing human life.

Mark turn the conversation back to Liz, asking about her life, which she summarized. Then she asked why he had never followed up with her grandmother. He answered that it had been impressed upon him that Grandma Steele was a coarse person and a woman of loose morals and he should avoid any association with her.

"It was wrong not to question such a statement, especially when I grew older. Even if the description had been true, as a grown man I really should have reached out and contacted her, but hey, I'm not perfect. It was easier to continue to erase her from my mind and focus on my own personal life."

Liz thought about what Judy Prichard had said: Luke's comment that it was her grandmother who had boys and Clarence. Mark said her grandmother was a woman of loose morals. She wondered what Matthew's story would be.

Turning to face Mark, she did not hesitate to say to this brother, newly met, "Yes, you were wrong. You really must contact her someday soon"

Changing the subject, she asked Mark if he was married.

"Here we are, speaking of loose morals. I am not married, but Raven Inuvik and I have been living together for six years."

Before Mark could wonder what reaction Liz might have to that piece of information, she laughed.

"So you see my brother, since you're a pot, you dare not call the kettle black. Incidentally I happen to see that woman is shiny copper."

This time it was Mark who laughed. They were going to get along just fine.

Not long after their laughter had subsided Mark drove up to a house made from logs, with a covered porch extending across the front. Golden light shone down from the windows and there was a whisper of smoke coming from the chimney. Mark parked the station wagon directly in front of the porch. As he carried her suitcase up the steps, a woman with long black hair opened the front door.

She was smiling and said, "I heard you drive up. Welcome sister of Mark. My name is Raven."

Liz was startled for a moment. She had assumed people living in British Columbia were of English ethnicity and then she realized how stupid that presumption was. This woman had a face as round as the moon, a flat nose and slit narrow eyes that became even more narrow when she smiled.

Raven noticed the fleeting look. She was used to that from strangers, who soon became aware they were many Eskimos and native Indians living in the area.

Liz asked Raven, "What is that marvelous smell?" The interest was genuine and the aroma was coming from the kitchen and was drawing her into the house.

"I was not certain if your plane would be delayed, so our meal will be of a simple soup, bread and salad. Time only makes the soup taste better," said Raven her speech was much slower than Liz are used to hearing. It had a lilting cadence.

"Come on, Liz" Mark encouraged her as he led her up a staircase made of a light colored wood with darker knots contrasting. "After you settle in and freshen up, come on back downstairs and we'll give you some of Raven's soup."

Her room had a quilt cover on the bed and another one hanging on the wall. The window was not covered with curtains, but you could see nothing in the darkness outside now; no lights in the distance, nothing but stars shining above. The headboard was made of curved branches and the bedside table was obviously homemade and roughly hewn. On the top of the table was a kerosene lamp, lit. The light shown on the small carving: a totem pole of a fish with a frog in his mouth: the totem was painted black, but there seem to be traces of red in the carved crevices. The carving intrigued Liz.

The aroma of Raven's soup called to her. She washed her hands and splashed her face, then descended to the main room. There was no wall dividing the areas of the kitchen, living room and dining area.

Mark was standing at the sink shredding lettuce and placing it in a large wooden bowl.

"May I help?", asked Liz. She was given the assignment of cutting up the tomatoes, cucumbers and scallions. It was such a wonderful feeling a family warmth, the three of them working together.

Raven was setting placemats of woven yarn on a table that was made from a huge plank of wood, highly varnished. The natural bark remained along the edges. Like the bed's headboard, the backs of the chairs at the table were also made of bent branches.

"What a wonderful place you have here," Liz said.

Raven responded, "Mark built the home and the furniture."

Mark countered, "Raven did all the upholstering, weaving and made our quilts."

"And the small totem pole in my room?" Liz queried.

"It's my mothers, but that's a long story" said Raven "First, let us eat."

The soup bowls were interesting ceramic pieces, oval, with one lip extended to serve as a handle. The entire pot of soup was placed in the center of the table within easy reach. Indeed, all three had second servings of the vegetable-beef soup. Raven had baked cracked-wheat bread and together with the salad Liz thought it was a perfect meal. The beverages offered by Mark were coffee or water.

After the meal was completed, Mark told Liz "Raven usually cooks so I do the dishes and clean up the kitchen."

Liz quickly offered to help Mark but he insisted, "You two go sit and relax. I can hear the conversation from here and, who knows, I may have a comment or two." The two women moved over to the pair of sofas that flanked the fireplace. Raven showed how Mark had made the sofas. "First he made benches for storing things like blankets and bulky jackets, then added a tilt-back support for comfort." Raven had covered the cushions in brown corduroy. There were a couple of small pillows decorated with quilt squares.

Raven added another log to the fire and they sat, feeling comfortable with each other. They could hear Mark running water at the sink. "Let me tell you about the totem" said Raven.

"My father is an Eskimo who came to British Columbia to find work. There was no food to be found in the rivers, seas or forest. There are some things a man desires that require money. But, more than that, he desired to find a wife.

"When he saw my mother, he was smitten. However, the tribe said to obtain their permission for this stranger to marry my mother, he must make a carving. The possibility of marriage would rest upon that carving and the Shaman's interpretation.

"At first my father could not decide what to carve. He carved a fish and painted it red. He did not know our legend of the Red Snapper, but decided red might be considered too bold, so he remove the red and painted over it with black. Then he completed the small totem with a frog image in the mouth of the fish.

"The frog was a favorite symbol of his Eskimo clan but he did not know what it might mean to my tribe. To us the meaning is "one who stays near the hearth" or "reliable "or "good wife". That he chose to carve a frog was a good sign.It was a very strange carving, very different from anything they had seen before.

"They knew he did not know our legends. It would be bad if he chose to carve a Dog/Shark. That would be a bad omen because the Dog/Shark had carried away the Chief's daughter and she never returned. But he did not carve a shark. It was a good thing, too, that he did not carve a moon, because that was an exclusive crest for only a few of the highest ranking chiefs. Another favorite is the raven, but everyone knows the raven is mischievous."

Mark interrupted the tale with laughter from the kitchen. "I agree Raven is mischievous."

She continued her story "Our legend of the Red Snapper is about a man who was looking for wife, so, as a token to the Goddess of the Sea, whenever he saw pale fish he would paint them red. Through the help of the Goddess he found a wife. Another is a legend of the magnificent Thunderbird/Lightning Snakes who are so powerful that they hunt whales. A man could paint a Thunderbird on his canoe then paint over it so the whale could not see it, but the power of the bird would still be with the fisherman. That my father painted the fish, and traces could be seen that he had removed the paint, was equated with the Thunderbird legend plus the totem included the frog was interpreted by the shaman as a very good omen. His simple miniature totem was successful in winning my mother to become his bride."

Liz said, "What a wonderful story!"

Raven replied solemnly "It is a true story."

Mark join the two women. His timing was right: he brought three cups of dessert: pears that Raven had canned in syrup plus a tin of cookies. He placed them on the table next to the women.

Liz got it from the sofa and leaned over Raven, giving her a hug. She moved to her brother and gave him a hug, saying, "I love you both."

She asked Mark about his work.

"I met a man who told me China produces most of the world's aluminum, but it is also a major industry in Canada. Aluminum is light weight, strong, malleable and conducts heat and electricity. When it comes in contact with air, aluminum rapidly becomes covered with a tough transparency or aluminum oxide that resists further corrosive activity.

"This element occurs combined with other elements in minerals such as bauxite, corundum, cryolite, feldspar and mica. Incidentally, the gemstones Ruby and Sapphire are corundum, and they consist mainly of crystalline aluminum oxide and have a relative hardness of number nine which is very hard. With my childhood interest in those gemstones, it seemed to me that should be the kind of industry I should get involved with.

"But enough about geology and enough about me. Cross-country travel is tiring, even though air travel is quicker than some other modes. I want to allow you time to rest. We'll talk tomorrow."

This time it was Mark who moved over to Liz. He gave her a hug and a good-night kiss on the forehead. The room was filled with warmth and love.

10

HOW DID YOU MEET RAVEN?

What a pleasure to awaken to the aroma of bread baking in the oven. Liz stretched one arm, one leg at a time, then tossed the quilt outside. She sat on the edge of the bed for a moment, her glance caught once again by the miniature totem carved by Raven's father. How lucky Raven was to have that family legend to hand down.

Liz wondered if Mark and Raven would ever get married. Why hadn't her brother already proposed to her? Or married her? Did he want children? Did Raven want children? Liz had many questions she would've liked to ask but knew it would be rude. Perhaps Mark would reveal more of himself today. Regardless, I already know I love my brother.

There was a chill in the air, so she didn't sit there any longer. She dressed, then went downstairs to the main room. Mark and Raven were sitting at the table, drinking coffee. They both looked up at her as she walked down the stairs and smiled.

"Good morning," said Mark. "How did you sleep?"

"On a cloud. I have never slept so soundly as I did last night nor feel as rested as I do this morning."

Raven stood and went into the kitchen area. "Coffee? Apple juice?"

"Just juice thanks, Raven." Liz sat the table.

Mark brought a cutting board with a loaf of still-warm bread. "Cut yourself a hunk, Liz. Here are a couple of fruit preserves to choose from". Mark continued "I thought today we would play tourist. Tomorrow, your last day, we will just hang around here or something. Is that OK with you, Liz?"

"That sounds great, Mark."

"Raven wants to spend a day with her parents, so I will drop her off there on the way to Vancouver. I have to make a phone call to my office this morning before we leave. Take your time and enjoy breakfast." Mark went into his bedroom.

The two women then discussed soup and bread recipes.

Liz asked Raven if she worked. Raven smiled and thought to herself that the question was very "American". She answered that she sold her quilts at the local arts and crafts fairs.

Mark returned to the room and, as they prepared to leave, Raven placed a loaf of bread and some home-canned items in a woven bag before they drove off in the station wagon.

About a half hour later, Mark turned onto a dirt road. On one entire wall of the house they approached was a gigantic painting of a fish, done in black and red. Liz sat with her mouth agape, stunned by the beauty of the painting.

"My mother painted it herself," Raven said in her deep and husky voice.

Two people emerged from the house. Raven got out, taking her woven bag. Her parents embraced her and approached the car. Raven introduce them and Liz enthusiastically commented on how artistic the entire family was. This embarrassed them, but they smiled and waved, as Mark drove away.

"They don't think anything they do is exceptional. They believe it is simply a natural way of doing thing. I agree with you, Liz. I think it is wonderful, too," said Mark.

"Family is very important to her and, since we are rarely apart, she suggested she stay with her parents overnight. I will pick her up tomorrow afternoon.

"How thoughtful Raven is! How did you to meet?"

"It's a strange story. I had gone camping with three of the men I work with. We walked to a nearby stream. A tree had grown with a strong branch jutting over the river. An Indian girl sat on the tree trunk, holding a fishing line. She was wearing a white blouse, pants with the legs rolled up, and swinging her bare feet. She'd been leaning over, looking into the water, her long black hair hanging down. When she heard us, she jumped up and ran into the woods.

"Suddenly I was looking at a stream with an empty tree trunk jutting out and woods and sky behind that. I wondered if, indeed, I really have seen the Indian girl. I just couldn't shake that image.

"A few weeks later I was driving around the area and noticed a craft fair. I parked my car. With bauxite here in Canada, it occurred to me they might be displaying corundum and maybe sapphires or rubies. It was worth a look. No, there weren't any gemstones, but I did see a jewel. It was that same Indian girl with the raven-black hair. She was at a quilting booth."

Mark continue driving silently.

"Don't stop the story there! What happened next?" asked Liz.

"Nothing, because I lived here long enough to know I just couldn't walk up to her and ask her out. Even if I did, she would say no. But I did inquire around and found out who her brothers were. It's a long story but anyhow, her brothers got to know me and trust me. I was finally able to meet her and ask her on a date and here we are now together six years."

Liz wanted to ask more, but the traffic was heavy and she enjoyed observing the area while Mark concentrated on driving. They parked and took a ferry boat. Liz was fascinated by the scenic ride to Victoria on Vancouver Island. There they visited the beautiful Butchart Gardens. Liz couldn't decide which variety of hanging begonias was her favorite. She wished her brother brought a camera so she could share the sights with her grandmother.

After several hours in the gardens, they walked along the waterfront in Victoria and ate a sandwich at a tea shop. Next they walked around the city streets, eating ice cream cones. Mark explained that the capital city was Victoria, on Vancouver Island, but the town of Vancouver was on the mainland. He insisted that have been done to confuse the tourists, but Liz just laughed at her brother. The ferry ride back to the mainland was just as thrilling to her as the trip over.

"I believe you are a true sailor," Mark observed.

"Certainly," agreed Liz, "Water is my sign. What is your sign?"

"Oh, I don't really know. Earth I suppose. What else for a geologist?"

11 MARK REVEALS HIS LOVE OF GEOLOGY

On the way back to Mark's house Liz talked about Grandma Steele. She told him what Luke's girlfriend Judy had said about poisoning and said she wondered what Matthew would say. She told Mark her grandmother had been strict while she was growing up, but now that Liz was older she was more of a friend.

"I love my grandmother very much and hope you and your brothers will get to know her sometime soon."

Mark agreed it was appropriate and long overdue.

When they arrived home Mark said he would be preparing salmon for dinner. He wrapped corn-on-the-cob and potatoes in foil and set them on a rack he had installed in the fireplace, high above the flames.

Mark talked about physical geology: mineralogy, which focuses on the forces that shape the exterior of the earth and, through time, the interior. He mentioned the drifting of continental crusts produced ocean basins, continents, plateaus and could fold rocks making mountains. He explained that the plates move a few centimeters each year, colliding and separating.

He went on to say there are igneous rocks like granite, sedimentary rock like lime stone and clay and metamorphic rocks. "The intriguing thing about metamorphic rocks is that they were formed from either very high temperature or, he continued, the huge weight of rocks above it. “Marble, slate, and quartzite are all metamorphic rock” explained Mark. “Isn’t that interesting?”

Mark stopped. He laughed and said, “I apologize I get carried away when I’m on the subject of rocks. Raven says I have rocks in my head.”

Liz smiled at her brother, and told him she learned quite a bit and assured him that he made it all very interesting.

Mark‘s response was to say that their dinner was ready.

That evening and the next day were spent companionably. Liz made some corn and potato soup from Grandma Steele’s recipe. She asked Mark if they could pick up Raven and bring her home for dinner together. She and Mark rummaged the refrigerator and freezer, putting together the meal. Mark set the table and plucked a bouquet from the yard. Liz asked the names of the flowers.

Mark answered. “I don’t know, just weeds.” He left and picked up Raven.

Raven was surprised by the preparations and made one change in the table-setting. She brought out soup spoons made from animal horns, the handles beautifully carved. Mark whistled and told Liz that she must’ve made a big hit with Raven, because those carved spoons were only used on special occasions.

Liz responded that she was surprised that the arts and crafts of the area had not been commercialized; all that amazing talent was a precious gem.

Raven smiled and caution Liz, “Be careful. Don’t mention the word “gem” or Mark will be giving another of his lectures.”

That signaled Mark to stand up. He held his hands as if he was reading from a book. He lectured, “We are burning fossil fuels fast, heading toward depleting the source.”

“You see!” said Raven. The three of them burst out laughing.

12
BACK HOME: CHILDHOOD MEMORIES

What a wonderful three days Liz had enjoyed with her brother Mark and his girlfriend Raven Inuvik. Now she was on another cross-country flight. If she were physically weary or emotionally depressed, she might sleep, but quite the contrary, she felt very well-rested and overjoyed and discovering such a wonderful brother. Time passed quickly, what was in-flight meals and snacks of Coca-Cola and peanuts that were served almost continuously.

Arriving back in the New Jersey airport Liz was surprised to see her grandmother plus Shirley and Shirley's mother and father. It was Sunday. The hardware store was closed, so Shirley's father had offered to drive everyone in their car to the airport. Liz, Grandma and Shirley sat in the backseat. She entertained them with stories about how Mark had surprised her with a big bear hug at the airport, and about the house made of logs, and Mark had made lots of the furniture too.

She told about how nice his girlfriend Raven was and said her parents had a beautiful painting on the side of their house, an abstract of a fish, in the manner of the NorthWest Indians. She told them about the beauty of the Butchart Gardens and how much she enjoyed the ferry ride.

She turned to Shirley and said, "I mailed a postcard to you but it probably won't arrive for a couple more days." Shirley thought it was funny that Liz arrived before the card. She started to giggle and both of them laughed and laughed until Shirley got hiccups.

Liz told her grandmother she had missed her and was glad she was back home. Grandma still seemed embarrassed and didn't know how to react to that comment. Instead, she told her that Shirley's mother had baked a cake for Liz.

Liz walked through the living room, continuing past the dining room where grandma displayed one of her few treasures: a Belleek China basket sent to her long ago by her sister in County Donegal, Ireland. The dining room was almost never used.

She remembered a dinner served there at one time, but she couldn't remember now who was there and what was the occasion. What had been impressed upon her was it was important to protect the surface of that wooden table. One must never place a sweating glass of cold liquid on the table, because it could leave a white ring on the wood. Before a dinner party in that room, Grandma would cover the table with a thick, protecting pad, and then a large linen tablecloth.

The next thing Liz remembered, as if a second snap shot in a picture album, was Grandma standing at the ironing board, a couple of days after the party. The tablecloth had been washed, hung on the clothesline to dry, then was moistened with a sprinkling bottle and left overnight to make certain that all parts of the cloth were damp. It required a very hot iron to get the linen material smooth of wrinkles. Liz never thought it was worth all the bother and had long ago vowed never to use linen tablecloth.

The group continued into the kitchen. Both Liz and Shirley saw it at the same time: a chocolate cake with shiny white boiled icing. Yum! The kitchen was cozy. Grandma already arranged plates and forks and paper napkins, plus a bouquet of her peonies. It was quite a homecoming. Liz entertained them with more stories about her trip, saying the only "sad" part was that she had not thought about taking along a camera.

After Shirley and her parents left, Grandma and Liz returned to the kitchen table to talk some more. Grandma handed her a letter postmarked "Mystic, Connecticut." It was a note from Matthew encouraging her to come to Mystic anytime. He said he wished he could invite her to stay in their home, but he was sorry there was no room, however there were several inexpensive motels nearby. Included was his telephone number and a photo of him and his wife and children. On the back of the picture were the names: Matt, Marian, Joey, Max and Halibut. Yes, there was a dog in the photograph also.

Since Liz had not been able to contact her brother Luke she placed another call to New York. It was Judy who answered the phone again. She said Luke had not yet returned from Key West, complaining that she feared Luke had caught "the island fever". He decided to stay at a few more days before returning to New York. Judy assured Liz she would remind him to phone Liz as soon as possible.

Grandma asked, "What do you think, Lizzie? What are your plans?"

"Grandma, I just don't want to stay up north for the cold winter. I think Florida is going to be my next exploration. I was thinking about looking for a used automobile and driving down to Mystic to visit Matthew and his family. And then, perhaps, I'll drive down U.S.#1 and travel south. See where it leads me. Who knows I may end up at the end of the highway in Key West, Florida."

Grandma voiced the argument that millions of people live in cold climates and they cope.

"I don't want to "cope" and I don't see why you do either, Gram. Come with me to Florida. That would be just perfect! I would love for the two of us to be together in the sunshine."

"You are young and you need to do this alone. Who knows, I might come and visit you someday, after you are established. When did you plan to leave?"

In three more days Liz had said her goodbyes. Five years ago she simply quit her job and bought an airline ticket to San Francisco. This time things appeared to be more final: she found a used car, a DeSoto, that fit her budget. She drove it around town to say her goodbyes to her classmates from high school and friends where she had worked five years ago, plus the people at the hardware store where she had filled in recently. She visited Shirley and gave her a glass snow globe that she had had since her childhood. It was a gift she wanted Shirley to have to remember her.

She had washed all her clothes and stored things in her closet in boxes. She packed summer clothing, a sweater and slacks in two suitcases. She put into her purse a copy of a nice letter of recommendation that she had from her old boss at the job she had in San Francisco, her address book, and a copy of her birth certificate plus some recent photographs taken of herself with Grandma Steele. She was ready to get on the road!

13 HALIBUT, THE FISHERMAN'S DOG

Liz drove her DeSoto to Mystic Connecticut. She didn't stop anywhere along the way, finally checking into a motor court on the Mystic River.

She phoned Matthew from her room. Marian answered, pleased to hear from Liz. She asked her to come right over to the house and stay for dinner. "It's only beef stew, but there's plenty" urged Marian. She gave Liz the directions on how to find the house. Liz was delighted with the welcome and decided to do just that.

Along the way she spotted a sign: "Ice Cream" and pulled in. She bought a half-gallon of Fudge Ripple and a half-gallon of Rainbow sherbet (orange, raspberry and lime) and had them insulate them with newspapers.

Marian's instructions were clear and she found the house without any difficulty. It was white wooden two-story, the door and the shutters painted red. There was a rather large black dog lying on the front steps that match the photograph Matthew had sent to her. Liz pulled onto the driveway. The dog approached the car.

Although he was wagging his tail Liz hesitated to get out, but then a woman, short and stocky, called from the doorway, "Hal, get in here."

The dog responded and went into the house. The woman said something to someone in the house, then walked to the car, smiling and extending her hand.

"You must be my sister-in-law. I am Marian. The kids have put Hal in the basement until we find out how you feel about dogs. Come on in, honey" she said with a dimpled smile.

Marian kept talking. "You must be tired. Did you drive all the way today? What did you eat today? Would you like something now? Supper won't be ready for at least another hour. Matt will be home soon. Come on in."

The two women entered through the kitchen doorway. Marian asked Liz how she felt about dogs and Liz said she love dogs. At that signal the two boys open the basement door. Hal came over to Liz. She leaned over to pet his neck. Hal gave a little jump, slobbering her with a juicy kiss.

The boys' mother apologized. "Oh, my goodness! Joey, bring a damp washcloth for Liz. Hal's name is 'Halibut,' just for the Hal of it. Get it? He's a good dog and the boys love him."

Joey returned with a washcloth and the two boys stood together staring at Liz.

"This is your Aunt Liz, boys" explained Marian. Max was going through a growth spurt, his wrists sticking out from his shirt sleeves. He had red hair and freckles and made Liz think of Tom Sawyer. The other boy was younger, topped with a blonde tousled shag the color of Marian's flyaway hair. In unison they said "Hi." That formality completed, they scattered, running out the back door.

"I wish we had room for you to stay with us, Marian said. Liz thanked her but explained she'd already checked into a motel.

A tall, skinny redheaded guy walked in the front door, the screen-door slamming shut behind him.

Marian called from the kitchen, "Matt, she's in here! It's your sister!"

He came towards her in a loping walk as if he had sea legs.

"Hi, little sister. It's been a long time" he said. The smile revealed one snaggle-tooth projecting a little in front of the other, center front. He extended his hand and they shook. He led them from the kitchen into the living room.

Matt and Marianne sat on the sofa, Liz on a chair. Marian led the conversation. Finally she said to Liz, "You two sit there and catch up with each other, honey. I'm going to check on my boys."

Conversation was a bit awkward, but finally the background stories were gone over. Max said he had been raised on what he called "the "Caleb Steele estate" by an aunt. She had lived her childhood in Salem, Massachusetts was taught to fear witches. She insisted his grandmother had bewitched Clarence away from his family. She demanded the grandmother never be mentioned in her house.

"I always meant to check up on my grandmother one day, but life has been hectic and I never got around to it."

They heard Marian shout, "Max! Joey! Come in the house and wash your hands. Dinner is ready! Leave Hal in the backyard. Hurry up, now!"

Matt told Liz he wanted to wash up before dinner, too. He wanted to get into the bathroom before the boys did. He said their house was a two bedroom one bath but he would hold the boys at bay if Liz would like to go upstairs to the bathroom first. Liz backed off, telling him for the three of them to go ahead.

She went into the kitchen to help Marian. The aroma of the stew was delicious plus there were hot rolls. Dinner was served and the ice cream dessert was a big hit with the boys, and for that matter, with Marian and Matt too. Marian was the type who chatted nervously with new people.

When there was a break in the stream of conversation, Matt said to Liz, "I was going to take the boys fishing tomorrow. Want to come along, Liz?"

Marian spoke up, "Oh Matt, you know that's my day to volunteer at the Children's Center. I have to show up. They are shorthanded. But I want wanted to go fishing with Liz, too."

Matt smiled at his wife. "Honey, you knew I was taking the boys out on the boat tomorrow. This way Liz and I can have some brother/sister talk."

She agreed, "You're right, of course, Matt. I'll make a big picnic lunch for the four of you to take on the boat."

Liz asked the desk clerk at her motel if they would give her a wake up call at 7 a.m. Up, showered, and dressed, with some milk and a donut from the coffee shop, Liz arrived at Matt's house five minutes before the designated 8 o'clock time. She parked her car in the street in front of the house, because Matt's truck was in the driveway with a boat attached to the hitch. Hal gave her a happy, wagtail greeting as she walked up to the front door. She could hear Marian inside the house, saying, "Come on boys, finish your breakfast"

Matt swung open the screen door and gave Liz a big smile. "I'm going to drop off Marian on the way" The two boys stood up from the table and spoke in unison again, "Good morning, Aunt Liz." She went up to each and gave them a hug, which seem to embarrass them, but Liz believed hugs were good for everyone, including shy kids.

Marian handed a shopping bag to Liz saying "Here's lunch." It was unexpectedly heavy and Liz almost dropped to the floor, but Matt swooped down and captured it in time. "I hope it's not brick sandwiches, Marian." he laughed.

The three adults got into the truck and the boys hopped in the truck bed.

"I don't know what kind of a sailor you are," Matt said to Liz. "It's windy today so we won't go out in the ocean. How about some freshwater fishing?"

Liz agreed anything was fine with her.

They stopped in front of a plain brick building with the sign that read 'Church of Jesus Christ of Latter-day Saints'. "Stay as long as you want Matt. MaryJane will drop me back at the house. Have fun, Liz" She threw kisses at the boys and entered the building.

"Marian believes everyone in the world is related, having come from Adam and Eve. That's one of the reasons her church opened this Children Center. She volunteers one day a week. She loves kids and loves her work here. She's a wonderful mother."

It wasn't long before they arrived at the boat ramp. He had the boys hold the boat steady by the dock so Liz could get on board while he parked the car and boat trailer.

The sun was warm, but there was a cooling breeze. Liz told Matt she could enjoy anywhere if it was on water. He smiled and said that was why he had become a fisherman.

The lunch bag turned out to have nine sandwiches: egg salad or meatloaf or bologna. There was a six pack of beer, four bottles of cream soda and four bottles of root beer. Liz chose an egg salad, Matt had meatloaf and the boys each had two bologna-on-white sandwiches. Liz drank one beer and later chose a cream soda. After they had been fishing a while and Matt had finished his beers Liz brought up the past.

"I had been four years old in 1934 and you, Matt, were 12. How did you adjust to the changes after they took you away?

"That was more than 20 years ago, Liz. It was a whole different world. I was devastated by our parents' deaths. I didn't adjust well to the fancy world of the Steele family in New Haven. The house was huge and gloomy. My aunt and uncle had four children, blonde with brown eyes. I grew up much taller than the other kids and felt awkward. I never felt like I belonged.

"I taught the girl next door, Deirdre Edwards, how to play tennis when I was 16 and she was 14. Off the tennis courts, she wouldn't acknowledge me in school or anywhere else. A couple years later she had gone out drinking with some boys and came home drunk. Her father met her at the door and was furious. He told her that he was canceling her Coming Out Ball, which was a big deal. I guess to spite her father, suddenly she started courting me. I fell for it and it wasn't long before I asked her to marry me. The marriage didn't last long. She started to cheat on me."

Liz glanced at the two boys in the boat, wondering if this was the kind of thing they should hear.

Matt understood the look and responded, "I think is important for my boys to know that cheating, whether it is on a math test or not being true to a spouse, is wrong. It is also important to choose the right partner if you want the marriage to last. Puppy love and physical attraction are nice, but if you were going to last for the long-haul, there had better be more to it than that.

"A lot of it was my fault. My grandfather sent me to college to be an economist. It was about money and wealth, things that didn't interest me. I was bored by Ceteris Paribus, Indifference Curve, Macroeconomics, Value Added, Market Failure, and the GNP.

"Deirdre loved spending her days at the Country Club playing tennis in the morning, next was lunch, and playing canasta there all afternoon. Then coming home to dress up in evening attire to return to the Country

Club for a late dinner, drinking and dancing. Every day, every night. Same place, same people.

"When she started cheating on me, I wanted out and she did, too. That was fine. She is married to a fancy Duke now. I'm not bitter. I'm glad she's happy because I am blessed, I've got Marian and the boys." Matt stop talking to reach for another beer.

Liz asked, "Where did you meet Marian?"

"I left New Haven right after the divorce and moved around the coast for a while getting a job in fishing. Finally I signed on with the company I've been with now for 10 years. Marian was the gal in the front office. I wooed her and won her and it was the best thing that ever happened to me in my life. Next to having Joey and Max. They're wonderful kids."

All the time Matt and Liz had been talking, the boys had been in the bow of the boat, successfully bringing up fish. "Look at this big one, Dad!" Joining the boys, the crew became more serious about fishing. They were able to take home more than enough fish for their supper.

When they returned home the boys helped Matt hose down the boat. Liz went in and talked with Marian about their fishing results. Marian had made baked beans and macaroni and cheese to go with the fish she knew her three men would provide. She also made gingerbread with lemon sauce for dessert.

After dessert Liz wanted to help her clear the table but Maria announced that Max and Joey were doing the dishes tonight. She said she thought it was important for the boys to learn how to take care of themselves so when they left home as adults they could fend for themselves.

"They will make better husbands, and my future daughter-in-laws will thank me" she said laughing. The boys didn't grumble too much and the three adults moved into the living room.

"Are those family names: Joey and Max?" Liz asked Marian.

"Yes," she replied. "My church encourages studying genealogy. Max is named for Maximilian Jackson, my great-great grandfather, and Joey is named after Josephus Fitch Packer, another great-great. You know like Packer Tar Soap. They left Mystic Connecticut around 1850 and move to Key West, Florida."

Liz looked startled. "This is too much of a coincidence. I am on my way to Key West. When I leave tomorrow morning that is where I'm headed. Do you still have family there?"

"Sure. My cousins Trish and Bubba Jackson. I'll give you their address and maybe you can look them up."

Liz mentioned their grandmother again, telling Matt that it was true Grandma had been strict with her when she was growing up but now she had mellowed.

"Like most fourteen-year-olds, no doubt I tested my grandmother's boundaries, making her seem like a witch to me. But she is such a wonderful friend now. I hope you'll be able to get to visit with her someday. She would love it."

She told about her visit with Mark in Canada and how she still hadn't been able to see Luke.

Matt said "What a lucky guy I am to have a sister like Liz, right, Marian? I am glad you looked us up." Then Matt did something out of character for him. He went over to Liz and gave her a big hug. It made Marian tear up with happiness.

Liz turned the mood into laughter by calling into the kitchen, "Joey! Max! Come here quickly!" The boys ran into the room, startled.

"It's time for a family hug" She gathered all five of them to together for one big hug.

"Oh, boy, Aunt Liz, you are a funny aunt" said Joey.

The timing couldn't be better. Liz said her goodbyes. As she drove off she decided as soon as she returned to her motel for that last evening she would telephone her grandmother and tell her about her good feelings with another part of the family clan.

14
ON THE ROAD AGAIN

Liz slept as if floating atop fluffy clouds, the sky overhead a pale blue, the sunshine golden. There was no need for an alarm clock, no wake-up call. There was no hurry. No drive to an airport, no scheduled take-off. She woke up slowly, remembering where she was and the happy time she'd had visiting with her brother Matt and his family.

She remembered Matt telling about being raised by an aunt in the town of Salem. She was haunted he had heard ideas about witches, disturbing thoughts to put into the minds of young children. Ideas instilled into youngsters were difficult to erase. That was the clever intent of some motivational speakers in politics, religion and other hierarchy.

Liz Steele, ever a positive person, was immune to such palaver. A sunbeam, shining through a slit in the closed drapes, had moved across her bed. She stretched and yawned, then threw off the covers. She was ready to start the day!

A quick trip to the coffee shop. No rules, she chose a glazed donut and a pint of milk. Not the best choice, but she enjoyed it. Suitcase in the car, maps studied and she began her trip.

Each time Liz stopped at a service station she would go inside the office and pick up one of their free State maps. The gas station attendant would fill her tank, check her oil, kick her tires to check the air and clean her windshield. While he serviced her car she had unfolded the huge paper maps and verified how her route appeared. She had chosen not to take I-95 down through the center of most states. Instead she decided to go entirely via US Highway One.

Her trip from Mystic to Key West was about 1,500 miles. She kept her radio on, humming or singing aloud to "Rock Around The Clock" with Bill Haley, "Come On-A My House" by Rosemary Clooney, "My Foolish Heart" by Billy Eckstine, "Hound Dog" by Elvis Presley and "How Much Is That Doggie in the Window". That reminded her of Matt's dog Halibut.

Time flew by and she realized she was already in Virginia. Liz considered diverting over to visit the "Living History" museum in Williamsburg to see where the stores and workshops were manned by persons dressed in Colonial attire, but decided she had much better enjoyed her visit with her brother Mark in Canada. There she had enjoyed real-life crafts within the log home he had built and was impressed by Raven Inuvik's quilts and carved spoons.

She stopped for lunch: a hot dog and cola drink, but their specialty was apple cobbler. Of course she had to try it. Singing her way through

North Carolina she pulled over when she saw a hand-printed sign saying "Try our home-made cherry cobbler." So she did.

By this time she knew she had to stop somewhere in the State of Georgia to find peach cobbler. Just over the Georgia border was Florida. Her latest map gave the information that Florida's highway, Jacksonville to Key West, was 533 miles long. The radio sang to her "Goodnight, Irene."

Liz pulled into the next motel, deciding it was time to eat something nutritious and go to bed. Tomorrow would be another day.

U.S. Route One had turned out to be just the kind of highway she wanted. In Florida it traveled near the Eastern coast line, but Liz moved over to Route A1A, which was even closer to the water. She set her sights on her next stop: she would stay overnight in Miami Beach and check out the beaches. Driving down Collins Avenue she compared the rates quoted on signs. Choosing one, she checked in and immediately went out to the beach.

It was a stupendous site! She saw a broad expanse of golden sand extending far to her right and left. The ocean was a gorgeous shade of turquoise. The glare of the sun on the sand and sea was more than Liz could take for more than a few minutes. She went back inside the motel lobby to the gift shop and bought sunglasses plus some postcards. For the first time since she started this trip she felt a little nervous about where her adventures may lead her.

Mealtime again. Was traveling merely driving and eating? There was no need to grab and eat something. No rush. She felt the need for a day off from driving. She wanted to find food she had learned to enjoy while living in San Francisco. Liz asked the front-desk clerk where she might find a Chinese restaurant. That night she was happy *not* have any cobbler for dessert.

Next morning she chose a Florida breakfast of ambrosia: orange slices with coconut sprinkled on top. She spent the morning lying on a chaise lounge. The shade of an umbrella could not protect her from the ultraviolet rays of Florida sun. She got sunburned. She retreated back to her motel room, showered off the useless suntan lotion and sand.

Thoughts about her grandmother came to her. When she was a

teenager and had too much New Jersey sun it was her grandmother who applied Jergen's Lotion to her back to cool the burning sensation. This brought her attention to the postcards. Her intention was to write a few lines, but the cool sheets were inviting. She curled up and slept: her first nap in many years.

Liz looked at the clock at her bedside. She had missed lunchtime? After a late afternoon meal of a corned beef on rye plus strawberry cheesecake she was sick of thinking about food. Even a cup of chicken noodle soup could not entice her. Dehydrated, she reached for a drink of water. Sun and sand, driving and eating, no one to talk with. She was eager to complete her journey to Key West, Florida.

Driving the last 50 miles of Florida mainland, she arrived in the Homestead/Florida City area. It was the last stop before the Florida Keys, so she filled the De Soto with gasoline. Service stations in this area were charging 25 cents a gallon, more than she was used to paying. She hoped the cost of living in Key West would not be high. She was ready: prepared for the final 130 miles along US Route One, leaving mainland Florida and island-hopping over 42 bridges.

15 HIGHWAY OVER SEAS TO KEY WEST

Movers and Shakers of the 1890s or 1900s had discussed ideas of linking North America to Cuba, the Caribbean Islands and Central and South America by a series of motor and ferry routes: an International Overseas Highway. Henry Flagler had retired from Standard Oil when he was 53. Twenty plus years later, at age 75, the multi-millionaire financier decided the time was right for him to push forward to the town of Key West where he built the Casa Marina hotel. Fishing was great, the tropical climate would entice Northerners, and a car ferry would extend the sugar, orange and cigar exports from Cuba.

On January 30, 1905 Henry M Flagler announced he would construct a railroad from the Florida mainland, across 130 miles, spanning the string of small islands to the final destination, the island of Key West. He had extended the Florida East Coast railway from Jacksonville to Miami. The Panama Canal was opening up soon. This new Miami-to-Key West leg would then extend onto Cuba via car and ferry boat, making the North and South American link closer to culmination.

Flagler and his chief engineer, Joseph Meredith, employed 3000 to 4000 men, including Greek divers. They worked long hours. Feeding, housing and providing water was in itself a mammoth responsibility. With no freshwater available in the Keys, drinking water for the men had to be delivered daily by barge from the mainland.

The men slogged through the Everglades marshes and the mangrove swamps. More than 75 miles were built over marshland or water. Concrete pilings had to be sunk into deep water. The mosquito swarms were beyond imagination, yet during the seven years of work, there were no epidemics among the workers.

But it was the hurricanes that were the nemesis.

A hurricane in October 1906 blew up to 125 miles an hour, blowing 70 men out to sea and destroying floating cabins and houseboats. The hurricane of 1909 blew away miles of track, slowing down the progress, but none of the completed viaducts were damaged.

Yet Henry Flagler and his crew of men did it! They completed the overseas Highway on January 21, 1912. The very next day Mr. Flagler now 82 years of age, rode his railroad to Key West, Florida. He was greeted there by a cheering crowd of more than 10,000 people. For 22 years it was possible to travel Miami to Key West and on to Cuba via rail and steamer for the round-trip price of $24... And that included meals.

Until the hurricane of 1935.

The Key West newspaper, "The Citizen", contacted Fred Johnson, Supervisor of Perky, Florida (later called "Sugarloaf"). Perky, located in the southern stretch of the Florida Keys, was not affected at all by wind or water during the 1935 hurricane.

According to the September 5, 1935 newspaper article it was Matecumbe area, in the northern section of the Keys, that had suffered extreme damage, as described by Fred Johnson. Mr. Johnson had surveyed the area from a low-flying plane. He told the newspaper reporter, "The Matecumbe area and surrounding territory presented the worst areas of destruction that I have ever seen."

"Matecumbe is flat. Nothing is left standing in that area except one building in Tavernier, and of the many thousands of coconut trees, only a few are left. Long Key is another scene which is evidence of the terrific forces of wind and waves." The newspaper article continued to quote Mr. Johnson, saying it would be difficult to estimate the number of dead because the train, which had been sent down from the mainland to return workers to Hollywood Florida, had blown off the track.

He said "About 10 cars have been washed off the tracks and some of the occupied cars look to be about 400 feet from the right-of-way. It was there I believe the greatest loss of life will be recorded. There were approximately 30 miles of track washed out all together. While the concrete viaducts were apparently standing and undamaged, there were many places on them where the ties and tracks had completely disappeared. In other places, the tracks were there, but warped and twisted as to be completely useless. At Key Vaca several miles of tracks seem to have disappeared.

"Other terrible evidence of the fury of the winds were a great number of automobiles at different points of the Keys, apparently smashed and twisted out of shape. I have heard of the destruction wrought by storms and winds and have seen the ravages of the elements here in Key West when I was much younger, but never have I imagined that such a beautiful and prosperous section of the country could be transformed into such a terrible picture of desert devastation, suffering, and woe as that part of the Florida Keys over which I passed this morning" said Mr. Johnson.

The railroad was not repaired and replaced. Instead, it was the State of Florida that acquired the Keys extension of the railroad. In 1938 the

Overseas Highway was completed on the road laid bare where the train tracks had been, but over the original viaducts, which had remained secure.

It was in 1955 when Liz Steele was driving down that overseas highway, on her way to Key West. Florida Keys does not lay in a straight line directly south. Instead, the string of Keys' islands curve until finally the road points west. There is an argument: in Spanish is Key West "Cayo Hueso" or Cayo Oeste". Any mariner will tell you the original and correct name is Oeste, Spanish for West.

The concept of the narrow islands is, in itself, a distraction. One continues to glance right and left, checking to see if it is really water they're going to be seeing just a couple of hundred feet behind a storefront or a small hotel.

Certainly when driving across the bridge it is the water that is the eye magnet. The color of the water defies description. Liz wondered how she could describe the colors to her grandmother: aquamarine, teal, turquoise, cornflower, sky blue, cerulean, blue green, sea green, azure. She knew words could not convey the astounding beauty of the seafloor that could be seen through the clear shallows, the reflection of the blue sky and puffy white clouds on the surface, and hundreds of sun-gold glints flickering on the wind-ripples of the water's surface.

Small metal mile-markers, green with white numbers, posted along the highway, told Liz she was very close. Mile-marker 7, 6, 5! number 5! A sign reading, "You are now on the island city of Key West, Florida".

16 END OF THE RAINBOW

Continuing along US 1, now named North Roosevelt Boulevard, she passed a couple of motels, but kept going until she saw "Simonton Street". On impulse she made a left turn. She remembered reading a blurb somewhere that John Simonton had purchased the island in 1822 for two thousand dollars.

Must be the main street, she thought. It wasn't, but it did lead her to a row of motels with the ocean in sight at the end of the block. She pulled into one, checked in, and dug her swimsuit out of the suitcase. She changed into her bathing suit. Tossing a cotton blouse over her shoulders, she slipped into her penny loafers, gathered up a motel towel and, like a lemming, she just propelled herself toward the water.

This proved to be a mistake. Nothing but an asphalt parking lot to her left and a bar on her right. Someone took pity on her, the dazed tourist, and redirected her around the corner to South Beach at the foot of Duval Street.

The magnetism of the water continued to draw her. She dropped the towel and slipped off her blouse and shoes. Liz walked directly into the ocean, still clutching her motel key. The water surprised her. It was warm and very shallow. She stopped when the sandy bottom turned into sea grasses. She sat down into the water until only her neck and head showed. Looking back at the beach, the view of the coconut palm fronds swaying in the breeze and the ocean gently lapping onto the sand made her feel as if she were in a South Seas movie.

A volleyball net had attracted a dozen or so people. Liz watched the activity, not following the game but looking at the players. There was a tall and tanned guy in faded flowered swim trunks and two men in white t-shirts and dark blue shorts: one a muscular blonde and the other sporting a crew cut. The fourth was a small fellow wearing a bandana covering his hair from forehead back to the nape of his neck. He was also wearing a white elasticized swimsuit, very skimpy.

Of the several girls, one was a tall blonde Amazon in a two-piece cotton bathing suit. Another gal had long black hair, wearing a black satin suit that could barely contain her voluptuous breasts. She was calling out the score after each play. One girl reminded Liz of her girlfriend in San Francisco. Liz was suddenly overcome with loneliness.

She wished her old friends were here with her. Or her brothers. Or her grandmother. Or somebody, anybody, that she knew. She was bombarded by self-questioning: What am I doing here? Where will I live? What kind of work will I get? What is my plan?

Her psyche dripping with self-pity, notwithstanding she was set in the picture of paradise, she slowly walked out of the saltwater and up on shore. There was a snack shop in one corner of the beach. She headed towards it to buy a Coca-Cola and a newspaper, but then remembered she had only brought her towel and key to the beach, but no money. She trudged back to her motel, the sounds of the volleyball players' laughter following her down the street.

Showering off the salt water, she dressed in shorts and a shirt and went out to the motel's pool/patio area, choosing a chaise positioned under a coconut tree. Someone had left a local newspaper on the empty chair next to her, so she reached over and picked it up.

There were only 12 pages, but the last page listed Want Ads. Not much there: receptionist, salesclerk, typist, waitress. No problem: tomorrow she would check with one of the employment agencies in town.

The next morning, dressed in high-heels, stockings, a dress, and a strand of pearls. Liz was too hot and sticky to don the white gloves that would have been appropriate for job interviews Up North. There had been no employment agencies listed in the telephone book, so she asked at the motel's front desk, but was met with a quizzical look and referred to someone else standing there, but they didn't have the answer, either.

Undaunted, she asked if the motel manager would know. He came to the desk and said that he only knew of the State employment agency, but mostly they just handled day-laborers for construction sites. She obtained the address anyway. She looked for a morning newspaper, but was told the local paper came out in the late afternoon.

Armed with a map of the island, she noted the Simonton Street, which ran across the island, spanned about two-mile width, going from the Atlantic Ocean/Florida Straits north to the Florida Bay in the Gulf of Mexico. It hardly seemed worthwhile to drive that short distance to the location on the State employment office, but the tropical heat was intense. Liz chose to drive her car.

There were no other women in the waiting room. It looked like the construction workers had found jobs; there were only two men lounging in the chairs, sitting with their legs stuck out, wearing the white rubber boots distinctive of men who were shrimpers.

Liz sat primly in one of the straight pinewood chairs until one of the workers, seen behind a long unmanned counter, looked up and asked, "Are you waiting for someone?"

Liz approached the counter and said she would like to apply for a position. Workers at the other desks in the room looked up at her in unison, as if that was a strange request. The woman beckoned her to come through the low wooden gate. Liz sat on the edge of the chair at the desk and handed the woman a copy of her work resume. The woman glanced at it and looked at the person at the next desk. Each raised one eyebrow.

"Is there something wrong?" Liz asked. She was assured nothing was amiss, but the woman patiently told her they had no listings for the type of position she might be interested in. Few businesses utilized the service of the State agency. Most jobs were filled by work-of-mouth within each company or by friends who knew someone. "Try the newspaper," was the suggestion.

Yesterday's newspaper was back at the motel but before returning there she found out the main shopping area was Duval Street. She wanted some open-weave sandals: her feet were too hot in her penny-loafers. She needed shorts and blouses without collars. Oh, yes, and sleeveless. Plus a loose skirt, to let the breezes blow and cool her legs. Taking her purchases back to her hotel room, she quickly removed the dress and stockings.

Now she really needed a job. No more buying clothes. But the languidness of the tropics had already infected her. Instead of job-hunting, she donned her still slightly damp bathing suit and her new sandals. Gathering together a towel, coin-purse, sunglasses, motel key, and yesterday's still salty cover-up blouse, she walked back to South Beach.

She went into the snack shop on the beach and bought a coke and ham sandwich. Moving back into the partial shade, she propped her back against a coconut palm tree, folded open her old newspaper and took a bite from her sandwich. The studying of the newspaper help-wanted ads was delayed by the distraction of sounds from the nearby volleyball area.

Some of yesterday's players were leaping at the ball, scattering sand and laughter. There were the Flowered trunks, the Crewcut, the white Skimpy suit, the Amazon and the Voluptuous one. Liz munched on her sandwich and watched the interaction of the group.

"Hi. Join us. We need another player." Liz flinched, startled. Some guy was standing next to her. "Hey, sorry, I didn't mean to scare you. I noticed you yesterday. Want to play?"

Several thoughts raced through her mind, the way thoughts can do in split seconds. One was she thought she might choke on that last bite of food. Another was that she did not remember this guy with the steel blue eyes from yesterday. Nor had she seen him approach her today. What was he, a Ninja, invisible? And his words "Want to play?" brought forth from the recesses in her mind hearing that same question from when she was a child. For a nano-moment she was five years old. Then she coughed on the bite of ham.

The Ninja guy, Juan, leaned over and passed her the Coke she had propped up on the sand. "Better take a swallow of this." He sat down next to her.

17

CLEAR WATER AND MUDD

A week later loneliness, housing and a job were no longer problems. Juan had introduced her to the VolleyBall crowd. Now she was living with the Amazon (Sharon Bergdorf) until she found her own apartment. Skimpy Suit (Don Rexford) seemed to know all kinds of scuttlebutt around the island; he referred her to the local newspaper where she did get hired as a proofreader and gofer. And Liz and the Ninja (Juan Robertson) had gone on a double date with Sharon and the Flowered Trunks (Rodney Rodriguez) to the drive-in movie.

Plus she had plans to go sailing to the Dry Tortugas next weekend.

She had seen a small notice in the local paper. The Audubon Society group had hired a shrimp boat to take the members bird watching at one of the clusters of island of the Dry Tortugas, located 70 miles west of Key West. There was room for a few more sign-on persons: $5.00, bring your own water, food, can-opener and blanket for the overnight visit. There was no refrigeration, ice or drinking water there and no fires could be lit. Liz signed-on and was given an Audubon membership card, too.

Later she wrote to her grandmother that the only introduction to the Dry Tortugas was a depressing description printed on the back of a local postcard: "Down the labyrinth of gloomy corridors inside Fort Jefferson, the visit can envision the tragedy of Dr. Samuel Mudd, sentenced there as punishment for having set the broken leg of John Wilkes Booth." She also wrote that she was impressed by the isolated beauty of the seven outcroppings of coral reef and sand that could scarcely be called islands. The fort was situated on Garden Key and on Bird Key was a wildlife refuge dedicated in 1908 to protect the Sooty Tern rookery. She sent Shirley a postcard of the birds.

The lighthouse and the fort were built in the mid 1800's, the light to warn ships of the coral reef shoals and the United States government's intent for the fort had been to protect commerce shipped from the Mississippi River to the Atlantic Ocean, controlling navigation in the Gulf of Mexico. The fort was never completed because, more than 20 years after construction had begun, it was realized that the fort was sinking. The weight of almost 16 million bricks was moving the sand and rocks away. The solid coral rock that was to have been its foundation, was not on the sea's surface but 80 feet deeper.

During the Civil War the Union Army utilized the isolated fort as a prison for captured deserters. When the fort's doctor died during the 1869 Yellow Fever epidemic, the prisoner Dr. Samuel Mudd was released from being chained to a wall, in order for him to care for the sick soldiers and prisoners.

On Monday, when she began her work at the newspaper, the editor overheard Liz telling about her trip. He asked her if she would like to submit an article about her adventures on Dry Tortugas. Here is what was published:

Forty Key Westers on a boat soon are all friends. It does not take long for one to find out that the amusing round man with the camera is Robert Hermes, a free-lance photographer whose specialty is nature studies; the attractive girl sitting on the stern of the boat is a school teacher, and the rugged man who looks like Burt Lancaster really runs the local beauty school.

The crew was friendly, too. They started to teach us how to make up the leaders and wind line around a nail in time to the tune 'Hot Ziggety, Oh What You Do To Me'. A crew member took out an immense hook big enough to catch a whale. We thought he was kidding but he baited it, tied the line to the boat, and one woman sat there fishing.

What excitement when she felt a bite on that line! The captain cut the speed of the boat and everyone got out his camera, scrabbling up on top of boxes to get a good shot. Oh, how disappointed we all were when the crew pulled in the baitless hook. At least one woman had a good excuse to tell a fish story about the big one that got away.

The approach to Fort Jefferson was a photographer's delight, as is the entire island, and I finally settled on a view of one corner of the fort, with a school of shrimp boats in the water behind it. To ham up the whole thing, I waited until we were passing a buoy with a frigate bird sitting on top.

Stories of mystery and intrigue about the island of the Dry Tortugas had been passed around the boat until most of the group felt like approaching the island with cutlasses clenched between their teeth and the Jolly Roger unfurled. A crew member offered to show me the fort, with typical sailor's tall tales of skeletons and gold sealed into hidden rooms. We toured the entire fort, peering adventurously into dark nooks by lighting a match. I felt like Tom Sawyer!

The gun room galleries, with small windows opening out to sea and the other side entirely exposed to the inner compound, were lighted dramatically by bright sunshine quietly pouring in the open sea. It was breathtaking to come around a dim corner of the six-sided fort and suddenly see twenty-two arched galleries consecutively diminishing to a minute frame for the next far-distant corner of this hexagon.

With perfect weather for outdoor sleeping, some of our party chose grassy beds, but most preferred the overhead shelter of the fort and established squatters rights by placing their blankets or sleeping bags or cots in the main floor galleries.

However, on my tour I had been very impressed with one particular tower and chose this sumptuous suite for my sleeping quarters. Three exposures looked out on Bush Key, over which the birds were soaring: the open sea, where a few shrimp boats had anchored; and a small, quiet beach with such clear water I could watch the fish come in close to shore. But most of all I like the slapping, splashing sound of the water up against the moat wall.

Although it would have been beautiful to wake up in my chosen Fort Jefferson tower, the light of a crescent moon made everything eerie, so I quickly moved my blanket down to a place where I was surrounded by lots of people. An active imagination is fun in the daylight, but trying to go to sleep with visions of skeletons sealed in the walls made my move to more companionable quarters imperative. Even my neighbor's snoring seemed soothing.

Just when night started to turn into morning, I awoke. Like the first sunbeams, I tiptoed around the corner of the fort. Choosing a spot on the edge of the moat where I could best see the sunrise, I attempted to capture the mood through penned words and sketches, but the grandeur so captivated my attention away from the paper that I sat in mute worship.

A pebble tossed into the moat splashed my hypnotic gaze away from the scene. I glanced up to a window in the fort where another passenger stood framed in the crumbling outline of a window, like a prince in an ancient castle. He waved a hello to me and saluted the sunrise.

I continued my sun-worshipping by watching a Man-of-War birds float on lifting currents as the breeze swept up from across the fort, but finally the scent of fresh coffee, boiled over a campfire, turned my attention from this beautiful scene to food. Like all the meals we shared on the island, breakfast was a party. Everyone sat cross-legged on the ground, exchanging tidbits of food and conversation and waving goodbye to the movie star Francis Langford as her Evinrude yacht pulled away from the island.

On Bush Key, the Terns were nesting. Superintendent Luis took photographers Hermes, who looks like Churchill, Allen Cruckshank of the National Audubon Society, who look, walks and talks like Gary Cooper, and Mrs. Cruckshank, with her broad-brimmed hat picturesquely tied down with a silk bandana, to the island to set up bird blinds. Mr. and Mrs. Cruckshank were taking photographs for the Audubon television show of the Roseate Terns and the Noddy and Sooty Terns. The Dry Tortugas is the most northern known colony where the latter two will nest.

Our boat took many of the group out deep sea fishing, but we lazy folks just stayed at the fort and swam, sunned, fished off the pier and talked. Time could have stopped on the good, warm, sunny day. We would have sat under the trees forever, enjoying a whiff of breeze, but our shrimp boat return and departure time was announced.

How sad it was to gather up blankets and water canteens to leave the island. But we have remembrances of the beauties of nature and of the fort, mysterious stories, the fun of the boat trip, and newly made friends. The only outward sign that we have made the trip is a slight sailor's swagger as we head home, walking down the street on our sea legs.

Mr. Bartlett, the newspaper editor, had assumed he would only receive a short report of the trip from Liz, but he liked the feature-story approach and he had her article printed in the Sunday issue of the newspaper. The Audubon members called him and gave him positive remarks about the article. Mr. Bartlett called her into his office.

Except for Mr. Bartlett's office, two huge rooms encompassed the newspaper building. The massive printing presses filled one area. The other room had many desks where the writers, reporters and business personnel worked. For the new person to have received a command performance call to the office of the editor resulted in everyone looking up from his/her desk. They watched Liz as she walked to his office.

She wondered what she had done wrong!

He started out telling her that he had expected only a short article from her.

She defensively started saying, "But you asked for my impressions..."

Mr. Bartlett interrupted her. "Wait to hear what I have to say to you."

She stood mute and nervous.

"How would you like to write an article a week for the newspaper?" he asked.

"About what?" she asked.

"Anything you like. You write it and submit it to me for review."

"How much do I get paid a linear inch?" Liz reported, having read somewhere that was how reporters got paid.

Mr. Bartlett laughed. He couldn't believe this young, new employee of his was so brassy. "Well, let's just see what you write first," he told her and he waved her away, out of his office.

She was perspiring and walked from his office to the restroom to wash under her arms, then returned to her desk to continue her proofreading for the next edition, saying nothing to the other employees.

After work, when she got back to Sharon's apartment, she told Sharon what had happened in Mr. Bartlett's office.

"Liz, you are a wild one! You are lucky he laughed instead of kicking you out. But here you are: a reporter!" and Sharon laughed, too.

The next several weeks, continuing with her proofreading job, but submitting one article a week to Mr. Bartlett, Liz had stories printed about beach volley-ball, what to wear in a tropical climate, and the problems of hunting for an apartment.

Liz understood that Sharon's offer for her to stay with her was short-term. Indeed, Sharon's mother was expected in Key West soon and would be staying in Sharon's apartment. As it was, Liz and Sharon slept in the one bed. Sharon had a postcard pasted on the refrigerator door. It was a picture of a very attractive woman in a two-piece swimsuit and a young man hugging her.This picture/postcard was taken in Mexico with her mother's current gigolo.

Sharon explained that her mother traveled a lot and always sent her postcards made from photos of her and her current boyfriend. Liz had assumed that Sharon's parents were divorced, but she said no, her father was older and his number one interest was working. He also enjoyed having a beautiful wife to show off to his friends (when she was home between trips). They had an understanding about her needs.

When Liz could not hide her bafflement about how a marriage could continue like that Sharon scoffed at Liz. "I suppose you expect to marry someone who is handsome and has a gorgeous build. You'll marry for love, even if he is poor."

"Of course," Liz insisted. "Would you marry someone you don't love?"

Sharon scoffed, "You are naive, Liz. You can love anyone if he is a nice person. You become more fond as you share life over the years. If you think you are in love you'd better keep your brain thinking sensible thoughts. Find someone you like and have fun in his company; make sure it's someone you can talk to and share thoughts with."

"Wow, some lecture! Okay, Sharon, I'll try that sensible approach. Actually, I have been thinking sensibly about my car. I don't need an automobile on this island. Do you think I could get much for my car? Then I'll just buy a bicycle."

Sharon asked what Liz had paid for the car in New Jersey, then told her, "Leave it to me Liz. I'm good at this, you wait and see." And with that, Rodney Rodriguez arrived to take Sharon out for the evening.

Liz realized she was inhibiting Sharon's lifestyle and knew both would be more comfortable when she found her own apartment. Liz started to scan the newspaper ads. As proofreader, she had first chance at the classified ads before the paper was released to the public. This didn't help too much, because the pickings were slim.

Like every town, some areas were less desirable than others, so Liz went on wild-goose chases that ended up at an unkempt shack with torn-out screens. Another was a house trailer where she could see the ground through holes in the flooring. One said "Bedroom, share the bath, "but it turned out to be a share-the-bed, also, with unsavory-appearing inhabitants.

Finally Liz chose a second-story apartment, sparsely furnished but overlooking Garrison Bight, a cove where the party-fishing boats docked. Sharon took her out for a celebration pizza and told her she had a buyer for her car. Rodney wanted a car and Sharon quoted a price $200 more than Liz had paid, and 'reluctantly' came down $50, so Liz would make a profit of $150! After she completed the transfer of the car, Liz bought a frying pan, a large and small cooking pot, kitchen utensils, paper goods, groceries and two wineglasses, installing everything in her new place.

That night she slept solidly, having the bed to herself.

Or so she thought. The next morning she was covered with pink welts. She wondered what bed bugs looked like, but when she peeled back the sheets she saw many fleas jumping about. Then she realized her ankles were tingling and saw little black dots, fleas, all over her feet and lower legs. She shrieked and ran into the bathroom.

Standing in the tub, Liz ran the water and filled it to the brim. She sat down, neck deep, immersing herself, and then shampooed her hair, too.

The previous tenant had kept cats in the apartment, which had been vacant for a month. Those fleas were hungry!

She went to work with wet hair and looked at the new classified ads.

During her lunch break she went to see a Mrs. Bates, who had a garage apartment available. The unit was tastefully decorated, including original oil paintings on the walls done by her daughter. Use of the swimming pool was included. The garden was lovely and Mrs. Bates and Liz sat on the brick patio fringed with hibiscus and frangipani, discussing the rent.

Liz loved the place, but the rent was double what she could afford and Mrs. Bates was living off her rental income, so could not reduce it to what Liz could afford. However, she said she knew of a small cottage on Elizabeth Street that might be right for Liz. Mrs. Bates phoned her friend and set up an appointment for Liz to see it after work that afternoon.

When Liz returned to work there was a small Colored boy sitting at her desk, doodling on a sheet of clean newsprint. He jumped up, alarmed, when Liz came up to the desk, but she recognized him as Shorty, the boy who Mr. Bartlett paid to sweep the sidewalks in front of the building. He arrived after school each day, pulling his wagon with him, and using his pay to buy a few newspapers that he quickly sold at a small profit in front of Sloppy Joe's or Captain Tony's bars.

He started to apologize but she was busy thinking about how she just had to find another apartment fast, so she smiled, and said, "Don't worry about it," She shooed him away so she could get back to work. She telephoned Sharon and asked if she could please spend the night with her, explaining why.

The cottage on Elizabeth Street was separate from the main house. Situated at the rear of the lot was a small, one-room apartment, with a shady porch off the living room that overlooked the garden. The double sliding glass doors gave a more open feeling to the room. In one corner was a small refrigerator, sink and small stove. The bathroom was tiny but clean. The best feature: the ceiling fan over the sofa bed. And the price was right.

The next afternoon Liz looked for Shorty to arrive after school. She went out front and would have missed him, but saw a wagon turning the corner of the building. Shorty was surprised to learn she wanted him to help her move her things from the apartment to the cottage after work.

Liz stuck out her hand, "Is it a deal?"

Shorty just looked up at Liz, blank faced. It was a new experience for him. Hesitatingly he stuck out his hand. Liz took his hand and shook.

No sooner had Rodney bought the DeSoto than he decided to drive to Miami for a few days. Liz asked Sharon what kind of a job he had and she answered "Bolita." This meant nothing to Liz, so Sharon explained it was a 'numbers game." You bet certain numbers with Rodney, who wrote them in a small notebook and the amount paid to him. The numbers were thrown in Havana, Cuba and announced on Saturdays on the Cuban radio station, which could be heard coming out of open doors and windows of Key West, loud and clear. You won, Rodney paid you. You lost, he gained.

Liz would have asked Sharon and Rodney to help her move her items to the new cottage, but with the DeSoto not available, she was glad she thought about Shorty and his wagon. It just seemed more "Key Westy" to her to do it this way.

Sharon had walked over from her place to Liz' flea-bitten apartment to help. When Shorty saw how badly Liz had been bitten on her legs, the ten-year-old boy would not let Liz go upstairs. He and Sharon brought down the items and loaded up the wagon. Actually, it took two trips, but they enjoyed the slow and companionable walk.

Shorty warmed up to having an audience and kept the two girls intrigued with stories about roosters having cock-fights and how to kill a rat (place a small bucket half-filled with water under the sink pipes coming from the wall, grease the pipe, the rat slips into the bucket head-first, cannot right himself and drowns).

Sharon instructed Liz to stay at the new cottage and start to put things away. She went back with Shorty for the second and final load. While there Sharon complained to the landlord about the fleas. He returned Liz' rent money to her. When Sharon handed the money to Liz, she insisted on buying lunch for the trio. Liz gave Shorty a few dollars for his help, then they went to the Two Brothers coffee shop. Liz bought three Cuban Mix sandwiches: six inches of Cuban bread with lettuce, tomato, cheese, roast pork and baked ham piled high. Shorty took his and said he had to hurry home.

Liz said, "Wait!" but Shorty had scurried off with his sandwich and his wagon.

18 SHORTY, HENDRY AND KIRK DOUGLAS

Liz worried she may have insulted her new little friend by giving him money. The next workday she looked for him and asked if she could take him to the Sunday afternoon movie matinee at the San Carlos theater on Duval Street. Hesitating for a moment, he answered that he could not go there, but would she like to go to his movie house, the Lincoln Theater, instead?

Finally the light bulb lit over Liz' head. Segregation. One day she had noticed two water fountains in the bus station, labeled "White" and "Colored" and was surprised such things still existed in modern 1955. Certainly she had never before been aware of any segregation while living Up North. She had seen the two water fountains but she was so shocked she had stood staring at them, understanding coming slowly. She took one step forward, toward the "Colored" fountain, but a man standing behind her said in a low and ominous voice, "Don't even think about doing that," and she had left the area.

She told Shorty, "Sure, the Lincoln Theater on Sunday."

Sunday at two in the afternoon Shorty Williams knocked on the cottage door. Liz was ready and two walked down Elizabeth to Petronia

Street. Shorty had said his Mama would like to meet Liz, was that okay with her? Mrs. Williams was seated on her front porch. Shorty introduced the two women.

Mrs. Williams said, “Shorty says you the lady who asked him to the movies.”

Another boy about Shorty’s size was peeping around the open front door. Shorty whispered to Liz, “That’s my brother Hendry.”

“Yes, Mrs. Williams. Is that all right? He was such a help to me when I moved.”

Mrs. Williams asked, “Where you goin’?” and Shorty answered that one: “Lincoln”.

Mrs. Williams shrugged. “If you want.”

Shorty whispered to Liz, “Can my brother come, too?”

Liz looked at Mrs. Williams, who shrugged again.

“Okay, Hendry, come on.” and Shorty led the three of them down Petronia Street toward Duval, then Whitehead Street and beyond.

When they arrived at the Lincoln Theater, there was already a long line of Colored adults waiting at the box office. At the approach of Liz and the two boys, the line of people all moved back, allowing Liz to be first. She was embarrassed and said no, but there was insistence from the crowd and she suddenly became nervous about being in a strange situation.

Shorty tugged at her hand and said, “Come on.”

Holding her hand, he led her to the ticket office where Liz said, “One adult, two children”.

At the inside doorway was a White man taking tickets. He said to Shorty, “I thought I told you you couldn’t come back here,” but Shorty pointed to Liz. The man’s mouth dropped open. He took the tickets and Shorty led them down to the aisle to seats.

Liz sat between them and gave them a motherly lecture. “Now you boys behave and be quiet” The movie was Kirk Douglas as Cyclops or Spartacus or something, but it had scarcely begun when the ticket-taker slid in the row behind Liz and tapped on her shoulder.

"Someone wants to see you," he told Liz.

That was a surprise to Liz. Who had she told she was going to The Lincoln?

"Who?" she asked, but he just repeated, "Someone wants to see you."

19

UPSETTING THE STATUS QUO

Liz told the boys to behave, she would be right back. She exited the theater. There was no one there. The man pointed out the door to the police car parked out front. "Him."

That worried Liz. Was her grandmother ill? How did they know to find her there?

The only person she might have mentioned the movie to was Lawrence, an Air Force guy she had met while playing volleyball, but he would have no connection with her grandmother.

She approached the car and went up to the policeman in the driver's seat, "Yes?"

He said, "Get in."

This made Liz quite wary. She had heard Tiki Gomez (the Voluptuous One) telling other girls at the beach a story where a local policeman had allegedly driven a girl out to a deserted area on South Boulevard and insisted he would not give her a speeding ticket if she performed a sexual act.

The policeman repeated to Liz more forcefully, "Get in."

She walked around the car, opened the door to the front seat and sat, tugging at her skirt to straighten it to cover her knees. She noticed he seemed nervous and watched her do that. The idea crossed Liz' mind: she wondered if he thought she had a knife strapped to her thigh and was going to attack him. The thought started a smile on her face until he suddenly pulled way, driving down the street.

"Where are we going?" Liz asked him. Now it was she who was nervous.

She thought, Oh, God, the Boulevard. "Where?" she insisted, but he wouldn't answer.

He pulled up to the police station and, for the first time, it occurred to her it must have been because she had gone to the Colored movie theater. Oh, well, slap my wrist and let me go home, for heaven's sake, she thought.

The policeman escorted her into an office where a fat police officer sat behind a desk that had a wooden name placard positioned where she could see: Chief Perez.

"Do you know why you're here?" he asked her.

"No. Why?"

"I'm asking the questions. Why did you go to the Lincoln Theater today?"

"To take my little friend and his brother to see a movie."

"But why to the Lincoln?"

"Because he said he wasn't allowed to go to the San Carlos."

Several policemen had gathered within the room and were standing behind Liz. One of them snickered at that answer. The chief raised his head and all were silent.

"Let me ask you, young lady, if you saw a Colored person on the street, would you speak to them and say 'Hello'?"

"Sure. Wouldn't you?"

More snickers.

"Show me your identification. You do have some identification, don't you?"

"Well, there's my library card, Audubon card and driver's license."

Chief Perez asked, "What else is in that purse? Can I examine it?"

"Certainly," Liz said, and handed it across the desk.

He opened it and removed one item. "What is rolled up in this paper napkin?"

Liz told the Chief, "You are welcome to open it up."

The Chief unfolded the napkin. Six Oreo cookies spilled out.

Liz explained, "I brought them for us to eat during the movie."

Snickers from the rear. The Chief stood up, glared at the back of the room, then sat back down behind his desk.

"Where were you last night?"

She couldn't figure out why that had to do with anything. Liz hadn't witnessed an accident or anything. Where was he heading? She answered, "The Cuban Club."

"Alone?"

"No, with a friend."

"A man?"

"Yes. He's in the Air Force, but was invited by member of the Club to attend the dance."

"Did you have any alcohol there?"

"No, I didn't."

"Can you prove that?

"Well, yes, if that is important to you. Are you familiar with the Cuban Club and the area where their bar is located?"

"Yes," answered the Chief.

"Well, everyone was ordering Cuba Libras, rum and Coke, but my friend is only 20, and since it isn't legal for him to have alcohol, we both ordered Coca Colas, and I felt like the bartender got mad that we didn't order something more expensive. I'm sure he will remember us."

Now it was an outright laugh from the rear of the room behind Liz. The Chief cut a mean glance at them.

"How old are you?"

"I am twenty-one."

"What about after the dance? Did you go drinking or home?"

"No. I had heard there's a wonderful ice-cream place next door at El Enon, but when we went there it was closed."

"So what did you do?"

"We went to Howard Johnson's for ice cream, but they had just closed."

The Chief was getting impatient. "Can we get to what the two of you did next?"

"He escorted me home!"

"So where were you at two o'clock in the morning?"

"In my bed."

"What were you doing?"

"Sleeping."

"Alone?"

"Yes."

"Can you prove that?"

Liz was getting tired of this. She said, "Actually, Yes, I believe so. You see, when we got to my place, we stood under the light over my door and while we stood there he gave me a goodnight kiss. I noticed the lady in the house next to mine. She had pulled aside her curtain and was peeping at us. She must have seen him leave and me to go into my place all alone."

The Chief sighed. "Have you ever been in trouble before?'

"No, sir. Am I in trouble now?"

"Yes. You were seen in Colored Town early this morning, soliciting. We've got you for prostitution."

Liz flared up angrily, "Oh, that's ridiculous, sir!"

"Well, it had to be you, because it was a White girl, and there aren't two white girls in town who would go into Colored Town. I have witnesses saying it was you, all right. Now what do you have to say to that?"

She shook her head. "I am sorry, but they are mistaken. Perhaps if they came here and saw me, they would see that I am not that girl."

"Good idea. Here's one now. Portier, come here. Didn't you say this is the girl you saw last night soliciting?"

A Colored detective came forward. He stared at Liz and she gave a steady stare back.

"Yes, that's her, sir," the detective said.

The Chief asked Liz, "What do you have to say about that?"

"I am sorry, sir, but he is mistaken. Perhaps you can bring in one of the other persons who saw someone last night."

The Chief seemed exasperated. He asked Liz, "Do you want to make a telephone call?"

"You mean a lawyer? I don't know any lawyers. No, there's no one I wish to call. Why? Am I arrested?"

The Chief sat back in his chair. "No! Get out of here! And don't you dare be seen going to the other side of Whitehead Street because the next time I will have you escorted right up to the County Line."

Liz retrieved her purse and identification cards. The police at the back of the room all moved, parting the way to the exit door. What made Liz even madder about the whole thing was that she walked out of the police station and it was very dark. She was leery about walking down the deserted street all alone on such a dark night with no one to protect her. Like a policeman.

Detective Portier phoned Juan Robertson the next morning. They talked but never used names. They recognized each other's voice, but if they were in a situation where they had to disguise voices, they had a prearranged code of phrases.

Juan answered his telephone. "Yes?"

No further acknowledgement was said. Since code phrases were not the response, the coast was clear, so Portier continued. "Saw you ten days ago with the new stuff. The Man had me corner her. Want to check?"

"Thanks," said Juan and he hung up.

20 THE GATHERING OF THE BAND

The "Brothers Assisting National Defense", a.k.a. BAND, met on a sporadic dates but always at 2:00 a.m. in a storage shed near the cemetery. It was located on a lot off a narrow alley that was traveled infrequently. BAND member Juan Robertson offered use of the shed. The building was placed in one corner, with no windows on the two sides that were closest to neighbors. The two other sides of the shed had small windows that were covered with wooden Hurricane shutters. The lot had high shrubbery surrounding it, with the remaining area covered with grass that Juan kept neatly trimmed so it would cause no concern to neighbors and be of little or no notice.

He made a point of being friendly with the neighbors, yet giving out minimal information. They did know his parents had retired early from a successful business Up North and had moved to Key West, living in a home on Henderson Street for eight years until both died in their mid-fifties, leaving some properties to their son Juan. Since he appeared to have no job, and his answers to their questions were somewhat vague, they believed him to be "a little simple in the head", not knowing he had graduated from the University of Pennsylvania.

Inside the shed were gardening tools, a lantern and other items that could seem to be innocent plus the usual hurricane supplies; canned foods, bottled water, candles and even an old canvas folding cot. If there was need to utilize light at night, the solid door could be covered from the inside with a blanket, to further insure no hint of light could be seen from outside. The roof had two air vents.

Each member of the BAND had a key to access the shed. When they met, they simply squatted in a circle or sat on the floor, using a small flashlight for brief moments until each person was settled in. The usual group included:

Oscar Boyd Fisher ("O.B.") age 38, an insurance salesman. Since checking accounts were suspect in those days. O.B. would visit homes on a weekly basis to collect cash for the insurance accounts. The small weekly payments were easier for low-income families to meet. The housewives loved the out-going, friendly insurance man, who always wore a white shirt and necktie, even on hot tropical days. Perhaps that is why he frequently requested a glass of water, which did require them to leave him alone in the living room for a few minutes. Other times he asked to use their bathroom. When the housewives would compare notes about this "safe" man who came to their houses every week, they decided if he drank less water, he wouldn't have to pee so much.

Joe Davidson, 32, who worked at the radio station as a sound engineer. He was quiet, sort of faded into the woodwork, and nobody really paid much attention to him. He had access to all the latest national and international news that became available to the radio station. Also he operated a ham short-wave radio from his bedroom at home.

Blackie Gomez, 24, was a driver for Keys Transport Trucking Company. He was very popular in the Cuban neighborhoods, especially with the girls, young and old. The grandmothers would tell him about news they received in letter they got from back home in Cuba. He drove his big truck to Miami and back three times every week.

Isabel Cothron, 52, worked at the Post Office. Although a female, the men considered her 'one of the boys', which secretly vexed her. She knew about everything that went in and out of the Post Office.

George Portier, 44, a Key West detective, a Colored man, was active and respected throughout the Colored community and with the White Conchs, too. Although he had not been to college, his IQ was the highest of the group.

Juan Robertson, 29, was considered a 'floater'; someone with no ties, free to travel wherever needed. Although the locals considered him a little 'different', all the diverse groups in Key West accepted him. Interestingly he could mix in with a gathering in town, but if you were to ask someone if they had seen Juan Robertson there, they couldn't really remember noticing him. He avoided having anyone photograph him.

William Fredericks, 67, was called "Mr. Bill" out of respect for the fact that he was their Chief Agent. He spoke with an Eastern European accent. He was slim, ate sparsely, and exercised vigorously. A loner, they knew little about him and none seemed brave enough to ask. He led their meetings and submitted any reports they had to Washington, where they had all undergone their training.

Their mission: Do what they were told by their Washington headquarters.

Juan Robertson's mother had been born in Spain, but her parents had moved to America when she was 8 years old. She spoke very little Spanish, but it was from hearing her accent that Juan did so well in his four years of studying Castilian Spanish in college. Juan had just returned from an assignment in Bogota, Columbia.

The group's next assignment was to contact some friends in Cuba who wanted to get Batista out of power. They supported a student activist, Fidel Castro. The BAND needed a courier, someone new, who would be above suspicion to take some information to their contact there. Juan reported that he believe he had found their courier.

Liz wanted to write her weekly article about her episode with the police, but when she discussed the topic with Mr. Bartlett he suggested she hold off on that one for a while. He asked Liz if she would write about a real estate deal he had been hearing about and told her to check at the County Courthouse about certain properties.

She found out that a large tract of land on the island had been confiscated by the government a dozen years prior, when the Navy needed land to build housing for servicemen. The owner had not wanted to sell, but he was told it was vital for the war effort and a patriotic necessity. That is, they would either acquire it as "necessary-in-time-of-war" take-over, or the owner could accept a token figure as payment. A man with a family, he accepted the pittance.

Since the housing was no longer needed by the government and had been abandoned, the local man heard it was going up for surplus sale. As the previous owner, he had started arrangements in Washington to buy back the property at current evaluation. However, an out-of-town corporation had made a surprise move, blocking the naive local, and the sale had just been completed to "Lucas, Inc."

The local's name was F. L. Jackson, living on Pigeon Lane. Liz wondered why that seemed to have some meaning to her, but she couldn't bring just what it was to the surface of her memory.

When Liz left the newspaper office that evening at quitting time Juan Robertson just happened to be passing by. He stopped and chatted with her briefly, and then asked Liz if anyone had shown her the awesome sunsets of Key West. No? "Come on, I'll show you," he urged.

As they walked along the street, Juan stopped in a small shop and bought two sandwiches and two Coca-Colas, plus for dessert: two *piruli* candies. These were hardened sugar-syrup with layers of red, green and yellow coloring twirled on a lollipop stick.

When they arrived at the end of Duval Street, Juan led her along the shoreline to a rickety wooden pier. They had to walk with eyes down, careful to avoid gaps missing in the planks. At one side of the pier a shrimp boat was docked. Several women stood at a table, talking and laughing, while their hands were working fast. They were heading shrimp; pinching off the head of the crustacean. Some wore tattered gloves in an attempt to protect their fingers from cuts and punctures from the spiny shrimp shells.

Juan moved near the edge of the wooden pier. He took the sandwiches out of the paper bag and tore the bag open. He placed it on the pier to protect her skirt from getting soiled, and beckoned Liz to sit. With her feet dangling over the side, they sat together, munching on their food.

Juan said, "Watch for the green afterglow, when the sun sets". Puffy clouds turned from white against the blue sky to golden, then orange, an amazing peach color, then lavender and purple. It was quite a show, the sunset over the expanse of water, a small nearby island with a group of tall palms as part of the composition, plus an occasional shrimp boat passing by.

When the sun had completely sunk into the water, Juan reached over and hugged Liz to him. He gave her a lingering kiss.

"Wow, is that part of the sunset ritual?" Liz bantered, trying to make light of the effect his kiss had made upon her. He helped her up from the edge of the pier, advising they should leave the area before it was too dark to see the dangerous holes in the pier.

Juan asked, "Where would you like to go now?"

"It's been a long day. I think I'll head back to my place," Liz answered.

As Juan walked her home, he said, "I haven't seen you lately. What have you been doing? Did you go anywhere yesterday?"

And that was when Liz told him about her visit to the Lincoln movie theater with two little boys and then the police station interrogation saga.

Juan interjected a few questions, as Liz went on about the incident. He wished he could have been in that room during the questioning to have been able to observe her reactions at that time. He might make a report at the next meeting of the BAND.

When they arrived at her cottage Juan embraced Liz again, giving her a warm kiss, hoping to go inside her cottage with her. Although she had enjoyed his kiss, or perhaps because she did, she smiled, and said goodbye, entering the cottage alone.

Liz closed the door but didn't move any farther into room. She leaned against the door, thinking about her life in San Francisco, when she was so in love. She had grown up believing in the myth that a girl fell in love, married, and lived together happily ever after. Well, she had fallen in love with Lee, but it had ended there. Period. Now where would her life lead? How does someone fall out of love?

She wondered, should she lie on the couch and not move until she wasted away and died? Or should she be realistic and try to get on with her life? Easily said, but hard to deprogram her heart. Juan's kisses had awakened her body, but her heart resisted that restart spark.

Listless, she moved away from the door and walked into the bathroom. She showered, put on her nightclothes and went to bed, although it was still early.

21 BORN IN KEY WEST = CONCHS (KONKZ)

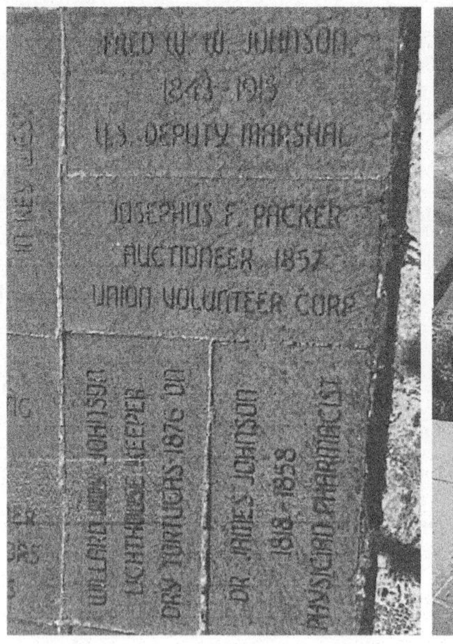

Sound asleep at two o-clock in the morning, she awakened suddenly. Jackson on Pigeon Lane? Wasn't that the name her sister-in-law Marian had given her? Matt's wife had told her to look them up;

they were descendant of Marian's great-great grandfather, but Liz hadn't gotten around to attempt to contact them. Could they be…?

In the morning Liz remembered that early morning thought. She phoned the Jacksons during her lunch-break. Mrs. Jackson told her to come by and see them anytime: how about after Liz got off from work?

Liz rode her bicycle to Pigeon Lane and found the address. It was a small white wooden house with green hurricane-shutters at each window. The roof was a shiny metal, perhaps tin, that reflected the sun's rays and deflected heat up and off the house. It was then that Liz noticed a wooden trim under the gutters across the porch; a lacy carving of graceful scrollwork..

She leaned her bike against the white picket fence and was met at the top of the steps by a woman who appeared to be about the same age as Liz or maybe a little older. She extended her hand and said, "Hello, I'm Trish Jackson. Let's sit in the porte cochere; it's shaded from the afternoon sun."

Attached to the side of the porch was a slanted roof extending out over a brick patio. A thick bower of flowering vines leaned on the roof, but allowed some of their branches to drip over the edge, making a fringe of crimson Bougainvillea and yellow Allamanda flowers. Trish gestured toward large wicker armchairs with poufy colorful cushions welcoming one to sit. On a low table between the chairs was a tray holding two tall glasses and a pitcher. Pink hibiscus flowers decorated the tray.

"Limeade?" offered Trish.

Liz had explained during her noontime phone call to Trish that her Mystic, Connecticut sister-in-law Marian Steele, had asked her to look up the Jacksons. She didn't want to mention the real estate connection yet.

Trish asked Liz about her trip to Key West and where she was working. She revealed that she, too, had come to Key West several years prior, and had met Bubba at a boat race. They wed four months later.

"It's been four years already. We have two girls: Fern age two and Heather, six months old." Trish pointed to the open window looking out over the porte cochere and said that both girls were napping right there. Bubba would be home from work soon.

"I'll tell you," Trish continued, "I couldn't have found a more wonderful, true-blue guy, my Bubba. He'll be getting home soon."

Liz asked, "Where does he work?"

"He is a plumber/pipe-fitter, working on piping the desalination plant. When you came to Key West, did you notice that big pipeline that runs along the highway? The U.S.Navy built that, bringing water to Key West from the Florida mainland 150 miles away. Before that everyone had to rely on their own home cistern. My mother-in-law tells me about how the Water Company used to come around and place small fish in her cistern to make sure the fish ate the mosquito larvae."

Liz asked, "What about the fish droppings in the bottom of the cisterns?"

Trish agreed. "I wondered about that, too. I suppose they didn't drink it when it got near the bottom of the cistern. It doesn't rain much in Key West so I don't how they ever managed to have enough water, especially when, in the old days, there were such large families in each house.

"This new desalination plant will process two and a half million gallons of fresh water every day by processing sea water through pipes, boiling it. The evaporation process results in steam: pure fresh water. Bubba has really been enjoying working on the complex piping system."

As if on cue, an old car drove up in front of the house and parked. "Oh, here he is now!"

Trish beamed a smile at the tall young man in a dark-blue coverall jumpsuit. "Hi, honey. We're over here" she said loudly and he came toward the two women. Trish introduced him. He said Hi and leaned over to kiss his wife. Then they heard a voice at the window.

A little blonde, blue-eyed girl, the two-year-old, was peering out the screen window and announced "I woke up."

Trish got up to go inside, but Bubba waved her down and said, "I'll see to the children, honey." He turned toward Liz and said, "Nice meeting you" as he went inside the house.

Liz remembered she meant to ask Bubba about the large tract of land on Ocean View. She mentioned it to Trish, who warned Liz not to mention it to Bubba.

Trish explained. "First, let me say that when Bubba and I got married, he carried me over this threshold. When I told him the house was nice, and when our family expanded we would of course move into a larger home. He got mad and told me that this house was Our Homestead. He would add on, but we would stay here.

"He feels his father had been pushed out of the family homestead, that property they owned on Ocean View. He felt betrayed, because he told an old school chum he was making an arrangement with the US government to get it back into the family. The school chum worked some politics and had the land presented to the city to sell at a profit. It would be better if you didn't bring it up, Liz."

Liz hadn't realized Bubba would have such intense feelings. She reached for her limeade and saw a mosquito about to land on her arm. She slapped at it.

Trish commented, "Oh-oh, fresh Yankee blood. We have been bitten so many times, I do believe it's like allergy shots: you become immune and no longer get a welt. At least we don't have as many now that the mosquito spray planes and trucks come by."

22

A TOWER FOR BATS?

"When my husband was a child his family lived about 15 miles north-east from here, where his father was the caretaker, postmaster, fishing guide and building superintendent for Mr. Perky. The mosquitoes were so thick in the evening they would form a black print on your hand when you put it against the window screen.

The insects would suck your blood right through the screen. He said his mama would get mad when the kids did that as a fun game.

"They told me about how life was, living on the Keys in those days. Only a few isolated people could stand it. Bubba went to a one-room schoolhouse on Big Pine Key and all grades totaled only nine children, all ages. Mr. Perky, a millionaire, owned 25,000 acres of land in the Keys. He chose one island, now called Sugarloaf Key, to build a resort and fishing camp, but when his rich cronies came down, they could barely tolerate the mosquitoes.

"Then Mr. Perky read a book by Dr. Campbell called "Mosquitoes, Bats and Dollars." The doctor had a large ranch in Texas and many cattle, but the mosquitoes bothered his cattle. Dr. Campbell had built special wooden towers to attract local bats to reside in his bat towers on his ranch, for relief for his cattle. Mr. Perky sent Bubba's father to Texas via train to purchase the bat tower blueprints plus a box of secret recipe bait. It was a horrible mix of ground female bats and guano droppings. It was guaranteed to attract the Keys bats."

Liz asked Trish a question. "Where do most of the bats live in Key West?"

Trish said, "That's the problem. There are large colonies of bats in the caves in Cuba and caves in Georgia, that flew between those geographical areas, but no structures on the Keys that would protect a swarm from hurricane winds and rain. Bubba's daddy said whenever there was trouble with the telephone service, the repairmen would find a few bats in phone transmission boxes, but no place for a swarm to roost.

The tower cost Mr. Perky over $10,000, which was a lot of money back then, and now, too," said Trish, but Bubba's daddy had ordered Dade County pine twelve by twelves for corner posts that were so hard you had a time getting a nail through them. The shingles were made of cypress, to last. He told me it's about 15 feet square at the bottom, and there are louvered openings running from one side to let the bats in and out. Inside he placed thousands of lathing strips, nailed horizontally four inches apart, for bats to hang on.

"Bubba's daddy built the thirty-foot wooden-slat tower elevated on four legs that had metal guards to stop rats from climbing up to the roosts. When the foundation cement was still damp, he told Bubba he had taken a sixteen-penny nail and inscribed "Dedicated to good health by Mr. and Mrs. R. C. Perky, March 15, 1929" because of the memory of the Yellow Fever epidemic thirty years prior. At that time about seventy people died, and Dr. Porter, the state health officer, said about 1400 people had been treated by the doctor, but he said the total cases of Yellow Fever may have been nearer 4,000, since many families cared for the patients at home, without contacting a doctor.

"A hurricane washed away the bait, but the bat tower has stood up well through all kinds of weather even today. The thing that makes Bubba's daddy mad is when people laugh and say Mr. Perky brought bats in. The truth is, Perky never imported bats. But he did send for more bait-mix. However, Dr. Campbell had died, and the project had been dropped.

"Now we spray poison to control the mosquitoes," explained Trish.

"Oh, my", exclaimed Liz. "That's some story." She had listened with intrigued wonder at the tale. "I didn't like the part about the ground-up female bats, but I guess male bats will be bats."

With that the two women heard the baby whimper. Trish stood up, "Sounds like Heather is waking up. I'd better go in. I'm sorry I took up so much of our time yakking away. Why don't you come back on Friday around six o'clock for supper with us and you can visit with Bubba, too" They could hear Bubba and Fern walking with the baby.

"Thanks, Trish. I had a wonderful visit today. I'll see you Friday," said Liz. She went out to her bicycle to continue on to her own cottage before the sun went down and those few hardy mosquitoes that were still around would find her Yankee skin.

Liz wondered how she could find out more about Lucas, Incorporated. Her friend Juan seemed to have a lot of know how about this island. She planned to try to get some information from him.

At that same time Juan was thinking he would like to try to get some more information from Liz about why she would go to the Lincoln Theater. He had listened to the interview that Chief Perez had taped, unbeknownst to Liz. She seemed to have a lot of gumption. She just might be the person the "BAND" needed to deliver the goods to Cuba.

He had "accidentally" met her outside the newspaper office one evening, so he would not use that trick again. He had watched her leave each night and knew she rarely deviated from the same route going back to her cottage. This evening he sat at a sidewalk cafe that just happened to be where he knew she would pass.

He hailed her, "Hello, Liz, is that you? What a coincidence: I was just thinking about out! Come and join me. Can I buy you a bouche?

"What's a 'boochy'? she asked, as she propped her bike against an empty chair at his table.

"It's just a mouthful of strong Cuban coffee. You must try it."

"No thanks. I don't even like American coffee. I always say it tastes like simmered burnt automobile tires."

Juan laughed, but he persisted. "I can teach you to like Cuban coffee. Are you willing to take a taste?" he taunted. He asked the waiter for a Cafe con Leche, then added even more cream and lots of sugar. He held it out to her. "Just try it."

She took a wary sip. Then another. "Mmm, it is good." She sat down at his table. "I heard the most interesting story the other day. My sister-in-law had asked me to look up the Jacksons on Pigeon Lane, Trish Jackson told me about a Bat Tower that is on one of the island north of here."

"Yes, I know the Jacksons and I've seen the Bat Tower."

"Juan, I do believe you know every person in this town. And all the stories. You ought to run for mayor."

"No, it is merely that this is a small town. Tell me, where did you live before coming here?"

"Oh, no place as wonderful as Key West" was her answer, although she had intentionally meant to be vague. However, she began some questions of her own. "How can I find out who the persons are behind a company, like 'Lucas, Incorporated'?"

Juan repeated the name aloud, 'Lucas, Incorporated'?"

"Yes, they or it just purchased the property that used to have housing for Service personnel," explained Liz.

"Oh yes, you mean the Jackson property on Ocean View Boulevard. That was a big piece of land. I heard they had lost it in the early 1940s because they didn't pay the real estate taxes on it" Juan said, baiting Liz for what information she might have.

Liz didn't say anything about the possibility of the right to commandeer property because she wasn't certain which story was the truth. But she tried Juan again. "How would someone find out the names of the persons behind a company?"

Juan knew he shouldn't tire of playing games — he should keep evaluating her for possible usefulness to the BAND. Instead, he told her he would get that information for her from an old friend. Then he asked her if should would go with him to Logan's for a drink and dancing under the stars. And they did.

Liz tried to remember what her sister-in-law had told her about the connection with Trish and Bubba Jackson. The children of her brother Matt and Marian, Joey and Max, were related somehow with a couple of "great-greats", but she couldn't recall just how all that lineage stuff went. She wondered if Trish was interested in genealogy.

Invited to Friday supper, Liz thought about taking a hostess gift. Perhaps a bottle of wine, but someone at work had told her that the locals, who were called "Conchs" after the hard-shelled mollusk in the areas' seawater, were stiffly moral non-drinking Methodists. Not sure, she decided to take flowers.

Thursday she checked with a florist, but discovered flowers were outside her budget. At the small "Tropical Nursery" she bought a flowering Hibiscus plant that easily fit in the basket of her bicycle. She rode her bike back to her cottage and placed the Hibiscus pot on the porch, giving it a drink of water.

Friday, after work, Liz went home, changed into a sleeveless blouse, a gathered skirt and her sandals, then pedaled the Hibiscus over to Pigeon Lane. There, Trish was sitting on the porch, rocking baby Heather while the two-year-old sat nearby playing with a little tea set and a doll.

Holding the baby with one arm, Trish waved at Liz as she leaned the bike against the picket fence. Trish thanked her for the plant and they sat on the porch chatting until the baby fell asleep. She would probably nap for a while, so Trish left Liz and Fern to entertain themselves. The two sat on the top step. Fern poured a tiny cup of water from her tea set and offered it to Liz who enjoyed leaping back into her childhood.

With the baby in her crib, Trish returned to the porch along with Bubba, his hair still wet from the shower. Bubba thanked Liz for the Hibiscus, saying it was a great choice because this variety was like one in his mother's garden.

Then Trish launched into a story about what happened when she met Bubba's family for the first time. As they were walking through Mrs. Jackson's garden, Trish had seen a large bush with orange fruit. Nervous about meeting the family, she began to babble about how wonderful it was to have fresh oranges growing in your own backyard. Bubba's father asked Trish if she would like to have a taste. He plucked one and peeled the skin, offering Trish several segments.

It was later that Trish recalled there had been a sudden hush over the family group — Bubba, his mother and two sisters — as his father offered the orange to her. She'd smiled and popped it in her mouth. It was so tart!

Bubba had told her, "Sorry, that was a joke. This tree is not an orange tree, it is a "Sour Orange" tree. The juice is used for tenderizing and flavoring pork roasts, and he told her to spit it out. His mother said, "Freddie, you shouldn't have done that." But after that initiation, Trish was part of the family.

After Liz drank another teeny cup of tea party water, Trish helped Fern put away her tea set and the group moved into what Trish called the Florida Room, which to a Northerner was the Family Room. It was a large room built at the back of the house, with many screened windows open to the tropical breezes, two overhead Hunter paddle fans assisting the cooking process. Liz thought the fact that there was no rug also made the room seem cooler and showcase the beautiful wooden flooring.

Several rattan chairs were positioned at one end of the room, cushions covered with colorful prints. The other end had a long white table that Trish said Bubba had made for her by putting legs on a six-foot door. Fern was placed in a highchair and handed a slice of "Cuban Bread" from a long loaf similar to French bread.

The meal was simple: Broiled crawfish (Florida lobsters)

Grits with a tomato gravy
Fried plantains
Chilled avocado slices
Cuban bread and butter
Limeade

Trish placed a plate with each item onto Fern's highchair and let her feed herself. Trish explained to Liz that Conchs called avocado "Alligator Pear" because of the shape, color and texture of the skin. Liz though the plantains were bananas cooked in maple syrup, but was told those were cousins to bananas. Plantains were ready for cooking when the skin had turned black. Although they were tasteless when uncooked, when fried in oil they turned sweet. Grits were something Liz had never eaten before. She thought it was similar to Cream of Rice cereal. Fern was spooning it up with enjoyment, although a little messy.

Liz had thought Bubba was either a quiet man or unable to get a word in because of Trish leading the conversation. He did comment, however, about the difference between lobster and crawfish. He said he had never eaten a New England lobster, but that meat was mostly in the claw. Crawfish, however, had a meaty body. He told her he had taken a bushel basket down to the Key West Bight area after work that day, leaned over, and plucked up enough for supper tonight. He talked about when he was a child the locals used crawfish for bait when fishing. He used to go door to door in his neighborhood, trying to sell crawfish for a quarter, but there were few takers, it was so plentiful.

Liz was intrigued to listen to the Conch accent, a little Southern, but a lot like a New Englander with added or dropped letter "R" to some words. Then she remembered that Marian Steele had told her about the Mystic, Connecticut connection.

Trish said she had done a little family research on Bubba's ancestors, easy to do because of the Key West library's genealogy section. She had read the microfiche of the city's census of 1850 and 1860. Also, she had taken the children for strolls through the cemetery and found the Josephus Fitch Packer monument.

Josephus was born in 1822 in Mystic and married Fanny Wilber of Groton, Connecticut. Trish had been able to trace the Packers back to 1537 and the Wilbers to 1482. When Fanny Packer died in 1850 Josephus brought his four-year-old daughter Harriet to Key West. He worked as an auctioneer, a busy occupation in those days of the wrecking industry when Key West was the richest town in Florida.

Trish told Liz that she wondered why he had moved from Mystic to Key West. Had he known someone here or simply was looking for a new horizon? "This old history is so intriguing to me," Trish exclaimed.

She continued with the background tale. She said that Harriet Packer married a Jackson, and that was where Maximillian came in. Trish said reading the old census documents was fascinating. They listed where a person was born, and where their parents were born. The first Jackson in Bubba's line was a brick wall, a mystery she had not yet solved.

The only thing she found out so far was James A. Jackson, an apothecary, came from Scotland in 1837. He married Laura Antoinette Dennison in New York in 1838, stopping en route according to a notation in the family Bible for their baby to be born "somewhere along the banks of the Suwannee River, Florida."

Liz was captivated by the story. She thought about how little she had known about her family and how little she had cared until recently. To know all this detail was a rich gift. Liz wondered if she could get some information about her own background. She would ask her grandmother about it. Meanwhile she understood that this was what her sister-in-law had been talking about. What a small world!

The two women had been talking while clearing the table and rinsing the dishes in the sink. Bubba had taken Fern in to check on Heather. He and the children went out to the bricked patio in the side yard. They were playing while Bubba was cranking the handle of an ice cream churn. Trish brought spoons and paper cups out to the patio and the women sat watching Bubba do all the hard work.

"Home-made mango ice cream for dessert!" Trish announced.

It was a glorious culmination to a delightfully tropical evening among newly found friends.

Juan telephoned a friend in Washington, D.C., asking him to check out "Lucas,Inc." The call back regarding the inquiry stated it was listed as an investment company headed by a "Luke Steele" of New York. However there seemed to be a problem surrounding Mr. Steele. He had been working at a New York City bank that was currently investigating a possible embezzlement fraud. Mr. Steele had been traced from New York to Florida, but apparently had left the country.

In exchange for this information, his Washington source asked Juan what he could tell them about that situation.

23

LUKE'S PLAN A OR PLAN B

Matthew, Mark and Luke had been driven in a big car to another state, to the home of their great-grandfather, Caleb Steele. As children they expected it was going to be life inside a rich man's castle. Upon arrival they were escorted into a brick building which seemed to be utilized as a processing center for the administrators of the Steele family estate. The first thing one could see upon entering was a huge oil painting of an old man with eyes painted so realistically they seemed to be glaring directly at the observer, frightening the children. None of them ever forgot that view of Great-Grandfather Caleb Steele.

The children learned Caleb had drifted into dementia. His many children had quickly organized against him, and before any outsiders knew they had divided the property between themselves into small domains.

Matthew was given to one son whose parcel of land did have a river running through it. Time spent fishing at that riverside was his happy spot. After tutors, he was sent to Yale.

Mark (given to another son) had private tutors, then sent off to Yale.

Luke, given to another son, had always been an angry child, believing himself to have been cheated out of the prestige and lush life of privilege that he could observe while being raised in his adoptive family, whom he felt were of a much lower social status than their neighbors on the sprawling estate. They were conservative with their money and he never had the flowing funds most of his classmates enjoyed. His paranoia that his acquaintances thought of him as lesser, caused him to have an attitude of low self-esteem: not quite good enough.

Money was always on his mind. He went to Harvard and then banking became his focus.

Working in the bank, men would come to Luke for advice on investing and other money matters. But instead of basking in an aura of prestige, Luke felt that he was no more than a bank teller who cashed the paychecks of common workmen.

Luke had learned more from Judy Pritchard, a secretary in the bank's real estate department, than he had absorbed during his four year of college academics. She had told him a person could get government grants to revive a slum area. He tried it on a small scale in one neighborhood and he reaped a profit that surprised him.

When his bank sent him to Key West to investigate on some government surplus land, the opportunity was too tempting to resist. Money from the winning bid had to be upfront and available He "borrowed' a huge amount of money from the bank, with the intent to outbid everyone, then move on to his Plan A or Plan B.

Plan A was to hold his winning bid as bait, offering the top four runners-up the opportunity to invest in his restoration/commercial site, each at much lower cost than they had planned to bid, but instead they would become partners in the profit he felt certain he could make for them … and him. Receiving a cumulative total from the investors as more than the bank had sent, he would return the bank's money before the next audit, and report to the bank that he had lost the bid. He believed the controlling officers at the bank were soggy-brained fat-asses who would believe him and never find out his mischief.

Plan B was even trickier. He would out-bid everyone, pay with the bank's money but sign with his name, and then transfer everything into his fiancee Judy Pritchard's company set up in banks on the Cayman Islands. Then he would disappear, perhaps to the Bahamas. His New York bank would look for him, but lose interest after their insurance company returned the amount to their treasury, and he and Judy would have a 'dummy company' develop the land and send them the profits.

Plan A failed. He went to Plan B, then began his journey by flying to the Bahamas.

24 ONLY YOUR MAILMAN KNOWS

Grandma Steele's mailman, Tom, had been on that same route for 15 years. He could tell a lot about each person's life just by noting the postmark or return addresses. Of course anyone who wrote a postcard shouldn't care if the mailman glances at the message. Tom knew that Liz had moved to San Francisco and after five years had returned home, but now was sending letters from Key West, Florida to New Jersey. He delivered the postcards from Liz to Shirley's house next-door, too.

But today he was carrying what appeared to him to be a very special letter. It came from Inneshowen, Donegal, Parish Inch, Eire. A letter from Ireland! Tom walked up the front porch steps to place the letter in the mailbox, but instead of that he rang Mrs. Steele's doorbell. He handed her the letter. She looked from the letter in her hand up to Tom's eyes, and was worried. Even after all these years, she could recognize her own sister's handwriting.

She asked Tom to sit with her on the porch while she opened the letter. She feared it was bad news. She slid her finger under the flap and tore open the envelope. Sheets of fine line-paper were inside, together with a Bank Note. She quickly read the message then turned to Tom and smiled.

"My sister, Fiona invited me to come to my mother's birthday party.

It'll be a surprise. Mum will be ninety-six next month. I haven't seen any of them since…" and tears suddenly poured down her face and onto the letter.

Tom didn't know what to do. He reached over and placed his hand on Grandma's arm, extending a gesture of caring and concern.

Grandma tugged the edge of her apron up and dried her eyes. She gave Tom another smile and thanked him for sitting with her. "I'm fine now, Tom. Happy tears. You know what? I believe I just might do it. I just might go to Ireland and see my family."

Tom could hardly wait to get home today to tell his wife how his day was.

Preparation for the trip were few: Get a passport, arrange for the ticket, and notify Shirley's mother that she would be gone for six days. She decided not to include any mention of the trip in her letters to Liz. There was no need to concern her. When she returned home from Ireland, she would write to her telling all about the trip. She shopped at the Saint Vincent de Paul Thrift store and found a like-new London Fog raincoat that would serve her well during the trip.

Pride stood in the way of Mrs. Steele depositing the Irish Bank Note, which would pay for the airfare and expenses, but she became realistic. Fiona had anticipated her sister's reluctance to accept the money, but had written that she and her husband, John Sweeney, had been doing nicely with their little inn. Never one to brag about money, the Sweeneys were doing nicely indeed. There "little inn" was a large and very popular resort in Ireland, west of Northern Ireland.

Although Donegal is the most northerly county in Ireland, it is a favorite vacation spot because of its beautiful glens and towering mountains, purple and green with heather. One area has a sandy beach surrounded by dramatic cliffs, carved out by storms' waves. People come to the area to trout fish in the many area lakes. Some want to visit Lough Derg, a lake where it was said that St. Patrick visited for forty days of prayer and fasting, staying in one of the caves on the island in the middle of that lake.

The town of Inneshowen in County Donegal is part of that popular vacation area. Fiona and John Sweeney had seen their small bar, *'Jack's,'* evolve into a very successful restaurant and lodging called *The Inn at*

Inneshowen. During the time their business was small, they had raised their six girls and one son, each learning to help, whether it was washing glasses, piling up the supply boxes in the storage room, scrubbing the floors, and eventually working the till, as well.

Yes, *The Inn* had become a popular resort complex. Within, there were two bars. One was still called *Jack's* and John Sweeney spent most of his time there. Care was taken to maintain the intimate feeling of a small Irish pub. The other bar was *Owen Isle,* a more sophisticated nightclub managed by their grandson Liam. Other children were involved with all aspects of running what was now a corporation.

Nellanore Elizabeth Doherty Steele knew Fiona would not be so free with her money if she could not spare it. Should she read more into the invitation? Was their mother ill? After all, next month Mum would turn 96. Mrs. Steele must not postpone revisiting her family. The Bank Note was deposited and the plane ticket purchased.

25 GRANDMA REVEALS TALES HER GRANDMOTHER TOLD HER

The widow Mrs. Clarence Steele (nee Nellanore Elizabeth Doherty) had left Ireland when she was fifteen years old, her overseas fare paid by the Steele family. She was to assist the other Steele family servants who were accompanying the Steele family on their trans-oceanic return trip to America. They never would have brought her along if they had seen the future — that their youngest son would marry Nell Doherty a year later.

Fifty-eight years later Nell Steele was en route to Ireland, soon to land in Dublin. It wasn't her personal history that she mused. She was recalling the stories her grandmothers had told her about the history of the Irish.

Her grandmothers had heard stories from their grandmothers, but there were no tales about Mesolithic or Neolithic people. Their stories started with the Celts, although those ladies did not know the time frame was about 600 B.C. They had told her about the Celts, who protected their group by building curved stone walls, with an outer, middle and inner ring-fort. They said there were many beautiful stone carvings done by Irish craftsmen, artists who had also made intricate brooches, handsome sword scabbards and collar rings in bronze and gold that revealed stunning artistry.

The grandmothers prided themselves on their ability to remember details of this oral history, but as children, Nell and Fiona often commented that the stories grew larger and longer each time they were told, embellished with comments of incredibly brave deeds.

The old grannies would tell about the Gaelic era when there were three classes of Irish: The Professionals — poets, historians, jurists, musicians and druids: Free Men — warriors, owning land and cattle; and Slaves — prisoners or descendants of prisoners taken in war.

Perhaps it was the romance of the Viking invasions that held the interest of Fiona and Nell, their interest flamed by seeing a book with a picture of the Gokstad ship. No squat and flat-bottomed boat suitable for fishing in lakes, this was a skillfully crafted vessel with a curved keep swooping up with majestic beauty. This design plus new improvements like the square sail made it easy to maneuver and maintain high speeds even in rough seas.

Nellanore Elizabeth Doherty Steele was surprised at how much Irish history came back to her. It must have been the grandmothers who had told her that Vikings were seafaring men from Norway, Sweden, Denmark, driven to seek lands that could sustain their growing populations. Their home countries were beautiful with lush forests, rocky mountains and fjords, but not enough farming land to provide adequate food. The first Viking attack in Ireland was in the year 795 and Viking invasion continued for 200 years. Dublin Castle was begun in 1200.

It was these thoughts of her Irish history that re-awakened in Nellanore Doherty Steele's mind as her airplane flew her closer to her homeland. How foolish of Americans to think of 1600 as 'long ago'. What a glorious thing to be Irish and have such an interesting heritage, she thought.

In truth, she could recall detailed account of her grandmothers' stories. However, her memory was obfuscated about what happened to her between the time she was living at home with her parents and when she was dusting the staircase in the Steele family's home in America.

All she could remember was the agonizing hunger that never went away. Hunger to escape from the Irish life of relentless drudgery and hunger for the non existent food. She became more aware of the gaunt look of her grandparents and even her ten younger brothers and sisters, and the staring eyes of the starved and starving. As her siblings died, one by one, Nell herself became a little deranged. It was the parish priest who had saved her sanity by finding the position for Nell with the Steele family.

Nell looked out the window of the airplane but misting rain that keeps Ireland green obscured her view. Customs went quickly. Her gaze swept the crowd, but then she spied two tall redheaded young women and short, white haired lady.

One girl had carrot-red hair plaited in two long braids. She wore bib overalls and a tweed jacket. The other girl had a mass of curly auburn red hair tumbling over her aran knit sweater. She wore riding boots with her tweed skirt. The elderly woman wore a wrinkled mackintosh and brogan shoes. Her white hair was twisted in a bun, but many wisps of her white hair had escaped, almost giving an illusion of a halo.

She gave them a smile of hello. As she walked toward them, the two girls waved frantically.

"Auntie Nell? Auntie Nell?" they called out simultaneously.

Nell's sister Fiona was the first to reach her. She clasped Nellanore's hand with both of hers and held it to her heart, smiling. "It's been too long Nellie, dear. Welcome home."

Nellanore Steele was afraid she was going to cry. She smiled but was speechless. Nell was in a daze from the long flight and emotion of this meeting, but Fiona tucked her arm through her sister's and guided her along as they walked to the parked car.

"The girls suggested that the ride up to Inneshowen today would be putting too much travel on you, especially with you having adjust to the time-change, so we're going to show you a bit of Dublin and stay here overnight. We'll head home tomorrow, if that's all right with you, Nellie," Fiona asked as she continued to gaze at her sister as if to make up for all the lost years.

Still at a loss for words, Nell nodded acquiescence.

"Sweet Mary, Mother of Jesus, I would have known you anywhere. You still look the same," Fiona exclaimed.

Nell laughed at that and the two sisters began to chat back and forth, each flooded with old memories and years of happening to relate.

The two girls sat in the front of the car, driving, with the sisters in the back passenger section and chat. Nell noted the car was a Rolls-Royce but made no comment, sensitive to the fact that "Pride" was one of the Venial sins and she wouldn't want to make her sister have to confess that next Saturday. Fiona inundated Nell with names of her children and grandchildren but so far Nell could only remember that these two girls were Maureen and Colleen.

Maureen, the driver, parked so they could stretch their legs. They walked down O'Connell Street; visited Trinity College Library to see the Book of Kelts illuminated manuscript. Walking along the north bank of the river, there were the Custom House and the famous Four Courts. But it was Dublin Castle that interested Nell. When they entered the heraldic museum Fiona had the Sweeney clan traced. She was delighted to hear the name came from the Irish *suibhne,* meaning 'pleasant'.

"John is pleasant," she laughed. "I think that's why everyone in his bar enjoys his company. That's what brings them back. That's why he couldn't come to meet you at the airport, Nell," Fiona explained. "All the regulars insisted he be there with them to watch the tellie in the bar. Today there's an important Hurling final."

Colleen interrupted to advise Nell, "Did you know that the Gaelic game of Hurling is over four thousand years old?"

Nell admitted that was a fact she wasn't aware of, but she recalled the furor of interest in the games.

Maureen asked the curator to show them the Doherty crest. There was a giant Red Deer standing up under a green band with three white stars. When asked the meaning of Doherty, the curator told them the original Doherty or *Dochartach* was the twelfth in lineal descent from son of Niall, the fifth-century king who supposedly kidnapped St. Patrick to Ireland. He then told them it meant 'unlucky'.

"Aha!" exclaimed Nell. "I see now where my luck came from," but Maureen insisted she was no long a Doherty but a Steele, and changed everything. Sorry for her negative outburst, Nell proved herself a quick-tongued Irish woman by agreeing.

"Yes, meeting Clarence Steele was my lucky day."

"Enough of heraldry for the day, Auntie Steele. Now how about a spot of tea?" suggested Colleen.

Before leaving Dublin Castle, Fiona had a copy of the Sweeney crest made for John to place in *Jack's* bar.

That evening the girls pressed the older women to enjoy an hour or two in a singing pub, where they each imbibed in more than one glass of Guiness stout. As each new round of *"Ulscebeatha."* the 'water of life.' was downed, their singing grew louder and the words to the old songs were remembered more quickly.

Did you ever go into an Irishman's shanty,
Where money was scarce and whiskey was plenty.
A three-legged stool and a table to match,
An old wooden door, that's hung by its latch.

It was a lovely evening on the Old Sod.

As Nellanore began the approach to a wakened state the next morning, she wondered why she felt so much pain in her head. Could she have a brain tumor? She opened her eyes and the shadow of sleep moved from her brain. No. It was a hangover. It had been a long time prior to last night since she'd had any alcohol.

Ah, but the evening had been so much fun. The last thing she remembered was the four of them trying to create a poem rhyming Maureen with *mavourneen*, Colleen with "my queen". Nellanore with "troubadour", but their difficulty was matching Fiona with some other than "Desdemona". It had all seemed too hilarious then, but when Nell attempted to rise from the bed, a moan escaped.

She turned quickly to see if that had disturbed Fiona, but there was no other bed in the room. This was not an American motel: no twin beds. Apparently the two sisters had slept in the same bed. Focusing a little better, she saw a piece of paper on Fiona's pillow: "Top of the morning to you, Nellie dear. Come to the Tea Room when you are ready."

Nell wondered what time Fiona had left the room. What time did we get into bed? I slept in my slip. I guess I didn't bathe last night. Where is my toothbrush? Did I pack any aspirin? I can't remember.

Both of her suitcases were at the foot of the bed. Nell found her things and hurried about, fearing she was a thoughtless guest, putting them behind on their scheduled time to leave for Inneshowen. She rushed into the hallway and found the Tea Room. Her family of three was there, enjoying breakfast and showing no concern about time. They greeted her with smiles, appearing none the worse for wear after a Guinness night.

"Bit of a headache, have you, Auntie? What you need is a good Irish breakfast. Do you drink our tea with lemon or cream?" encouraged Colleen, but Fiona patted Nell on the arm.

"I'll get you some coffee and a scone. You'll feel better soon. Sorry, dear. We should have come back to the hotel a bit earlier, I fear. But what does it matter, after all. We're here together and in no rush. The ride home will only take a few hours and we'll be settled in for a nice long quiet visit."

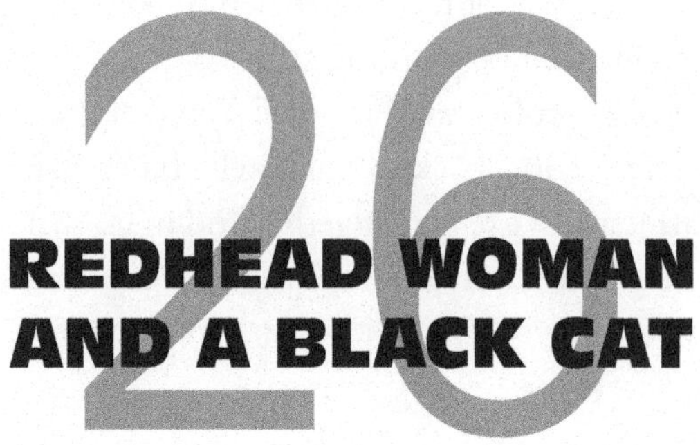

26 REDHEAD WOMAN AND A BLACK CAT

Seated in the backseat of the Rolls once again, this time on the left, the better to enjoy the view unobstructed by passing vehicles, Nell was surprised at how quickly she had recovered. There was no pressure, no rushing, just a relaxed family outing.

Actually, Nell had never seen any of Ireland outside her parish boundaries, before she left at age fifteen. Whatever sights she had passed, between home and boarding the ship with the Steele family, were a forgotten memory.

Colleen drove the car this time. They left the luxury hotel and big city area. Colleen ambled in no direct route, for the pleasure of Nell. The diverse lush green valleys, lakes with fishing boats, sharp cliffs, sandy bays, quiet farmlands, bogs, small villages, monastery towers and moss-covered ruins of old castles. In the distance, there was a haze over a mountain with flowers of gold and lilac and blue, like the colors in Monet's impression of Rouen Cathedral.

Maureen had been identifying various birds as they flew past. Suddenly she shouted "Watch out! Black cat!" and Colleen swerved to avoid hitting the cat.

Instead, the front wheel jammed against a pile of rocks, a cairn, marking where someone had died. With a bang, the car jolted to a stop.

"Jesus, Mary and Joseph!" Colleen yelled.

"Don't swear, Colleen," her grandmother scolded.

"I wasn't swearing, I was praying. Thank God no one was hurt. I think we have a flat tire."

Maureen was first to recover her sensibilities. Still dressed in bib overalls, she checked the boot of the car and brought out the jack. Squatting down, she began to jack up the car, but stopped. "Better get out, ladies. This will take a bit of time and you might as well enjoy a few minutes walk to stretch your legs." Then she quietly told Colleen, "This is a one-woman job. Stay with them and keep them out of trouble, would you?"

The two sisters had already started a jaunt down the road, with Fiona pointing out a stone farmhouse with a small family cemetery in the field next to it. "At least the rest of the day should go well. Things come in threes. The black cat, the cairn, and that wee cemetery. Yes, all should be well now."

Nell thought the flat tire should be counted, but that would make four, so she said nothing. They were passing the farmhouse when Colleen caught up with her grandmother and aunt. A man was climbing a ladder to the thatched roof, apparently to do some mending repairs. His wife was seated outside, knitting. She looked up at the passers-by. The three on the road waved and kept walking but the woman hailed them.

She waked to the roadway and asked if there was any trouble. Colleen told her they had a flat tire, but her sister was fixing it. The woman flinched as if in shock and called up to her husband.

"John, come down, these ladies have a flat tire and a girl is trying to fix it!" Then she turned to the three strollers and issued commands. "You, girl, go get your sister. I've some dinner ready and she's to come to the house and eat. My John will fix your tire." and turning to the older women she told the, "Now come along inside and sit. Tell me, where ye be going?"

Fiona attempted to decline the offer, but the effort seemed futile, and soon the five women were seated at the kitchen table, chatting. Anne Rafferty introduced herself and was intrigued by Nell, whom she identified as an American.

"Oh, no. I'm Irish, from County Donegal," Nell insisted, but her

American accent and clothing, especially her shoes, made her stand apart. She realized it had been about 50 years since she had been back in Ireland, so she had expected to see an iron kettle hanging over a fire in the hearth. Instead, Mrs. Rafferty had a black cast-iron stove with a large pot of dinner she insisted on sharing.

"Me mother always said there's enough to share, even if you have to add a potato to the pot," and with that she began to ladle out a bowl of her stew for each person.

Nell was the first to comment, asking for the recipe. Mrs. Rafferty laughed and told her, "Fill the pot with water and add some onions, carrots, cabbage, turnips and lots of potatoes. If you have some beef or mutton, toss it in. Simmer it a long time, and it's ready. Do you have that, now?"

Nell smiled and said, "Yes." She wished her granddaughter Liz was with her right now.

When they had finished sopping up the last drop of gravy with Mrs. Rafferty's homemade wheat bread, John Rafferty appeared. Mrs. Rafferty got up from her seat and John sat in it. She gave him a bowl of the stew and set the loaf of bread in front of him.

Fiona thanked him for helping them and apologized for interrupting his work on the roof.

Mrs. Rafferty laughed, and told them he had probably sent the cat out to jinx them so he would not have to fix the roof today.

Colleen asked, "You knew it was a cat?"

"Ah, there's a devil Manx cat around here. We don't fed it and it belongs to no one. He's caused more than one accident. We can't find him to catch him and do away with him. Perhaps he's a leprechaun, do you suppose? They're so mischievous, you know."

Maureen prided herself on being a new and modern young woman with the ability to do anything a man can do. She was peeved that John Rafferty insisted that he fix the flat, and that she was told to leave him alone and 'go back with the women.' To taunt him, she asked him now, "Do you believe in leprechauns and brownies and fairies, Mr. Rafferty?"

He scoffed, "Of course I don't believe in fairies, even though they do exist.

Maureen was unable to restrain a snicker.

He looked at the four women and said, "Anyone can tell you, red-headed women in the car is bad luck."

Fiona felt Maureen's teasing was inappropriate, but as a guest in the Rafferty home, having received their hospitality, agreed with his statement. "Yes, my husband would have driven us to Dublin, but the girls insisted on coming. He, too, commented about red-haired women in the car, but we have to ignore that. All of our girls and granddaughters have red hair."

Everyone laughed, including Mr. Rafferty. It was a good day. They continued their drive to Inneshowen with no further delay, promising to send some jam to the Raffertys as soon as possible.

The tree lined road wound gradually until it burst free of greenery to expose a dramatic first view of *The Inn at Inneshowen.* There was a clearing for the convenience of arriving automobiles, made beautiful by a long hedge of roses, flowering profusely.

There was a stone cottage with a thatched roof. The whitewashed walls shone brightly in the afternoon sun. The cottage was nestled between two large wings of red brick buildings, the mixed architecture highlighting the stone cottage.

Nell, having lived alone for a long time, was neither a babbler nor a person quick to reveal her emotions. She stared with widen eyes at the panorama.

Fiona explained, as she had to so many tourists, "We started with the cottage, as a Bed-and-Breakfast, but it just grew."

Finally, Nell found words. "I never expected anything so grand."

"Ah, Nellie girl, it's just a pub grown big. Jack and I don't live here, you know. We live down the road, in the same house since we were married more than 55 years ago. Mum lives with us, and, of course, you will be staying in our home. But come inside the Inn and meet some of our family."

The tour encompassed the cottage's registration area. To one side in that room were two overstuffed chairs next to a lace covered table set with the makings for hot tea. It was there that Nell met Fiona's grandson David. They continued on through the gift shop, large dining room, and a library with doors that opened to a patio overlooking a golf course.

Nell met Monica, Nora, Peter, Rosaleen, Anthony and Catherine. They continued to the horse stables to greet Shannon and Brian. Fiona said she was sorry Bridget was not there at the time. "She's the one with a gift to tame wild horses," Fiona said, "She's been away at a horse show for the past several days."

The two sisters walked past a large greenhouse, back to the main buildings. As they approached a door, men's voices could be heard.

Alarmed, Nell told her sister, "It sounds like they are fighting."

Fiona chuckled. "No, it's just Jack and his friends. The Hurling game would still be playing, but maybe we can get a word in," and she led Nell into the darkened bar, *Jack's*.

"Jack!" Fiona yelled over the noise, "Come welcome your sister-in-law. Nellie's here!"

The men in the room fell quiet. All eyes turned to examine Nell, to her intense embarrassment, but the moment was brief, and everyone turned back to watch the television set except for a ruddy faced man with gray hair of kinky waves sparking out from his head like electric wires.

"Holy Mary, Mother of God, it's true! You've finally come. Welcome home, Nell," and Jack put one arm around Nell's shoulders, squeezing her in a bear hug.

Before Nell could respond, Fiona asked, "Could you come to lunch with us, Jack?" but he gave the answer she expected.

"I would love to, dearie, but the boys are counting on me. Besides, I have a wager on this game. Set a spot for me tonight, though. Bridget says we're having lamb."

Nell lifted her hand in a wave of Hello, which turned into a wave of Good-bye, as Fiona led them back out of the bar.

"No more than I expected, but it's always nice to ask. But he'll come home for food, just like any good Irish Wolfhound. Tonight will be just our children so as not to overwhelm you so soon, but tomorrow is Mum's birthday party, when all the family will be there. Let's go back to the front cottage. Colleen and Maureen will have left the car and I'll drive us to our house."

"I didn't know you knew how to drive."

"Oh, it was that or use a donkey cart. It's a busy life here, but it keeps one moving about."

Nell wondered how much her 96-year-old mother could move about. She was soon to find out.

Fiona drove a short distance from the Inn property and parked in front of a stone house, this one with a roof of tile. Nell wondered if their mother was bed-ridden or sat in a wheelchair. Who stayed with Mum and fed her during the times Fiona was away?

They walked toward the half-door. The top was open and as they approached, a sprightly woman appeared and swung open the bottom half.

"I saw you drive up, Fiona. Come, Nellanore, give your Mum a hug."

Tears started down Nell's cheeks. Sagging flesh obscured the old woman's jawline, but the daughter recognized the eyes and cheekbones of her mother, not seen for more than half a century. Observing her mother's fingers, twisted with arthritis, Nell put both her arms around her mother, but was careful not to squeeze too vigorously, recalling the jolt of discomfort that Jack's bear hug had given her.

"Come along, girls," Mum urged her daughters. "The table is set and I've made some creamed salmon and peas. There's cake just out of the oven for our dessert. You don't have a sugar problem, do you, Nellanore?" Mum asked.

Nell stood, shaking her head negatively and Fiona laughed, "Cat's got her tongue, Mum", and turning to her sister, said, "I can't keep Mum out of the kitchen. I see she has our noon meal ready. We'll get the bags after we eat."

Having heard tales of luggage being lost, Nell had carefully tucked an envelope of photographs in her purse, as insurance against the possibility of her suitcases being mislaid. Strangers at first, after all these years, the conversation started out with questions of "How was your flight?" and "When do you plan to return?" Then Nell brought out the photos. She showed snapshots that her granddaughter Liz had taken of Mark inCanada and Matt in Connecticut. Nell showed several pictures of Liz and even one of her neighbor's little girl, Shirley.

The afternoon quickly became at ease and full of laughter as Fiona told anecdotes about her large family, with Mum adding terse witticisms to each tale. The telephone rang several times; children and grandchildren checking on the plans for the evening and the birthday party the next day, offering help.

When Mum stood up and began to clear the table, both her daughters quickly pushed their chairs back and helped, but Fiona quietly cautioned Nell not to stop their mother or she would get a tongue-lashing from the old woman, telling them "I'm not helpless yet." However, Fiona knew to get to the sink first and began to wash the dishes. Nell picked up a towel. Mum saw that she was outnumbered and outmaneuvered and announced that she would go to her room for a while. "Not to sleep, just rest me eyes."

Her two daughters each gave her a kiss on her cheeks and their mother left the girls alone to talk.

27 LIFE IS NOT ALWAYS A BED OF ROSES

The two sisters sat at the kitchen table. Nell told Fiona how impressed she was with the love and attention and consideration her children gave to each other. Fiona agreed that she was blessed, and said to Nell, "Children are such a comfort in my old age. I'm sorry your son Charlie and his wife died so young. It's too bad you and your husband had only one child."

With that, Nell burst into tears. Fiona was quick to come around the table and kneel beside her sister. "What's the trouble, Nellie? Tell me. What is wrong?"

"Oh, Fee. I've never told anyone," and she cried some more.

Fiona retrieved a large cotton handkerchief from the pocket of her skirt and pressed it into Nell's hand. "Come on girl, wipe your eyes and blow your nose, then tell me. I'm your sister; you can tell me anything, you know."

Nell took a deep breath, wiped her eyes, and, indeed, she blew her nose. She told her sister about how as a servant in the Steele home she had witnessed the way Clarence Steele, as the youngest son, had been the one child the domineering father, Caleb Steele, had chosen to continuously belittle.

"I had been scrubbing the marble stairway outside the room where Clarence was suffering another scathing and sneering tirade from his father when he could tolerate no more, and he ran out of the room," said Nell. "He tripped over me, and his father stood over him, enraged his son had walked away from him. I tried to help Clarence get up. That kindness goaded the father to say, 'Get out, I disown you, and take that bitch with you!' Clarence grabbed my hand and we ran."

"It wasn't easy. No money, nowhere to turn, but we did it, somehow. We married but Clarence was unprepared for the life of the working poor. Our son Charles was born but Clarence succumbed to the solace of drink and loose women, finally dying from a disease that affected his mind."

"You mean syphilis? Oh, dear Nellie, I've seen in others what that can do," Fiona said. "I understand."

Nell said, "Our son Charles was my reason to carry on. Years go by but eventually they grow up and marry. He did find a lovely girl, Agness, and the three of us lived together. I wrote you about her. They were a good match together."

"Yes, Nellie, you wrote to me, but all your letters were cheerful. Life sounded good." insisted Fiona.

"No sense writing sad letters to loved ones far away. Write about the good days, I believe. And there were good days. Charles and Agness had four children and they bring happiness in everyone's life. But then the scourge of tuberculosis was everywhere. The epidemic was killing so many people. Agness succumbed to TB, then so did Charles."

Fiona asked, "What about your four grandchildren? How did you get by?"

Nell answered, "Caleb Steele hard, and sent men with a letter insisting he had the right and the resources, so was taking the boys to be reared correctly on the Steele estate. But he did leave the youngest, Elizabeth, with me, thank God."

"And where are the others now?"

"Matthew is a fisherman, married and with two boys. Mark works for an aluminum company in British Columbia, Canada. Luke is a banker in New York City. Elizabeth works for a newspaper in Florida."

"Ah, there's a blessing. A four healthy children," Fiona said. She pulled her chair up against Nell's. "But all children are a gift from God. You see, Nell, you are blessed, too. And know that I love you."

Nell laid her head on her sister's shoulder and held the handkerchief to her nose, sniffling. Fiona said nothing, gently rocking her sister back and forth.

Finally Fiona spoke: "I'm no priest or someone who can give advice, but you must accept the fact that the past is past. Lock that memory in a wee little corner of your brain and leave it there to gather dust and cobwebs. Now, it seems to me, what will bring you the most happiness is to get close to those four grandchildren as best you can, and give them your love. Everyone can use a little more love. And you know, what you give, comes back a hundred-fold."

Nell kissed her sister on the cheek. "Just having you to talk with has lifted my soul. But selfish me — tell me about you and your family, Fee."

As an introduction to the evening's dinner with all seven of the children of Fiona and Jack Sweeney, Nell's sister gave a briefing regarding each.

"Grace is 55 and never found a husband, but she has been the backbone of our business ever since we expanded from "Jacks" bar. She has the gift of management.

"Angela is 53, a bit morose and bitter that she never married, but certainly she has an artist's flair that would have been extinguished if she'd catered to a husband and children.

"Ellen, 51, and her husband David have eight children ages 32 to 20.

"Alice, 49, and her husband Peter have eight children, ages 28 to 10.

"Oh, I skipped Dorothy. She is 50 and has one child, Susan, who is 25. Dorothy met a Chinese engineer Hong Tan Ha, when he was hired to evaluate cracks and other damages done to structures by the bombings. The company had wanted someone who was not Irish. I think Dorothy and H.T. are the happiest of my children.

"Then there's Eileen, 45 and single. Her fiancé was killed when a coffee shop was bombed. It really doesn't make any difference who threw the bomb. He died, and they were to marry in three weeks. She was pregnant. Now she has her son Neal who wants to be a famous chef!

"Our son is Sean. He's 40 and not married yet. You know how Irish men are. It takes them a long time to wrench themselves away from the single life. But then, it never really does change, of course. The men still spend all their time with their friends, in bars or at sporting events, returning home for food and the comforts of the marital bed.

"That's why we look to our children and grandchildren for love and happiness," Fiona said sardonically. When Nell made no comment, Fiona continued. "So you see, we all have our stories. No family can avoid the mountains and the valleys as they travel through the journey of life. But we had better stop all this talking and save some stories for…"

Before Fiona could finish the sentence, her mother entered the kitchen, looking refreshed and ready to run a mile. She cut Fiona off with words similar to what Fiona had been say, as happens when two family members are close.

"You two had better stop all that talking and save some of that chit-chat for tonight."

Nell chuckled as she observed the vigor of her 96 year old mother and told her, "Mum, you look like you are ready to jog."

Mrs. Doherty was quick to respond. "No, but I do feel ready to dance a jig."

Nell agreed. "I believe you! As for myself, I am a bit tired, and turning to Fiona she ask, "Where…"

Fiona said, "Oh, saints preserve and protect us, where are my brains? You'll be wanted to go to your room and settle in. Here we go, Nell," and she led her out of the kitchen.

The meal that evening was later than Nell was used to back in the States, but what a meal it was. Grandmother Doherty, whom everyone called "Mum", had planned the meal and prepared much of it, saying something like, "What's the fuss about. Nellanore is only one more mouth to feed than usual." However, each of the girls had contributed something, except Angela, who had requested she be assigned to kitchen clean-up duty.

Everyone arrived more or less on time, even Jack. The exception was Sean, who made a grand entrance just when Mum said they could delay no longer. In contrast to usual quiet meals that Nellanore had when home, this was a noisy gathering, with back-and-forth bantering between everyone there. To herself, Nell wondered how much more boisterous tomorrow night's birthday party could possibly be.

28

KEY WEST PARTY PREP

In Key West, Liz was eager to play the role of hostess, even through her apartment was so small. She wanted to have Rodney and Karen and Juan come to her place for dinner, but she knew there was no room, until she remembered they could eat out on her porch. It would be cozy, but adequate. Then there was the problem of a table and four chairs.

As she rode her bicycle home from work, she passed an empty lot two blocks from her place. Men had been replacing telephone wires in that neighborhood and had left an empty wire spool out by the curb. Liz decided it was a wonderful find — the table she needed — but she had to get it home before the trash truck picked it up. She parked her bicycle back at her apartment, walked back to the empty spool, and turned it on its side. She rolled it home, like a double hoop, and with a little difficulty, was able to manipulate it around the path and onto her porch.

Having saved money on the table, Liz checked out a used furniture store and the Salvation Army thrift shop. Each place had two matching chairs that were cheap enough for her to afford, but neither place would deliver them for her. As she left the second shop, she wondered if she might ask Shorty, with his wagon, or Rodney with the car he had bought from her, but there was Juan, standing outside the shop. He kept popping up everywhere. She wondered if it was always accidental, or was he persistently courting her? Better than Shorty or Rodney, Juan had an old Ford pickup. And there he was.

"Hi, Liz. Find any treasures in there?" Juan asked.

"As a matter of fact, yes. Two wicker chairs, a little battered, but just what I need. How would you like to help a lady in distress, and truck them home for me?"

"Why not? Let's do it," Juan agreed and they went back inside to complete the purchase.

When he had the chairs up in the truck bed, Liz decided to push for a little more moving assistance. "I could have you and Karen and Rodney to my place for supper on Saturday, if I had two more chairs."

Juan looked quizzical. "What are you saying? Do they have more chairs here?"

"No, but the shop on Bertha Street has two folding chairs that fit my budget. Could we stop by there, too? I hate to put you to more bother."

"You just have to ask. Get in the truck. I'll put your bicycle in the back with the chairs. Let's go. I'll do anything for a free meal," he told Liz, laughing.

When the four chairs were set around the spool-table, the setting looked lovely to Liz. Juan kept his opinion to himself. The chairs were mismatched. The spool wood was splintered and dirty. He thought Liz was a big weird. Nice, but strange. Certainly different from the hometown girls, which made her intriguing. Much better, in fact.

He said, "Dinner here Saturday sounds great. Now how about going with me to Chino's Drive-In for hamburgers, fries and a milkshake, then maybe a movie?"

When Liz got home that night, she stayed up for a while, writing a letter to her grandmother about her news of the past week. She felt sorry for her grandmother, sitting all alone in New Jersey, with no excitement in her life.

29 IRISH PARTY: MUM IS 96

Her grandmother was having a wonderful time in Ireland. Although Fiona and Nell had fought like sisters when they were young, the years had mellowed them, and during this brief visit they had established a close bond and great rapport. Also, what truly warmed the cockles of Nell's heart, was to see her mother so active, alert and full of life.

Nell had brought from America a few gifts: a bottle of Jack Daniel's whiskey for her brother-in-law Jack and for her sister a bottle of Maple syrup from New England. To her Mum she gave a silver-framed photograph that Shirley's mother had taken of Nell and Liz in the peony garden.

For Mum's 96th birthday present, saved for the night of the party, Nell had made up a basket containing some of her own homemade jams — blueberry, pear, and strawberry. A large picture book, *Gardens of America,* was also in the basket, plus a Kelly green silk scarf tied on the handle like a huge bow. Well-padded to survive the trip, the presents had taken up a lot of room, which was why Nell had traveled to Eire with two suitcases.

The evening of the birthday party, Mum emerged from her room looking handsome in a Chanel-style suit made in a powder blue boucle. She wore a large silver Claddagh pin and no other jewelry.

"You look wonderful, Mum. You must be the Queen of Ireland!" Nell exclaimed. Indeed, Mum carried herself in a stately fashion, smiling and nodding to everyone in the room. There was a special table set up for her in the main dining room of *The Inn,* and as each guest arrived, they went to her and gave her a hug or kiss or handshake (being careful of the arthritic fingers). It was obvious that Mum was genuinely loved by all.

As the guest who had traveled the farthest, Nell was seated at Mum's table and the introductions became overwhelming to Nell. It was a blur of faces and names: Colin, Caitlin, Fiachra, Renny, Aengus, Jarlath, Aideen, Cahir, Fergus, Shauna, Niamh, Darrash, Garrett, Triona, Brianna, Aoibheann, Susie, Michelle and Shelby.

Nell questioned her mother, "Those last few great-granddaughters, are their name Irish?"

Mum answered philosophically, "My children wanted to name their children Old Irish names, but the next generation wanted a change to something more modern. It's the way of the world."

Everyone carried in a platter or bowl of food from home and placed it on a long banquet table that extended along one wall. Nell couldn't remember what some of the items were, but her mother identified them with ease: Barm Brock, Soda bread, Brown bread, wheat scones, marrowfat peas, potato pancakes, curry-hot rice, leeks and parsnips, seared salmon, lamb shanks, lemon chicken, colcannon, beef stew, spiced beef, oxtails, creamed rice, fruit truffle, Mileeven whiskey cake, Bewley's porter cake, chocolate roses and Celtic Irish-cream after dinner mints.

Nell's mother whispered to her, "Take a little of each. Now you wouldn't want to hurt anyone's feelings, would you? Not after they brought all this wonderful food to the party," and she piled her own plate high, the arthritic fingers finding the strength to carry the dish of food back to her table.

Three men stood at the end of the dance floor, playing fiddle and pipes. First the very young, then the very old came out to dance. One man danced a lively jig. Mum was beaming her lovely smile; Nell feared her mother might join the man on the dance floor and jig herself into a heart attack, but Mum simply sat and clapped her hands to the beat.

Of course there was an open bar of whatever you wished to drink on the other side of the food table. Nell chose only to sip a little Bailey's Irish Cream after her dinner.

It was a wild and wonderful gathering. When Nell kissed her mother and wished her a happy birthday, Mum said, "Well, I hope you will plan to come to my 97th party next year! I'm sure it'll be even better than this one."

The birthday party was wonderful, but the highlight of Nell's trip back to the Old Country was the time she and Fiona spent talking with their mother about when Mum was a child. Even though times were harsh and they were poor, Mum talked about her childhood with her brothers and sisters and parents and grandparents. Nell wished she had tape-recorded it.

30 A CHICKEN FARMER NAMES FIDEL?

In 1898 the United States Army joined the fight in Cuba against the Spanish dominance. The U.S. lost 2,500 Americans, most not from fighting, but from Malaria and Yellow Fever. By the 1920s U.S. companies owned two-thirds of Cuba's farmland and businesses. Cuban Blacks formed their own political party, but when President Jose Miguel Gomez banned that party, there was a rebellion and 3,000 Afro-Cubans died in the rioting.

During the twenty years between 1913 and 1933 Cuba had three presidents,. Their governments were noted for corruption and fraud, so much so that each president left office a wealthy man. Colonel Fulgencio Batista took office briefly in 1940, and initially he had the support of all Cubans, but his administration was corrupt, also. He became wealthy, but lost the democratic elections.

On March 10, 1952, Batista and a few of his officers entered, Cuba's largest military installation, Camp Columbia in Havana, and took control of the Cuban army in a bloodless coup. With the army supporting Colonel Batista, in just seventy-seven minutes he overthrew the presidency of Carlos Prio Cocarras. Cuba was now controlled by the harsh and cruel dictator, Batista. Observers on the island noted that most Cubans shrugged their shoulders as if revolt against another corrupt leader was futile ... except for a young lawyer, Fidel Alejandro Castro Ruz.

Fidel Castro was the son of a well-to-do planter who leased large areas of land from United Fruit, then sold the sugar cane crop back to the same company. Fidel attended the University of Havana law school, but even as a student was a rebel, plotting against Dominican dictator Trujillo.

Batista's motivation for wealth and acceptance stemmed from being the mulatto son of a poor cane-cutter. After the Havana Yacht Club voted against accepting him into the elegant club due to his mixed race, his craving for money and power grew into a massive accumulation of sugar plantation, cattle ranches and even his own airline. His lust for food was so intense that he would sit down to lengthy meals, interrupted periodically for self-induced vomiting, so he could eat more. In an attempt to keep a watch on his enemies, the secret police gave him daily reports of information made from wiretaps. But his political power was declining.

The time was ripe for someone to replace Batista.

Fidel Castro and Abel Santamaria leased a two acre chicken ranch they called *El Siboney* because it was near the vacation resort Siboney Beach. They gathered a band of followers, enthusiastic supporters who acquired guns and ammunition for the revolt. The attack was planned for the Sunday morning after the carnival night of Santeria, with the assumption the soldiers would be sleeping late. And they were.

On July 26, 1953 Fidel Castro and his anti-Batista revolutionaries convoyed into the Moncada Barracks. Although Castro's group secured the Civil Hospital, the revolutionists divided into three areas, were outnumbered by one thousand highly disciplined, heavily armed soldiers. Fidel, and the others who were not killed in the raid, were taken prisoner and brought to trial. During the trial Castro spoke out, saying, "History will absolve me" and denounce Batista, stating everyone should receive an education and the large property should be divided up so every family could have their own piece of land.

Although he was sentenced to 15 years imprisonment and sent to the Isle of Pines, a small Cuban island south of the main island, when Batista was declared president for another term he felt confident his position was strong enough to release the political prisoners in April 1955. Fidel and a group of his followers went to Mexico and met with Ernest "Che" Guevara of Argentina, a doctor who joined with Fidel to help create the Rebel Army, whose purpose was to return to Cuba and overthrow Batista.

The U.S. State Department debated about Batista's effectiveness in supporting American investments in Cuba, particularly with increasing demands for social change. CIA agents that had assisted in a political coup in Guatemala were drawn from their experience to help assess the current Cuban situation. David Halberstam, in his book, *The Fifties,* suggested that in the 1950's "those who posed legal and moral questions about clandestine operations were considered naive."

31 "SAVE THE BOTANICAL GARDEN" TEA PARTY

The long-neglected Botanical Gardens, located on Stock Island, one island up from Key West, was the site of an afternoon tea party. Many community leaders attended; it was a good opportunity, politically, to be seen and heard.

The Garden Club was a small group of women (and two men) who were interested in learning about flower-arranging and the local flora of the tropics. The Botanical Garden was a separate entity that had no direct connection with the Garden Club; indeed, it was a forgotten area. Originally 55 acres of land, with 7,000 sub-tropical exotic plants donated by the Department of Agriculture, the city fathers, blind to the value of a hardwood hammock, had nibbled away at the property. Now only a little over a dozen acres remained, full of weeds and vines and encroaching plants that were smothering the once-beautiful spot. The Garden Club members were hoping the city and county politicians would budget some money to help get the area vibrant again.

A group of three ladies went to see the editor of the newspaper, Mr. Bartlett, and sweet-talked him into giving them a small, free, public-interest announcement about the "Save the Botanical Gardens" meeting. The same three women spoke briefly to the members of the Rotary Club and Junior Chamber of Commerce, urging them to attend. Most effectively, each of the Garden Club ladies coerced their husbands in going.

The local Garden Club members had voted to attempt to build interest in rejuvenating the area and had publicized an open-air meeting in the Gardens. The women had set up a few card tables with their kitchen tablecloths. They brought Kool-Aid, paper cups, buckets of ice, and their home baked cookies and brownies, decorating the table with small branches of flowering trees.

The Mayor and other members of the City Commission and County Commission dutifully attended. The Commander of the Naval Station, the Colored preacher from the AME Zion church, the White preacher from the Methodist church, the owner of the local radio station, the manager of the local water company, representatives from many smaller businesses, and the editor of the newspaper were there, plus many locals, those who were interested in the garden, or mingling with the community leaders, or wanting something to do on a humid Sunday afternoon.

William Fredericks was there. He saw several men talking with Mr. Bartlett, the newspaper editor. He ambled toward them and casually joined the circle. They were discussing Cuba and the politics of Cuba's president, Batista. One man volunteered to go to Havana at Mr. Bartlett's expense, saying he would then write a column for the paper. All the men guffawed. Each of them had made several trips to visit the prostitutes in that city. It was an opening William "Mr. Bill" Fredricks had hoped for.

"I agree that an article about Cuba would be of interest to your readers", said Mr. Bill. "Why not send that new reporter you have? The girl who wrote about the Dry Tortugas." He said no more. Others agreed half-heartedly and changed the subject. The seed was planted, so Mr. Bill left the mosquito infested Botanical Garden to those who enjoyed being seen.

Nellanore Steele's suitcases were heavier on the return flight to the United States. Her sister had insisted she accept a set of Royal Doulton dishes, Waterford crystal stemware and many Belleek items 'for Elizabeth's dowry'. Nell herself had purchased for Liz a Claddaugh ring and for Shirley a picture book of lovely fairies, plus a small Belleek vase for Shirley's mother. At the goodbyes her mother had pressed into Nell's hand a rosary made of small green stones: Connemara marble.

Grandma Nellanore Steele was delighted to find several letters awaiting her arrival home. Without unpacking her suitcases, she sat down at her kitchen table and read them.

Liz had written: "Love my job and am making new friends. My wee apartment is cozy, but my porch overlooks the landlady's tropical garden, so my entertaining takes place there. I recently acquired four chairs and a table, so will serve three friends my condensed version of a Thanksgiving dinner this weekend. Our November weather continues to be hot and sunny, so outdoor dining is delightful, Gram. Wish you were here. What have you been doing lately? Love, Liz."

From Canada came a letter from Mark: "It took a visit from my sister Elizabeth to awaken me to the years I have neglected writing to you. No doubt she told you about my house in British Columbia, where I work for an aluminum company. I really enjoyed her visit and hope it is one of many more in the future. Warm regards, Mark."

Matthew, the eldest, sent a brief note, with a longer note enclosed from his wife Marian: "My sister Liz came to visit my wife and children and gave us your address. I'm sorry we'd lost contact and hope to make amends. Sincerely, Matt." From Marian: "Matt is not much with words, but he and I want to invite you to come to our home in Mystic for Thanksgiving dinner. It would add so much to the holiday to have you here with us. Love, Marian."

No word from Luke in New York or his girlfriend that Liz had met while there.

The Key West cuisine, Conch cooking, seemed to have lots of fried fish or roasted pork with garlic or a ground meat dish that was something like a Sloppy Joe but called Piccadillo. Then, too, there was rice and beans and avocados and plantains. Liz had invited Sharon Bergdorf, Rodney Rodriquez and Juan Robertson for dinner, but all she knew how to cook was what her grandmother had raised her on…it would have to be a Yankee dinner. She figured she could put most of it in the oven all at once:

she would bake a stuffed chicken, acorn squash and whole potatoes and, maybe, add some zucchini for color.

Dessert was a problem. She wanted to make her grandmother's prize-winning Lemon Meringue pie, but locals were hung up on Key Lime pie. In addition, she would have to make a pie crust and she had no rolling pin. She decided on a cool and easy Jello with red cherries and made with half water and half wine. The opened wine bottle was set aside to serve with dinner. She had no wine glasses but paper cups would suffice.

She had painted the two wicker and two folding chairs with some Woolworth white paint a few days ago. The telephone cable spool was covered with a clean pink bedsheet folded in half, and for her centerpiece decoration she snipped a branch of cerise bougainvillea from the landlady's bush. Liz had wanted some background music, but she had no record player and no radio.

The neighbors who lived on the other side of her place had been arguing all afternoon. She was afraid it would ruin the party's ambiance, but then she heard a door slam and a car pull away. Right after that, she could hear the woman humming, and then through the open windows came music, with the local radio station playing current favorites.

"Luck of the Irish!" she exclaimed out loud to herself. It was an expression she heard her grandmother say frequently when she was a child, forgetting it was Grandma's birthplace.

It was getting close to the time they should arrive, and she was getting nervous about whether everything would be ready on time and would they like it or what would they talk about and ... then stopped that trend of thought by going back out into the garden, this time to pick one hibiscus flower. She bobbie pinned it over her left ear, wondering which side signaled 'available'. She thought Juan was very attractive.

Sharon and Rodney arrived first. Sharon handed a box of after dinner mints to Liz, and received a hug from Liz. She immediately invited her two guests out of the hot apartment onto the porch. Sharon was gushing about how pretty everything looked when Juan walked in carrying a long loaf of Cuban bread and a pound of butter. Liz set that out on the table, and the two men immediately sliced chunks, buttered them and started talking about a Key West high school football game during their bites of bread.

Sharon went back into the kitchen area to help Liz. The two women decided to portion out the food in the kitchen, then carry the four plates out to the porch. The meal went well. The food was enjoyed. The men got up to take their plates back inside to get more chicken. The wine bottle was emptied, the bread finished and even the Jello mold was scraped clean. The four felt very comfortable with each other. Everyone helped clear the table and rinse the dishes. Then Rodney suggested a ride in the DeSoto.

32
A MOONLIT DRIVE

Juan and Liz sat in the backseat. Juan casually draped his arm over Liz' shoulder. The foursome drove down Duval Street, waving at friends and acquaintances they spotted promenading down the main street, which ran north and south across the island's mile and a half width.

The length of the island of Key West is about four miles, east to west. A three-mile road had been built along the northern length of the island. It circles around, then extends another three-mile stretch at the water's edge on the south side. It was there, on South Boulevard, that Rodney drove the car and parked. No streetlights marred the favorite spot for lovers to meet.

The two couples got out of the car and slowly strolled down the wide sidewalks that banked the water's edge, enjoying the romantic vista: a long line of coconut trees lined the beach as far as your eyes could see.

"Sometimes you can see the Southern Cross constellation from here," Juan told Liz.

He pointed straight out to sea and told her, "Cuba is right there, 90 miles away."

She gazed at the horizon, half expecting to see the landmass across the sea. The view was a panorama of ocean and sky, with more stars than Liz had ever seen before. A crescent moon shed just enough light to scatter diamonds on the water ripples.

She heard the car doors slam. Looking back at the DeSoto, she saw that Sharon and Rodney were back in the front seat of the car.

"Are they leaving?" Liz asked Juan.

"No," he told her. "I think they are doing this," and he placed his left hand on her back and gently pulled her to him. Juan touched her cheek with his right hand, then slid his hand under her ear, around the back of her neck and spread his fingers through her hair as his lips gently touched her lips. Then both hands drew her closer and his kiss became more intense. He released his hold and took one step back. He looked into her eyes, trying to gauge her reaction.

Her body gave a brief tremor.

Worried, he asked her "Are you cold?" and pulled her to him again.

Her answer, "No", came out a low, husky tone. Although her hormonal response was affecting her body, her mind was still clear and active. She thought "Where is this leading?" She backed away, took a deep breath and said, "Let's slow down, Juan."

Following her lead, he asked, "Do you want to walk some more?"

Juan and Liz walked along the wide sidewalk that had been built during the 1930s by WPA workers. When they reached the East Martello Tower, a Civil War brick fort, they turned back, retracing their steps to the car.

Liz said, "Perhaps it's time to go home." The long walk and the casual conversation had banked the fires. The attraction was still there but the bodily insistence had been staunched.

The four drove back to Liz's apartment. Rodney pulled the DeSoto up behind Juan's truck. Liz and Juan got out and said their good-byes to the couple, who waved and drove away.

Juan walked Liz to the door of her apartment, not knowing if he would be spending the night with her or what her feelings were.

She unlocked the door and turned to him. "You are very exciting, Juan. But, good night."

He stood there, looking at her. Liz leaned forward and gave him a quick kiss on his lips, smiling and said, "Goodbye."

He turned and slowly walked to his truck, remembering the evening, the supper, the car ride, the walk on South Boulevard, and, oh, those kisses.

Travel was wearying and now that she was back home Nellanore Doherty Steele just wanted to be alone for a while. It felt good to get back in her own house and her old routine of very little socializing, except for an hour or so once a week with Shirley and Shirley's mother. Grandma had some thinking to do.

She thought to herself: Friends and family — those are the important things in life.

Her thoughts continued: It's not about getting up in the morning to go to work to make a lot of money, nor studying books to compete for the highest grades. Family should not be neglected, but closeness nurtured. Petty grievances must be ignored for the bigger picture of maintaining close ties with family, whether it be mother, father, sister, brother, grandparents, aunts, uncles, cousins, and the entire family 'extended', 'nuclear', or the common, everyday, plain old 'Just Family,' whomever that may encompass.

She berated herself, physically cringing with the pain of embarrassment when she thought about how she had neglected her grandchildren. It is true that she believed them to be well taken care of physically, but she realized that they must have asked themselves why she had abandoned them. Why hadn't she kept in touch? She wondered about that and mentally thrashed herself, vowing to do better.

And friends … she remembered an old song they would sing: *Make new friends, but keep the old ones; Some are silver and the others are gold.*

Edith and Clyde Chapman were old friends. Such good friends that Elizabeth had called her grandmother's friends "Aunt" and "Uncle" ever since she was little. When Grandma Steele's son Charlie had died, she had gone into a deep depression. It was her next-door neighbor of that time, Edith Chapman, who had helped her when she needed emotional support.

They had been so close that they had called each other by nicknames, back then in the early days of their friendship. Edith called Grandma Steele 'Grouch' and she was called 'SourPuss' in return. Grandma Steele chuckled to herself as she remembered now that Edith had continued to contact Grandma Steele periodically, but the return correspondence from Grandma was negligible. She decided to write to her now.

Grandma Steele wrote to Edith 'SourPuss' Chapman, but avoided the old nickname. Even so, she knew that her friend would not be angry that the correspondence had been sparse for so many years…that's how close the bond of friendship had been, that time could not wear it away. She wrote a newsy letter about her trip to Ireland to see her sister and she wrote about her granddaughter Elizabeth, now living in Key West, Florida.

The letters to her grandsons were much more difficult to start.

Delaying the actual moment when the composition of the letters must begin, Grandma went to the stationary shop to decide upon the appropriate notepaper she would use. Yellow paper was too chipper; not personal enough. Gray was dignified but too stiff and cold. In trying to convey warmth and love, she picked out small notecards with flowers on the front.

The message to each should be identical, she thought. She should not go on and on. The small notecards would keep it brief. She wondered how she could convey how sorry she was that she had allowed them to grow apart. She decided she would say just that.

Dear Matthew, (Dear Mark, Dear Luke) Recently I traveled to Ireland to visit my 96-year-old mother and my dear sister Fiona. That visit re-emphasized to me the importance of family.

I am sorry I did not feel, after you suffered the terrible loss of your mother and father, that I could keep you four children all together with me, at that time.

When it seemed you were going to live in better surroundings I felt it was a blessings. Now, I wish you all could have stayed together.

I pray that you are happy, and hope you will contact your siblings, because family is the most important thing in life. God bless you.

Know that I have always loved you and always will. Grandma N. D. Steele

She wrote a postscript to her letter to Matt and Marian, thanking them for the invitation to join them for dinner on Thanksgiving. She asked them for a "raincheck".

33

THE PROOF READER

The desk for the newspaper's proofreader was adjacent to the printing press room. Liz was distracted by the clacking noise from the old presses. Eventually her brain protected her concentration by turning the metal reverberations into a meditative hum. Her articles were written on a typewriter. Busy one day, distractions masked by the noises, Liz was startled to feel someone tap her shoulder. She looked up and saw an old friend, Jim Hannigan, smiling at her. Conversation was impossible in that area, so she beckoned him to follow her into the business office.

"Jim! What brings you here?" She had met Jim Hannigan while she was working at the San Francisco television studio. He had been part of the crew on one of the yachts being featured about a yachting race from California to Hawaii. The televised interview had included owners and some of the crew members.

"My Captain, Lars Olson, decided to sail his ketch, the 47-foot "Viking" down the Pacific from Los Angeles, across the Panama Canal, up the Atlantic ocean to Norway. He headed to Key West for supplies. While here the Captain is having a Holiday Party for friends and crew.

"When I read the local newspaper article by Liz Steele I hoped it was the Liz I had met. And yes, here you are! I came to invite you to Captain Olson's holiday party."

Liz asked, "A party on the "Viking"?"

"No, Liz. The Commander of the U.S. Navy Station here in Key West has arranged for us a safe harbor off shore Key West. Captain Olson is having his party at the Key West Yacht Club on Roosevelt Boulevard."

"Jim, what a wonderful surprise. Yes, I'd love to go. Thank you."

The surprise last-minute invitation to a gala at the Yacht Club had Liz wondering how local ladies dressed up for a night on the town. She had one item in her wardrobe that might work: a long black skirt, an old faithful from San Francisco. She topped it with a simple white cotton tank top, then added some of her chunky rope of beads. Done and ready.

Jim arrived at her cottage apartment at the time they had agreed upon. During their walk to the party they had time to chat about their adventures since last they last met. He said he had finally found a woman who would understand the life of a sailor: gone for long periods of time working for Captain Olson. Married, their base home was in Los Angeles.

Liz skimmed over her travels, mentioning her visit with her grandmother and then her solo drive down U.S. Highway One to Key West.

Upon arrival at the Yacht Club Jim introduced Liz to Captain Olson. Liz glanced up at the Norwegian. (Much later she confessed to Sharon what she had seen was a very tall, slim man with unruly blonde hair, very much sun-bleached. Wind and sun had also darkened his skin, which served as a contrast to his hazel eyes, fringed with dark lashes.)

More arriving visitors pulled the captain's attention. Jim and Liz moved closer to the sound of music. The entertainment for the evening was Key West's own version of Nat King Cole, the smooth sound of 'Coffee Butler' singing current songs while playing the piano. 'Coffee's' low, throaty voice kept them captured nearby.

Several times throughout the evening Captain Olson did stop by the table to speak with Jim and Liz briefly. When it grew late Lars Olson asked Liz for the next dance. During that time he mentioned he had, indeed, read her newspaper articles and was impressed with such an adventurous young woman. He explained he was often busy traveling but asked if they could begin corresponding. "Would she send him a copy of her articles?" She nodded and the dance was over. He returned her to Jim and said Good Night.

34 HOW TO TRAP A SPY

The weekly articles Liz wrote for the Key West newspaper, *The Conch Courier,* were receiving positive feedback. She had written with a newcomer's wonderment about some of the tropical flora: bougainvillea, heliconia, jasmine, frangipani, hibiscus. One of the members of the Garden Club wrote Mr. Bartlett a "Letter to the Editor" praising the newspaper for running such an article and requested more items "from that girl reporter".

The independent agents of Brothers Assisting National Defense (BAND) were doing their work, too. They wanted Liz to be sent to Cuba and believed they could use her, unbeknownst to her, to get a message to a Cuban underground agent that was being carefully watched by Batista's men.

"O.B." Fisher was a talker. Wives loved his visits to collect the insurance premiums. They could catch the latest goings-on about town. He mentioned to a couple of the ladies he had heard "that new girl reporter was going to write about vacations in Cuba". The ladies stayed home all day, dusting and vacuuming and washing clothes. It was nice to have some news tidbit to mention to their husbands in the evening.

There was a little rivalry going on between the local radio station owner and newspaper chief. When Joe Woodson, owner of the radio station, heard from his sound engineer that there seemed to be a lot of mention on the radio teletype about Cuba, Joe sat next to Mr. Bartlett at the next Rotary Club meeting and suggested he'd better get some up-to-date stuff in that paper if he wanted his newspaper to be on the ball.

Blackie Gomez went to the dances every weekend at the Cuban Club. He acted a little drunk and belligerent and went on and on about there not being much news in the paper about Cuba. It was just local news or things going on in Washington, D.C.

Each member of the BAND did their part to start the ball rolling — to get Mr. Bartlett to send Liz to Cuba on an assignment to report her views as a tourist. The words got back to Mr. Bartlett through many different avenues. Sometimes called "the Conch telegraph", news (or gossip, true or untrue) could be passed around the island like wildfire.

Mr. Bartlett decided he thought it might be a good idea to send Liz to Cuba. He thought of that all by himself. He decided it was such a good idea, he would pay her expenses for a whole week. He called her into the office and told her so. She was surprised and delighted, ready to leave the following week.

Miss Geraldine was told by Mr. Bartlett to write out an advance for Liz Steele so she could arrange her flight to Cuba. Miss Geraldine was pissed-off; she had worked for Mr. Bartlett for 20 years and he had never paid her way anywhere. She told that to the printing-press setter, who told the guy that delivered the rolls of newsprint, who told Blackie, the driver for Keys Transport Trucking, who told Juan Robertson.

Yes! Just the word they were waiting for!

Juan went directly to George Green's bookstore. It was a small shop, with double-doors kept open to the street. In the center was a large wooden desk where Mr. Green sat, piles of books obscuring him from his customers. Of course he could not keep an eye on potential shoplifters, but he wouldn't have seen them anyway, for three reasons. One, he was terribly near-sighted; two, he spent his time reading books; and three, nobody ever stole from Mr. Green, because everyone liked him.

The English-Spanish dictionary selection was limited to five books. Three were compact paperbacks and two hardbacks. Of the hardbacks, one was a large and comprehensive English-to-Spanish/Spanish-to-English dictionary and the other was a slim book called "Easy Spanish Phrases". Juan bought the slim hardback.

Two of the BAND agents met that night in their shed near the cemetery. One held a small flashlight while the other carefully sponged inside the back cover of the phrase book, then peeled back the paper lining. The microfiche with names, dates and plans for the Bay of Pigs invasion was laid in place. It was made larger than usual so it would rest just inside the paper lining. A smaller film would have shown outlines. Quick-drying glue cemented the paper back in place.

The next morning Juan took the Spanish phrase book back to Mr. Green. He asked Mr. Green if he would help him with a girl he was dating. Juan said she was an independent Yankee girl. He had intended to present her with the book he had purchased the day before, but she probably would want to pick out the book herself. Would Mr. Green keep Juan's selection in his desk, and suggest it to her when Juan brought her in later in the day? Then it wouldn't seem like Juan was pushing his preferences on her.

"You know how stubborn women can be, Mr. Green." Juan said, smiling his beguiling smile. Mr. Green was delighted to be involved with a little bit of a love story and placed Juan's book in his desk drawer.

Once again, Juan "just happened" to be in the neighborhood when Liz came out from *The Conch Courier* offices after work. She was delighted to see him and quickly told him the exciting news. She was going to Cuba next week!

Juan asked her, "*?Que quiere decir esta palabra? Recuerdos?*"

"What?"

"How are you going to get along? Do you speak any Spanish?"

"Oh, Juan, you could teach me a few sentences. I just need to know "I want a room with a bath" and "I would like a menu, please" and "How much does that cost?"

"Yes, I'll teach you a few words, but don't you think a translation book would help?"

"Do you think I need one?"

"Let's see what Mr. Green has available in his bookshop, Liz."

When they walked into the bookstore, there was no one at Mr. Green's desk but his tabby-cat, sitting on the tallest pile of books. Juan's heart skipped a beat, but then Mr. Green emerged from the back room. He didn't say anything to Juan, either because he couldn't see that far or he was enjoying play-acting his role in what he imagined was a romantic encounter.

Liz quickly discounted the large dictionary as too heavy and cumbersome to carry on a vacation and was trying to decide among the three paperbacks. Juan was quietly commenting that he worried it would be difficult to communicate while only looking up one word at a time, which Mr. Green walked over to them. He handed the small hardback to Liz and suggested she consider this Spanish phrase book.

She was delighted that the bookstore owner took interest in her quest and said, "I'll take it."

Juan said, "Let me pay for it," and hastened to Mr. Green, now at his desk. He handed Mr. Green one dollar for the already-paid-for book, and said, "Thanks."

Mr. Green pressed a key on his old-fashioned cash register. It chimed and the cash-drawer opened. Mr. Green placed the dollar bill inside and pushed the drawer shut. He was smiling. He felt like Cupid.

Liz was smiling. She was pleased with the book she had chosen.

Juan was smiling.

Juan spent the next seven days in a flurry of intense romancing of Liz.

It wasn't necessary. The mission of the Brothers Assisting National Defense was assured: arrangements had been completed to have someone deliver the secret message to their contacts in Cuba; and that person was not suspect by authorities, nor did she have any knowledge of the BAND, or that she was carrying any information.

But Juan felt unsettled. He was worried about Liz. He cared about her. She was not like anyone he had ever met. She was interesting, intriguing, exciting. It was a new feeling, but he wondered, could someone be true to the stringent rules and requirements of a member of the secret organization and also be married?

He worried that he was sending her to the wolves, unarmed except by her innocence. To assuage his guilt, he thought at least he could assist her with the Spanish phrases.

She listened to his Spanish words and wrote them as it sounded to her, phonetically.

Juan told Liz, "To prepare the person to listen closely to you, because of your pronunciation, start each sentence with *'Por favor'*."

She dutifully wrote on her 5 x 8 card *pour 'fahVOR'*.

For lunch, he suggested she find a small shop and order a *"batido de fruta bomba", a* milkshake with tropical fruit. And for dinner *"arroz con pollo"*, a chicken and rice meal every restaurant would have on the menu.

It was important to the BAND that Liz include in her travels the small Cuban town of Trinidad, on the south of the island. Mr. Bartlett was pleased with the articles that Liz had been submitting each week, and decided he would not suggest what she should write in her column about her impressions of Cuba.

However, he did tell her that for the short period of her visit she should travel no more than 200 miles east of Havana, then back. His brother-in-law had some financial interests in Havana, Matanzas, Sancti Spiritus, and Cienfuego. Based on his brother-in-law's interests, Mr. Bartlett gave Liz those towns as her assignment.

The town of Trinidad was not included. The BAND would have to think of something.

Liz wanted to go all the way to the eastern end of Cuba, but Juan knew Fidel Castro was in that area. For her to visit there could make some persons suspicious about her. Juan suggested that traveling that far was stretching her short visit into hurried days, and said she would be busy enough in the brief time she had.

"Enough study-time," Juan announced. They had been sitting in his apartment, he in one armchair and she in another. She was sitting cross-legged, with a notebook and the 5 x 8 cards on her lap. He longed to hold her in his arms, but feared it might feel like he was jumping her if he moved in so rapidly. Instead, he said, "Let's go dancing."

He drove her to Raul's Nightclub, where the musicians were playing romantic Hispanic songs. Juan and Liz danced to *Quizas, Quizas, Quizas* (Perhaps, Perhaps, Perhaps) and *Sin Ti* (Without You). By the time the group got to the song *Besame Mucho* (Kiss Me a Lot), their bodies were dancing so close together there was no thought to the movement of the dance: they danced as one unit.

Another evening he drove her down a street on the eastern end of the island and stopped his truck in front of a dark house. The front yard showed that it was in the final stages of being built. There was a sapling tree that appeared newly planted, propped up with three supports and a circle of rocks at its base. Stickers on each windowpane indicated new glass. Juan led her up the brick path and inserted a key in the shiny brass doorknob.

He swung open the door, lit a flashlight, and invited her inside the house. "No electricity connected yet, but I wanted you to see it. I wanted to know your impressions. What do you think of this house?"

Liz was afraid to answer. She thought, What's this all about? I'm no architect. Juan never discussed this house before. What does he want me to say? Why didn't he show me this place in the daytime? He is standing so close…is he going to kiss me? Is he going to propose? Do I want to marry him? This is all too fast or am I jumping to conclusions? What is the right answer?

She asked, "Whose house is this?"

"It doesn't matter. I just wanted your opinion of this place."

Liz hedged her response, unsure of what the real subject was. "Oh, Juan, it is so hard to look around the place in the dark. Can we come by in the daytime? I would love to see it then."

Juan quickly stepped back and re-opened the front door, shining the light on the floor so she could make her way out. He said nothing as they walked back to his truck.

"Are you mad at me, Juan?" Liz asked.

"No. You are right. Perhaps I'll bring you back here sometime in the daylight."

He drove her to her apartment, angry with himself for not proposing. The house was being build on one of the pieces of property he had inherited from his parents' estate. He had planned to propose to Liz tonight, even though his Chief Agent and sometimes father figure, Mr. Bill, had strongly cautioned Juan against it.

He was sending the woman he loved on a dangerous assignment in Cuba. She had no defense except her ignorance of the entire scheme. Was that enough to protect her?

35 WHAT SHE DOESN'T KNOW CAN'T HURT HER

The day of the flight from Key West to Cuba had arrived. Juan had told Liz that he would take her to the Pink Flamingo for lunch, then get her to the airport in time for her afternoon flight. She expected Juan to arrive at her apartment in his truck, but it was Mr. Bill who knocked on her door.

"Hello, Liz. Ready for lunch? I'll take your suitcase. Let's go," and he turned and walked down the narrow path toward the street. Bushes of hibiscus and other flowering shrubbery obscured her view past the shoulders of Mr. Bill. When they arrived at the sidewalk, Liz saw Juan seated in the front passenger seat of Mr. Bill's sedan.

Mr. Bill opened the back door of the car, indicating Liz was to sit in the back seat. He continued around the car and placed her suitcase in the trunk. Juan said nothing.

"Juan happened to mention that you are flying to Havana today, so I asked if I could join the two of you for lunch. I have been to Cuba myself, and thought you might like to hear some of my stories about the sights to see. We couldn't let you go to the airport in his old truck, could we? What if your suitcase bounced out the back? Oh, here we are, 'The Pink

Flamingo'." Without allowing anyone else to say a word, Mr. Bill parked his sedan in front of a small pink house.

The trio entered the front door, which were two wooden louvered doors painted white. The slat door swung in or out, like the old wild-west barroom doors. In addition to the kitchen, the house consisted of two rooms for dinner or sitting on an outside patio overlooking a small pool. Without asking their preference, Mr. Bill led Liz and Juan outside.

The decor of pink tablecloths, pink napkins folded into flower-shapes and tucked into stemmed goblets, white carnations in silver bud-vases, all made a lovely setting amid the lush tropical greenery. The bottom of the pool was painted a cool turquoise. Mounted in the center of the pool stood a large metal flamingo, its pink coloring appearing iridescent in the sunshine because of fine sprays of water spurting up from its base.

Mr. Bill chose a small table with two chairs. He sat in one and the waiter, bewildered by the choice of that table for what appeared to be three diners, pulled out the opposite chair for Liz.

"Bring another chair over here," Mr. Bill directed Juan.

The waiter urged them to move to a larger table, but Mr. Bill insisted they were comfortable where they were. It was obvious Juan and Liz were not happy with the arrangement, but both seemed unable to overcome Mr. Bill's commanding presence.

Mr. Bill gave the waiter for food order for all three, again without consulting the wishes of the others. Liz was dazed by Mr. Bill's attitude and also by Juan's zombie-like affect. She thought about what might have brought about this changed in Juan's behavior, but came up with nothing that made sense to her.

The meal continued with Mr. Bill talking non-stop. It was like a jangle of noise in Liz' ears, yet she heard nothing. She looked at Juan, but he was looking at his plate, as if hypnotized. He poked the food with his fork. Liz, too, ate little and was so distraught at the tension going back and forth that she was unaware of what was on her plate.

Finally Mr. Bill called for the check. He paid, the three returned to the sedan, and Mr. Bill drove to the airport.

Mr. Bill and Juan walked Liz to the airport counter. Mr. Bill handed her the suitcase.

"Do you have everything — your money, your identification, your Spanish phrase book?" Mr. Bill asked.

Liz nodded..

"Have a nice trip," Mr. Bill said. He turned and walked back towards his car.

Juan stood facing Liz. They stood still, saying nothing, looking into each other's eyes.

"Come on, Juan," Mr. Bill shouted.

Juan mumbled, "Have a nice trip," and turned away.

Liz reached out and grabbed Juan's arm. She took a step forward and kissed him, then turned to the ticket agent.

"Juan!" shouted Mr. Bill.

Juan walked toward Mr. Bill and the two men got in the automobile.

36 KEY WEST, AN INTERNATIONAL AIRPORT

Henry Flagler had extended his railway down through Florida to Miami and continued across stretches of sea extending from one small island to another, constructing a total of forty-three bridges. One bridge covered an expanse of seven miles. But the 90-mile stretch of ocean between Key West, Florida and Cuba required boats.

However, the Wright brothers' flight in 1903 had introduced another mode of transportation.

Things moved along quickly, and in 1909 the first overseas flight was made: twenty-one miles across the English Channel, flown by Louis Beleriot. The next year Robert Lorraine flew fifty-five miles across the Irish Sea.

In 1911 a test pilot for Curtiss Aircraft, J. A. McCurdy, hoped to make a record over-water flight of the ninety miles from Key West to Cuba. However, he ran out of gas just short of land, although within sight of the remains of the sunken battleship Maine in Havana's harbor.

It was May 19, 1913 when a man born in Key West, whose parents were of Cuban descent, made the first successful Key West to Cuba flight:

Augustin Parla Orduna. A statue was erected at the Key West airport to commemorate the overseas/international flight.

Another Key West first — the first **commercial** flight between the United States and a foreign country happened on November 15, 1919, with a small company using decommissioned Navy 'flying boats'. There was no radio communication in the planes, but carrier pigeons were utilized. They had been trained to return to their coop when released. When nearing Key West, the birds were released. The arrival of the pigeons was the notification to the ground crew and waiting relatives that the seaplane would be landing soon.

In 1925 Pan American World Airways formed its company, opening in Key West, Florida. There were no American international airlines at that time. A Key West investor, Malcolm Meacham, bought most of the land on the northwestern end of the island, then leased the land to Pan Am for a dollar a year. According to Geoffrey Arend in *Great Airports* "Pan Am flight operations in Key West inaugurated not only the airline, but also American International air travel into the big time".

When Liz booked her flight from Key West to Cuba in December 1955, it was the Cuban airline *Aereovias Q* that was the major airline passenger carrier.

She now had her round-trip airline ticket, some money for expenses (changed into Cuban money by Mr. Bartlett), her packed suitcase, her *Easy Spanish Phrase Book,* plus a few words she had written phonetically on cards. Her adventure had begun.

Day One of her trip from Key West to Cuba had not been proceeding in the way Liz had dreamed. She had anticipated that Juan would come to her apartment and sit there for a little while. It would be delightfully intimate, just the two of them — cozy, like a married couple.

That image jarred her. What am I thinking? she wondered. Could it be that I really want to marry Juan? But, she wondered, if that were true, why had I felt so skittish when he showed me the new house a few days ago.

She felt so confused. But it really didn't matter. Mr. Bill had burst that bubble today.

No, not Mr. Bill. It was Juan's actions — or non-actions — that had confused and frightened her. She had thought they would hold hands across the table and Juan would tell her some more stories about when he had visited Cuba in the past. He seemed to have many friends on that island.

He had told her that the Cuban people had suffered from years of political greed and graft. One evening he had asked her what she would say if someone asked her what she thought of Batista..

She had asked Juan, "Who is Batista?"

He answered, "Their president."

"Oh, in that case," she replied, "I'll say that he is wonderful!"

"Wrong!" he said firmly. "He's the leader of the faction that controls the graft. What their government should focus on is better schooling for all and health care for everyone. Instead, Batista puts the money in his own pocket!"

"Okay, okay, I hear you. But I couldn't say 'Your president is a stinker'. That is too rude."

Juan smiled. "Maybe you could simply respond in your own sweet way, 'Tell me about him'."

But that was last week. She didn't feel sweet today. She was still sulking under the dark shadow that Mr. Bill had cast over her morning.

She wanted to erase the shadows from her thoughts, so Liz strolled out of this small shack that constituted the Key West International Airport's processing area. Her flight to Cuba wouldn't leave for another twenty minutes. Adjacent to the airport was the Civil War fort. Liz walked over to the fort and took a photograph of the picturesque entrance. It would make a nice Picture Number One in her series of photos of her trip.

Liz continued across the boulevard and sat on a low retaining wall overlooking the sea. She remembered the night Sharon and Rodney had driven Juan and her out to the boulevard. It had been dark that night, but Liz wondered if this was the exact spot where Juan's kisses had caused her to tremble.

To distract her thoughts from Juan and the changes in his behavior she tried to enjoy the beauty of the vista: water, water everywhere. But ninety miles due South was Cuba, a large island 44,000 square miles. Right now she stood on a dot of an island that measured one-and-a-half miles by four miles wide. Quite a difference!

The stroll had done its job of lifting her mood. She returned to the airport and joined the other passengers who were about to board the plane.

Liz had expected to see a predominance of men traveling to Cuba. Her friends at the newspaper told her there were two types of men who went to Havana. Because the majority of businesses in Cuba were American-owned, company officials frequently traveled there. The focus of the other group of men was to utilize prostitutes or view the nightlife.

However, persons climbing the steps into the plane were a diverse group. First there were eight older ladies, each sporting their tour ID badge 'The Miami Beach Widows'. Then a young couple herded their two children up the ladder. Each child held a miniature wooden crate of candy 'oranges'. Next was a couple who appeared to be about fifty years of age. They were holding hands. Liz followed them on board the plane.

Two couples who spoke Spanish had bought a songbook with the words of currently popular hits. They were laughing, trying to emulate the sound and phrasing of the artist who had popularized each particular song. Next up the ladder was a young woman who wore an outfit that showed off her breasts to advantage. She swung her hips from side to side, giving maximum exposure of her thighs, much to the enjoyment and delight of the three sailors who were last to board.

The two motors of the airplane revved up and the plane lifted off for the short trip over the salty waters where the Gulf of Mexico and the Florida Straits merge.

Liz had studied the attire of her fellow travelers when they were boarding. The ladies from Miami Beach wore cotton muumuus printed with huge colorful flowers. Their shoes were open sandals worn with white socks. The young couple with children were conservatively dressed. The older couple each wore dark slacks and silk shirts. The woman's shirt was powder blue and his was a very pale yellow.

Liz began to question her own choice of traveling outfit. She had some preconceived notion of what Cuban women wore and tried to dress in the same manner so she would not look "American". She wore a dark pink gathered skirt made more full by the use of a crinoline slip. This was topped by a "peasant" blouse, white cotton with a drawstring neckline.

For shoes, white sandals, her bare feet and painted toenails showing. In addition she had golden earrings in a seashell motif. Now she felt overdressed, as if in a costume.

The two Cuban girls each wore a skirt that was slim line, straight to the knees, then a bias-cut flounce that extended below the kneecap. Their full-bodied figures filled their cotton blouses, which were buttoned up modestly. The young Cuban men had on dark trousers and colored Guayaberas, shirts with pleats stitched down the front.

Seated in the back of the plane, the gal with the well-endowed breasts had scarcely covered them in a thin knit top that criss-crossed in front, rounding her curves to maximum advantage. A short knit skirt and very high heels completed the outfit. The sailors were in their summer white uniforms.

The sailors and the gal were seated in back; Liz could hear an occasional giggle and an exclamation in a male voice. Everyone on board kept his or her eyes facing front. Whatever was going on back there, all four sounded happy with the action.

Photo Number Two that Liz took was from the window of the airplane. As the plane banked low over the outskirts of the city of Havana, Liz could see mansions with tennis courts and swimming pools within each estate. She took a picture of what was her first impression of Cuba.

The Havana airport building was busy filled with passengers who had recently arrived in planes from New York and Miami. Like a swarm of bees hanging from the hive, hordes of people were pressing to get into buses that would transport them from the airport to downtown Havana. Unlimited alcohol en route on the planes had caused many of them to lose their sensibilities. They were speaking loudly and coarsely, already complaining about the Cuban food that they had not yet tasted.

"I'll bet these Cubans don't know how to cook a good American breakfast of eggs and bacon and ham and toast," one booming voice said to no one in particular.

As an American, Liz was embarrassed by the foolish man, and turned in her seat in the bus to glare at him.

The man seated next to the loudmouth man nudged him and said, "See, you made that Cuban girl mad."

Liz turned back, facing front. She stifled a smile, thinking that her "costume" had fooled the American. He had the same wrong stereotype of idea of what women wore in Cuba that she had believed.

37 HAVANA AIRPORT TO HOTEL VIA TAXI

Juan had suggested several places to stay in the towns where she would visit. In Havana, he had told her about the Ambros Mundos hotel, adjacent to a famous old cathedral.

When the bus unloaded everyone in the downtown square, she hailed a taxicab and asked for the Ambros Mundos.

The driver nodded his head, but before he could start his engine, a man opened the front door on the passenger side and sat. He said a few quick words to the driver, then turned to Liz, in the back seat, and smiled broadly with his crooked, cigarette-stained teeth.

"I espeek Englis," he told her.

"Ambros Mundos hotel," she repeated.

The man, no bigger than a jockey, turned to the driver and said something more. Liz did not hear the name Ambros Mundos mentioned.

"Why are you here?" he asked.

"I am a tourist."

"Yes, but why did you come here?"

"I came to visit your beautiful country."

"You are solo? Alone?"

"Yes, alone."

"I know of many doctors," he whispered.

Confused, she explained to him, "I am not sick."

"Ah, yes, but in this country it is all right."

"To be sick?"

"The operation is not legal in your country, but we get many young girls who have come here to see a doctor. I know some good ones I can take you to", he insisted.

Finally, she understood. "No, I am not here for an abortion. I am simply a tourist, here to enjoy your beautiful country."

Abruptly, he turned to the driver and said something curt. The driver stopped and the little man stepped out of the taxi and slammed the car door. The driver drove off.

A little frightened, a little angry, Liz said in a loud and firm voice **"Ambros Mundos, por favor."**

The driver said, "Si."

Liz did not know if the taxi driver was taking the direct route or if he was taking her for a ride, literally, but now that the little man was gone, she sat back and enjoyed the scenery.

The drive continued along a seawall overlooking the ocean. Intermittently, a wave would send spray over the seawall. The view was beautiful. Next, they drove through lovely neighborhoods graced with elaborate homes that appeared to be possibly 200 years old. She snapped a photograph of an especially handsome estate painted a pale peach, made more dramatic by its lush plantings of a variety of palms, bamboo and huge pots of philodendra.

Suddenly the taxi turned a corner and the driver pointed. "El Morro", he said.

Liz vaguely remembered something in her history books about the Spanish-American War of 1898. Anchored in Havana Harbor, the U.S. Battleship *Maine* sunk: America blamed Spain for the onboard explosion and declared war. After four years of American control, Cuba became independent in 1902. (It was later suggested by US Navy officers that the explosion was caused by fire in the ship's coal bunker. A war for naught).

She mumbled to herself, I'm surprised that I remember that teeny bit of Havana trivia. I really should have done a little studying about this country before I started this trip. Too late now. Then she realized the driver had stopped the car.

"Castillo del Morro," he said, insistently. He pointed to her camera. He had parked the taxi so she could take a photograph of Morro Castle, a Spanish colonial fort constructed with limestone in 1590.

"Oh, grahs-is," she said, mangling a Spanish thank-you. She wound the car's window-handle, lowering the glass so she could get a clear picture of El Morro, then thanked the driver again. He smiled and seemed very pleased that she had shown interest in the fortress.

They had been able to complete this communication but Liz was wondering if her list of Spanish words would be adequate to get her through this Cuban adventure.

When the taxi pulled up in front of the Ambros Mundos, Liz was surprised that the front of the hotel presented a modest face to the street, unlike some American flamboyant extravaganzas. She was surprised but not disappointed. This was the kind of local character that said to her she was somewhere foreign to that of her prior experiences. She looked forward to settling into her room and beginning to record some of her impressions in a journal. This would be the basis for her Key West newspaper articles.

The next morning Liz awoke to the sound of church bells. The mental fog of being awakened at six o'clock in the morning blurred her vision. The veil of mosquito netting, hung from the ceiling and surrounding her bed, also blurred her vision. In a moment of panic, she flailed at the netting, her legs kicking and her arms waving frantically. Liz leaped from the bed, then stood looking at the gauze barrier that had protected her from voracious insects throughout the night. She started to laugh and later wrote in her journal that she was sorry a movie camera had not been in place to record her hilarious acrobatics.

The church bells continued to peal. Her room's casement windows were swung open. Liz looked out at the rooftops. Pigeons were perched along the rain gutters, gently nudging each other aside for their neighbor's spot, which must have been a better position for the pigeons to continue their bird-watching. Three green parrots flew past her window, calling out noisily.

Leaning out the window, with no screening hindering her, Liz gazed down on the street below. A young man was walking along, carrying two loaves of bread, the long thin loaves of Cuban bread. Liz was startled that he looked up at her. He said, "Buenos dias, senorita!" She quickly pulled her head back through the window-frame, like a turtle into its shell.

Turning brazen, she leaned out the window again, her shoulders touching the wood on each side. She was going to return the greeting, but he was gone. Leaning out the window made her feel like Rapunzel. Unfortunately, her hair was cut very short. It wouldn't work. She couldn't 'let down her hair', like the old fairy-tale. No, it was time to brush her hair, brush her teeth and get dressed. She needed to start her day. Her plan? Simply wandering around Havana.

She decided to leave her journal in the room so she wouldn't be encumbered by too many items throughout her walk. She read what she had written the night before:

I can't believe it was simply hours ago I was having lunch with Juan and Mr. Bill in America and now I am sitting in my own hotel room in Havana, Cuba. Last night I ate in the hotel dining room. For my beverage I ordered "leche", but then remembered some warnings about drinking milk in foreign countries. Was their milk pasteurized? So I then told the waiter 'aqua". But I wondered if the water was pure. I didn't want Montezuma's revenge. Or would it be Batista's? So finally I asked for "cerveza", hoping beer would not upset my stomach. The only thing it upset was the waiter. He seemed to think I was crazy in the head. Thank goodness Juan had suggested "Arroz con Pollo"; I ordered it for supper and it was delicious.

During my meal the hotel manager came to my table and told me that his "good friend Juan Robertson" had told him about my visit. He asked if my room was acceptable to me. (Si. Si.) Then he asked if he could presume to introduce someone whom he could vouch was a gentleman, a young German named Harry. I don't know whose idea that was, but after a few moments I gave Harry the deep chill, and he bowed and left me alone.

Liz went down to the cafe for breakfast. She ordered bread (Cuban, of course) and hot tea (that would be boiled water, so no Revenge possibilities, she hoped). Many others in the room were having eggs and bacon and ham and toast. She hoped the smart-alec wise guy on the airport bus was too hung-over to tolerate anything other than black coffee. When her breakfast arrived, so did Harry.

"Buenos dias, senorita Liz," said Harry, a heavy German-sounding accent to his Spanish.

"Hi, Harry. How are you this morning?" Liz asked.

With that encouragement, Harry pulled out a chair and said, "May I join you?"

From there the day progressed to Harry showing Liz the town.

First he took her to Morro Castle, "the proper place to begin your tour," Harry said. Then they walked back to the town of Casa Blanca. There was a brief rain-shower, so they sat at a sheltered table at an outside cafe, looking back toward the town. When the rain stopped, Liz took a photograph of the view. They continued on, visiting an art gallery. Harry purchased an orange from a street-vendor and they ate the segments as Harry took her window-shopping along the Pradeo and Naptune and Galiano avenues. Another shower started, so they walked back to the hotel, where Liz gave a firm "Thank you: goodbye" to Harry in the lobby and returned alone to her room to write the day's activities in her journal.

The telephone in her room rang. It was Harry. He asked if he could take her out for dinner. Liz said 'No'.

Harry persisted and wore Liz down. She agreed. He said he would meet her in the lobby and they would eat at LaFonda Cuba. However, when the time came, he whispered he had changed the plans. They went, instead, to La Bodcita del Medio and had a delicious meal. Several people at Bodcita knew Harry.

Later, Liz wrote in her journal:

Harry seemed much more relaxed and carefree during the evening. I had a wonderful time, but I'm glad Harry can be such a proper German gentleman. Sometimes it seems like he will click his heels together and give a curt bow. At least I was able to get rid of him at my doorway with a handshake. Tomorrow I'm determined to look around the city by myself.

The next morning Liz leaned out her casement window. She saw an old woman carrying a live chicken upside-down, by its legs. A young boy was holding about a dozen newspapers, calling out in Spanish, perhaps the name of the paper. A man came out of the building and gave the boy a coin for the newspaper. She heard a parrot squawking in the distance, but couldn't see the bird. It looked like another beautiful day.

For breakfast she tried 'cafe con leche' in the Nanking restaurant. With enough sugar and milk, she thought she just might get to like drinking Cuban coffee. Empowered by this caffeine, she went shopping. She bought two blouses at French Brothers.

On to El Encanto department store. She purchased another blouse and admired a leather purse. She wanted the larger one, but it was $8.00 and the smaller one was marked $4.50, so she told the clerk she would take the smaller purse. The clerk spoke Spanish to her, trying to explain something but Liz purchased the smaller one. Then she found out that the Spanish way of writing the number seven was with a line through it, making it appear like the number four to her. The smaller purse was $7.50. She was too embarrassed to say, "Oh well then I'll take the larger purse, the $8.00 one." She decided philosophically that it was a lesson learned.

On the way back to her hotel, she stopped at a restaurant for her evening meal. Checking her *Easy Spanish Phrase Book,* she found words for liver, goose, oysters, sardines, sausage, cabbage, pimentos, and of course chicken; none were of any help to her. She tried to ask for a menu, but failing to communicate she simply asked for Arroz con Pollo. Again, it was tasty.

38 TRAVELING SOLO

The next morning was time to move on to her next town, Matanzas. She used her list of phonetically written Spanish words to tell the taxi driver her destination: the bus station. She picked a more subdued outfit for the day: a tailored white cotton blouse and a dark blue skirt, plus her white sandals. Even so, she felt like the men were ogling her.

She was able to purchase a one-way ticket to Matanzas and sat in the waiting room, choosing a bench next to several older women. There was a soldier in tan uniform in the room. He was talking to a short young man of slight build. The young man had a thin mustache. The two men were looking at Liz. She looked away and opened her journal, re-reading what she had written so far.

When it was time to board, one of the women asked Liz, "Matanzas?" When Liz nodded, the woman beckoned to her to follow. Liz planned to sit next to one of the women, but the driver pointed to her ticket and a number above the bus window. Each ticket had an assigned seat. She sat in her assigned seat. Many other passengers got on the bus, but no one sat next to her. Finally the bus driver sat in his chair and the mustached young man got on the bus. The driver nodded to him, and the young man sat in the chair next to Liz.

Smiling the young man said, "*Buenos dias. En cuanto tiempo se llega a*

Matanzas?" Although she knew the words "no comprendo", she didn't even want to start any kind of conversation with this man. Although rude, she turned and looked out the bus window. They traveled like this for about 15 minutes.

When he said to her in English, "Would you care for a stick of gum?" without thinking, she automatically answered "No, thank you" and then the conversation she had hoped to avoid began.

"I wish to practice my English on you; do you mind? You are going to Matanzas?"

There seemed no way to get out of that question. Liz said, "Yes."

"Where is your husband?"

"I'm not married."

"You are traveling solo?"

"Yes".

"But where is your father, your brothers? How is it they allow you to travel alone?"

"My father is dead, I have no brothers. I am traveling as a tourist to see your country. Alone."

"But your mother, she did not send a 'duenna' to travel along with you?"

"No."

"How very…how do you say it…modern", said the young man. Apparently this shocking piece of information left him speechless until they neared Matanzas.

"Where are you staying in Matanzas?" he asked.

Liz lied and said, "At the home of my uncle."

"Oh, what is the name of your uncle?" he persisted.

Exasperated, Liz turned full-face and told him, "I really don't think that is your business," and she turned away and stared out the bus window. The scenery was beautiful with lush trees arching across the highway, branches meeting.

When the bus stopped in Matanzas, the young man walked behind Liz. She asked a woman at the ticket counter where Hotel Yaya was. The woman pointed down the street. The young man grabbed Liz' suitcase and said he would show her the way. Liz wanted to yank the suitcase from his hand, but he had already walked ahead. She followed, silently, but fuming mad.

When planning the trip, Juan had directed her to ask for a certain desk clerk in Hotel Yaya, but in response to her requesting that person, she was told something in Spanish. Her 'friend', still holding her suitcase interpreted as "It is his day off". The room was finally arranged. Liz tried to take the suitcase out of the grasp of the man, but he smiled and said he wold carry it up to her room.

Liz said, "No. Thank you. You have been very helpful. I won't need you anymore. Goodbye."

He kept his grasp on her suitcase. Liz looked at the other men standing around the desk. They stood still, observing but not interfering. Apparently they felt it was a lover's quarrel and they would not get involved. It was her loud insistence that he leave that finally deterred him. He sat the suitcase next to her.

She picked it up. Alone, Liz found the assigned room, unlocked it, and placed her suitcase inside. She locked the door but still didn't feel secure. There was a wooden chair next to a small table. She remembered seeing in an old movie where someone staying a New York fleabag hotel had jammed a chair under the doorknob. Liz took the chair, and as she placed it under the knob, she saw a deep scaring on the wooden door where many others had done the same thing.

Liz looked around the room. On one wall there were French doors made of glass panes. She went to those doors and peeped through the lace curtains that covered the glass on the other side of the glass panels. She could see tables and chairs in the next room.

She went back downstairs to the front desk and said she would like a different room; the one she was in had doors to a restaurant. The clerk, now proficient in English, said it was merely a storage room. No one ever went in there. There were no other rooms. Liz returned to her assigned room.

The bathroom was within the room. It was U-shaped, had no door, but was entirely marble — the floor and the three walls. The shower was at one end. There was no shower-curtain, but with the entire area marble, it was no problem if everything got wet. Also there was a washstand, toilet and what she imagined must be a bidet.

She had never seen a bidet before. She looked at the knobs and tried to figure out how it could be used. There was no seat on the porcelain rim.

She wondered if the women who had used it might have had a venereal disease and if someone could catch it by sitting on it.

With that thought she quietly exited back into the carpeted part of her room. Near the ceiling was a hoop with mosquito netting draped around it. She wondered how one got the netting down and around the bed at night. Thee were so many strange things to see. Intending to jot down some notes in her journal, she placed her suitcase on the bed. Unlocking it, she removed the notebook, but decided to have dinner first.

She went downstairs again this time to the hotel dining room. Liz had the feeling everyone was surprised to see her without her 'friend'. The waiter handed her a menu. She had not brought her Spanish Phrases book to the restaurant and didn't feel like taking a chance on the strange names, so simply ordered Arroz con Pollo. That evening she wrote in her journal *"I expect I'll be eating a lot of chicken and rice this week."*

Liz would have walked back to the Town Square that she had noticed on her walk from the bus station. However, she feared her lecherous friend might still be looking for her, so she chose to take a shower and go to bed.

When she returned to her room, she saw that the mosquito netting had been lowered. Also her nightgown was laid out on the bed. Her suitcase was on the small table. She took off her blouse and placed it on top of the suitcase and started to unzip her skirt, but she stopped. She thought she had heard some scuffling coming from the curtained glass doors. She went over to the doors and tried to peer through, but that room was dark.

She went back to the bed and took off the rest of her clothing. As she turned to walk into her marble bathroom stall, she heard a collective gasp. She was certain men were watching her from the glass doors! She grabbed her skirt and clutched in front of her. She turned off the light in the room and went back to those glass doors, but again she could see nothing.

She went into the marbled area, where she felt she would be safe from peering eyes, and sat on the available seat, the toilet. She was trembling, angry, yet could prove nothing. She felt it would be of no use to complain to the men at the desk. She sat there until she stopped trembling, then showered. Wrapped in her towel, she found her way in the dark back to her bed. It was a long time before she could go to sleep.

39

DON'T DRINK WATER BUT EAT CHICKEN AND RICE

At 4:00 in the morning, Liz woke up from the few hours of fitful sleep. She decided it might be safe now to turn on her bedside lamp and write in her journal. Maybe that would make her tired, and then she could sleep some more.

When coming from Habana to Matanzas ('What?' everyone exclaimed. 'One goes <u>*from*</u> *Matanzas to Habana, but never vice-versa') the bus drove through a small town called San Jose. It was my first small town and I was intrigued. I wish I had been able to get a picture of the thatched cottages snuggled near clumps of trees in the areas between the next town. The rest of the towns after San Jose pleased me less.*

I would like this room if I weren't so certain I had been spied upon through those French glass doors. Now that I'm used to mosquito netting, I feel like a princess in a canopied bed. I love the high ceiling with plaster scrollwork around the ceiling light-fixtures. What is best is my little balcony. I would love to sit with a Cafe con Leche in the morning, out on my balcony, but I am not happy in Matanzas. I am not interested in visiting the nearby caves and seeing the bats, even though it would be a good follow-up on our Bat Tower back home in the Keys.

When I get up in the morning, I believe I'll arrange to leave for Sancta Spiritus as soon as possible. On the map it looks like a long distance, but I don't care to travel here at night. It isn't so much that I'm afraid as it is that I cannot stand the raised eyebrows and the question 'Solo?'

This hotel must have been a beautiful building before someone chopped up the large rooms. I am lucky the person in the next room (a man, I think, from the sound of his cough) does not snore, for the wall between us does not extend fully to the ceiling, but allows 4 inches of sound to escape between our rooms.

Hotel Yaya has three grandfather clocks, but only one of them chimes on the half-hour, too. It is now 4:30 or as I heard someone say yesterday, 'four and a half'.

Oh-oh…the man next door was being kept awake by my light, I guess. In a great big angry-sounding voice he said something gruff in Spanish. I'd better turn off my light. However, I must be careful not to press the wrong button. The left-hand one is the buzzer for the hotel boy. Goodnight, Journal. I must let that man get some sleep. I hope I can sleep a little, too.

Liz was awakened at 6:30. She heard telephones ringing throughout her area of the hotel, apparently wake-up calls for businessmen. She opened her eyes but did not move her body. With her head slightly elevated by her pillow, she was able to see the glass doors. At the far end in that room were windows that allowed in enough light to show her there were no silhouettes of any persons standing there.

With heightened awareness of hearing, she listened for any sounds coming from that area. She slowly lifted the mosquito netting and swung her legs over the side of the bed. No sounds were heard. She went to her suitcase and selected clothing. She carried them into the marble bathroom, believing that space was safe from peeping eyes.

The hotel restaurant was filled with men, presumable ready to go to work. She ordered a Cafe con Leche and some Cuban bread. At a nearby table six men got up and left the room, clearing her line of vision to a table in the corner where the mustached man from Havana sat. He was looking at her. Liz took one sip of the coffee and wrapped her bread in a paper napkin. She hurriedly left the restaurant and returned to her room.

Liz brushed her teeth and quickly packed her suitcase. She went down to the desk and checked out, then walked the short distance to the bus station, where she obtained a ticket to Sancti Siritus. She drew a woman for her bus-partner this time. The woman gave Liz her Spanish fashion magazine. The Havana man did not get on the bus.

On the drive out of Matanzas, about a block from the central square, Liz saw a very old building, perhaps a church. She fumbled to get her camera, but the bus drove by before she could snap a picture. However, she was able to get a photo of some bohio huts with straw roofing. She took two other pictures she later described in her Journal:

There was an old tired horse with fancy trappings pulling an old tired cart full of old tired straw, with one priceless-looking old tired man. Later, at a rest stop at Colon there was a man playing a sort of homemade guitar. A young girl has two wooden blocks she hits together to provide the rhythm She sang — a beautiful voice. But then the old man sang (definitely not a beautiful voice).

Shortly after noon the bus stopped in Santa Clara for lunch. Everyone was getting off the bus. The woman next to Liz pointed to a nearby restaurant, then spoke with the bus driver and the bus conductor. A man who had been seated in the back of the bus spoke to Liz. In English he asked if she needed him for anything. Liz said, "No, thank you", and walked toward the restaurant.

The driver and conductor were staying in Santa Clara, as was the woman. The new bus crew pointed to Liz and spoke Spanish. The new crew nodded. Liz imagined that they were saying, "Watch this crazy American girl who is traveling solo."

At the rest stop in Colon, Liz had chosen a sweet pastry. She would have p referred a light lunch, but noontime meals here seemed to be what she considered a large evening meal. The menu was meaningless to her, as if it were written in hieroglyphics. She pointed to one item that didn't look like "pollo". However the waiter said, "Oh you don't speak Spanish. Do you like chicken?"

She had hoped to branch out into other entrees, and could see what was coming, but said, "yes." For lunch she had roasted chicken, but did say to the waiter, in her poor Spanish, "No arroz, por favor." To cater to her strange American tastes, he brought her a small plate of potatoes, but she said, "No, gracias." She saw a large red sign that said "Coca-Cola". That solved her beverage problem for the rest of the trip. No more milk, beer or water concerns.

Back on the bus Liz had a change of seat-partners, this time a man.

She ignored him until just before arrival in Sancti Spiritus when he began to speak to her in English. He said he was a printer from Santa Clara who was going to Sancti Spiritus for advice from a printer friend of his whom, he said, was a 'better printer than I am." The man said he printed the timetables for the Santiago-Habana bus-company.

Liz was concerned she would not be able to lose him. She didn't want another 'helpful' man like the one in Matanzas. However, she was able to find a taxicab. Back home Juan had recommended "Perla de Cuba" hotel. There were many men standing by the front desk in the hotel, but no one in the room spoke English. One man kept telling her, in Spanish, that there was no room available. She tried looking helpless, but to no avail. Finally she looked in her Spanish phrase book and said "*Que debo hacer?*" (What am I to do?) He pointed to another hotel across the street.

She trudged across the street. Her suitcase was beginning to feel heavy. The man at the Hotel Plaza said "No room try Perla de Cuba." The printer who had been her bus companion walked up. He told her that the biggest affair of the year, the National Cattle Fair, had filled up the town. The Cattle Fair would go on all week. There was no where to stay. She tried to look pitiful and asked if there was a family who would take her in for the night. He shook his head.

He told her the best thing for her to do was to continue on to a nearby town, Trinidad. (When Juan had suggested she visit Trinidad she had asked him, "You mean the Caribbean island off Venezuela?" and he told her "No, just the name of another town in Cuba.") There she could find a nice place.

Miraculously, just at that time, a taxi pulled up in front of the Hotel Plaza. The printer led Liz to the cab and spoke to the driver in Spanish. He told Liz the cab would take her back to the bus station so she could continue on to Trinidad. Shen she arrived back at the station, the driver indicated the printer had pre-paid for her cab. She tipped the driver and continued on her journey, this time to Trinidad, a small town on the southern coast of Cuba. (Mr. Bill had reached his agents in Santa Clara, and arranged this successful scenario. Liz would now be staying in Trinidad and the microfiche could be obtained from her Spanish phrase book.)

40
THE AMERICANA CARRIES THE BOMB

The trip to Trinidad was in a small Volkswagen jitney-bus. A capacity crowd of ten persons was constant. At first there were four men with tanned, weathered skin; a young couple sat up front with the driver; and in the middle were four women: two elderly women, one middle-aged lady and Liz. The crowd fluctuated at each stop, but that ratio remained about the same.

It started to rain. Then the rain came down harder, pounding on the leaking roof of the jitney. A steady stream of water poured on the right shoulder of Liz. Pressed together as the four women were, there was no way for Liz to move away from the water. It began to hurt, like Chinese water-torture. She placed her left hand over her right shoulder to protect her skin's nerve-endings. One of the workmen in the back of the jitney placed his leather jacket over her shoulders. She gratefully said, "Gracias".

While continuing to drive down the road, the driver turned his head and looked at Liz. He said something to her in Spanish. She replied, "No comprendo". This got laughter from the others in the jitney. "Ah… Americana" was the response.

The rain lessened, but the water continued in a slow drip on her shoulder. Liz looked out the window and was impressed by the beautiful countryside. She wanted to take pictures, but knew the rain would obliterate the shots. She hoped she might return to Cuba some day, so she reached into her purse and took out a piece of paper and a pen.

She jotted down the sights that she wanted to view again, on a sunny day: "Especially to the right, a little before marker 22; before going over two hills preceding marker 32; the tower at 59; a ravine on the right near marker 63." The passengers observed her strange notes with interest.

Apparently there were no routine stops along the route. The jitney-bus stopped when a passenger voiced a request. The three ladies exited the bus. The driver asked the couple to sit in the middle section and he beckoned Liz to sit in the front seat next to hm. Liz returned the leather jacket to the man in the backseat. When the three women had gotten out, someone had handed the driver a white box. As the driver started up again, he handed the box to Liz to hold.

There was a lot of Spanish conversation and laughter between the men in the back seats and the driver. The driver turned to Liz and said something in Spanish about a *bomba* and *bombardeo.* Everyone laughed. Liz shrugged her shoulders and smiled.

Not far along the road they came near a place where several people were standing in the street. The driver stopped and took the box from Liz. He walked over to the group. He handed them the box and pointed at the jitney. Moe laughter. The rest of the ride to Trinidad was uneventful.

Upon arrival in the town, Liz asked the driver if a taxi was available, by asking one word, "Taxi?" He answered, "Si" and pointed to a boy standing nearby.

The boy picked up her suitcase and said *'Donde?"*

She said "Hotel?" and he nodded his head. He kept walking, holding her suitcase. She finally realized the boy himself was the "taxi". As they walked along, the boy kept speaking Spanish to Liz, asking her questions. She kept saying "No comprendo" but the questions kept coming.

They continued to stroll along, slowly, passing through a town square with many trees shading the area. Hung from the branches of the trees were small birdcages. Canaries and other colorful birds were inside each bamboo cage. Old men who were apparently the owners of the caged birds sat on benches nearby. The boy walked into Hotel Canada and set down her suitcase with a smile. She handed him some American money. He seemed very pleased and ran away with the dollars clutched in his fist.

The card she had prepared with Juan, listing several useful phrases phonetically, was stuck inside her Spanish Phrase book. The book had not been helpful, but Juan's list had included the words she really could use. She said, "Por favor" in her poor American accent, and then continued with the Spanish words for "I would like a room with a bath". The man at the desk nodded and handed her a heavy ring. Attached to it was a key and a large brass plate with the room number engraved into it. He nodded toward the staircase.

The staircase was grandiose. The steps were wide, the railings massive with rococo carvings. At the top of eight steps was a landing where the staircase turned, continuing up another flight. On the landing, facing the entry lobby, a huge mirror looked down at the foyer. Liz was impressed.

Her room was large. The bed had the usual mosquito netting draped high from the ceiling. There was a desk and chair in the room, plus an upholstered chair with footstool. Two wooden louvered doors swung out onto a balcony that overlooked the wooded park in front of the hotel. The bathroom was very large, also, with very high ceilings and a window that was propped open, fastened up and outward, allowing fresh air, but not the rain. She was very pleased with Hotel Canada.

Liz showered, changed into fresh clothes, then sat in her softly cushioned chair. She put her feet up and took out her Journal.

I feel so much more relaxed, here in Trinidad. I hope Mr. Bartlett won't mind if I skip Sancti Spiritus. My room is on the right-hand side of the front balcony. My key identification tag for Room 19 must weigh one full pound. There is a loudspeaker in the park spouting Spanish words and music. In addition there is a jukebox downstairs and one across the street, playing conflicting music. But the three sounds, all mixed together, simply seem like part of the ambiance of this place. No problem.

Refreshed, she went downstairs to the hotel restaurant. She was determined not to get chicken. The menu said *bistek.* That sounded like "beef steak" to her, so she ordered it. It came with fried potatoes. She decided on *cerveza,* whatever the local brand of beer might be. It was a very satisfying meal. Then the waiter brought to her table a small custard and asked her, *"?Flan?"*. She said "Si," and enjoyed the custard with caramelized sugar as a delightful and fitting end to a wonderful meal.

Liz was about to get up, but a young man stopped at her table. He introduced himself as Lazaro Eclasias. He said he understood she had signed into the hotel, giving her home as Key West, Florida. He said he was a lawyer in Trinidad and had a close friend in Key West, a lawyer named Julio Rockman; did Liz know him? Liz said she didn't know him personally, but she had heard of him. Mr. Eclasias sat down on a chair at Liz' table.

"Why are you in Trinidad?" he asked.

"I am a tourist, enjoying your beautiful country," she repeated, as always.

"And you are traveling solo?"

Liz was aggravated by that question, again. That must have reflected in her face, because Mr. Eclasias hastened to say, "There is little to see in this town, but I wondered if perhaps you might be interested in seeing the local tuberculosis sanatorium we have here. It is very modern. No, you won't see any of the patients. It would be very safe for you to visit. I will arrange for a driver to take you tomorrow at 8:00 in the morning. Just ask for Father Antonio."

Liz seemed unable to resist the snowballing effect of someone as persistent as Mr. Eclasias. She agreed to visit the hospital.

When she returned to her room, she saw that the mosquito netting had been lowered around her bed. Although that was merely the routine responsibility of the maid, Liz thought of it as mysterious and miraculous. Indeed, there were watchful eyes everywhere. This time, however, Liz was not frightened. She felt very relaxed and slept well that night.

The next afternoon Liz wrote in her Journal:

5:45 in the morning and I hear Reveille! The sun was coming up. About a dozen men in blue uniforms stood on four corners of the plaza and played some wonderful, fast tune. The last two times were from father away, then the band returned. One of the trumpeters got fancy and put in some tricky notes to the song. However, I learned to expect, at the end of each tune, a loud rocket to be exploded.

Trucks came to take the townsmen to the fields. They had to push the second truck in order to get it to start, then all jumped on-board. The sun was silhouetted against a background of blue sky, then low pearl-gray clouds, next mauve mountains, then purple mountains, brown hills and the sand and terracotta colors of the building of Trinidad.

Lazaro had mentioned Father Antonio, so I went to the Catholic Church. I only had to ask about ten people for directions to the church. When I asked for Father Antonio, they told me he was in the hospital. I assumed they meant he was sick. Then I realized they meant he was the priest on duty at the hospital.

Before I forget...while I was waiting for the drive, the man who had spoken to me at dinner last night, Mr. Eclasias, talked with me some more. He said he liked Havana better because Trinidad was so quiet. I held back my chuckle and soberly agreed, while remembering the noisy music during the evening and the children on roller skates and all of the men talking so very loud.

The cab driver arrived in front of my hotel at 8:00. His name was Rigoberto. He drove four men and myself up the mountain to this hospital. Trinidad was quite warm but as we progressed up the mountain, it became cooler. It was foggy, but that did not obscure the magnificent scenery through which we passed. I was glad I had brought my sweater. I have learned to cover up more modestly, because all these men really look you over!

On the way up it was discovered that I am an Americana. There was one man in the taxi who spoke a little English. He had taken it in school many years ago but no one in his town spoke it, so the language had fallen into disuse. The taxi driver spoke to him...somehow I was able to understand the meaning of some of the Spanish...and he asked the man to stay with me during the tour. The man said, no, no, he couldn't. He needed to 'take a shave'. Then he agreed, so it was arranged that if I would wait in the lobby for a few minutes, he would get a shave and we would tour together. I was confused about why this clean-shaven man 'needed to take a shave'. Perhaps he meant to use a different word.

When we arrived at the sanatorium, a pompous and conceited little man with head thrown back and chin sticking out met me at the door. The man asked for my papers. I told him the lawyer Lazaro Eclasias had referred me to go on a tour of the hospital. He asked what clearance Lazaro had arranged. He asked if the taxi driver had papers for me. Thinking the man from the taxi might be better able to discuss this with him, I asked him to wait for the man. He asked where the man was. I told him he was getting a shave.

"I see", said the man. "Then I assume that you are connected with a

hospital in the United States that is the reason you are interested in this sanitarium".

Forced into a corner, I crossed my fingers hoping my visit to the church in the morning would wipe out this untruth. I said nothing. Then my friend, now shaven, reappeared and together with the other three men, we began the tour.

The pip-squeak man said Batista had wanted this hospital to be his monument showing how he cared about the Cuban people. Construction was begun in 1938 and completed in 1954. Capacity 1,000; present patient population: 478. If a patient's TB was too advanced to be helped medically, he is refused. If someone is brought here who does not have tuberculosis, he is sent down to the small Trinidad hospital.

The little man turned to me and said in English, "Your country believes in placing TB patients in a hot and dry climate, but we know better. We find that this cool and damp atmosphere in the mountains is much better for a cure."

Judged by the expression of our tour guide the highlight of our visit was being able to see the kitchen. There were two huge cauldrons that we were invited to look into. I had to stand on my tiptoes. The sides must have been five feet high. Inside one was cooked rice, the other had black beans. That was the only food I could see that was going to be served.

When we returned to the taxi, the cabdriver introduced me to some American-looking man in khaki trousers, tennis shoes and a print sport shirt. This is Father Antonio.

He is not a happy man. His mother's name was Williams. She is from Virginia in America. He is leaving the hospital's church to go to the New Orleans, Louisiana, USA, diocese. He would rather go to Tampa "to be near Palm Beach". In New Orleans he says he is afraid he will be called a 'spic' but his mother wants to leave Cuba.

On the drive back down the mountain, the men said something to Rigoberto. He drove the men and myself to a rest stop. The men went inside a small shack selling beer. I would have followed but Rigoberto put his hand up as if to caution me against joining them. I didn't want to question in my mind what problems that might have entailed.

Luckily, it was then I noticed a waterfall. It cascaded down into a valley and made a stunning vista I just had to capture on film. To show the right proportions, I needed a person to stand in the foreground, so asked Rigoberto, in my sign language, to please pose for me. I snapped the picture and said in my English, that he couldn't understand, somehow I would get a copy sent to him. I could say 'casa' for house and gave him my pen. He wrote his name and an address on the paper.

When we continued our drive, I noticed another panoramic scene. I asked Rigoberto to stop for one moment 'por favor' *and I added another photograph to my collection of lovely Cuban scenes. He drove each of the men to their homes first, then gave me a short tour of the town before dropping me off at Hotel Canada. My portion for the shared taxi ride was $2.50, which was much less than if I had hired a private car.*

After the morning at the sanatorium, Liz looked for a place to have something to eat other than her hotel. There was a shop with a sign "Cafeteria" but it seemed to be a simple coffee shop. She ordered a ham sandwich and a Coca-Cola. The shop had multiple doors that folded out to the sides, inviting breezes and strollers to enter. Liz sat at a table near the sidewalk and enjoyed the view of the central park.

When she finished her lunch she decided to walk around the tree-shaded plaza. Across the street from her hotel was a sign 'Farmacia'. She looked on the shelves, trying to find something that looked like hair shampoo. Always falling back on sign language, she demonstrated to the pharmacist: washing her hand by rubbing them together, then ruffling her hair. At first he showed her a cake of soap, but she demonstrated a pouring motion. At last a bottle of shampoo was shown to her and she nodded. The two of them were delighted with themselves that they had circumvented the language barrier.

When she returned to the Hotel Canada, a man at the desk stopped her. He dialed the telephone, then handed it to her.

"Hello," a man said. "This is Father Antonio. It occurred to me that since you are solo, perhaps it would be of help to you if my cousin and his friend showed you a little of Trinidad. I hope this does not offend you. I can say to you they are of the utmost gentlemen."

Liz was flattered that Father Antonio had called. She simply responded, "Thank you, Father.

He seemed very happy and began to speak very fast. "My cousin Jesus Hernandez and his friend Jorge Fernandez will pick you up at 2:00 today for a walk through Trinidad. I am so happy to have met you. I am sorry my mother was not here. Thank you very much. Goodbye."

Stunned by the sudden addition of plans for the afternoon, Liz handed the telephone back to the hotel clerk and walked up the grand staircase to her room. She decided a short siesta before meeting "Hay-sue" and "Hor-hay". The hair shampoo could wait.

41

JESUS AND JORGE GIVE A PRIVATE TOUR

At 2:20 p.m. there was a knock on her door.

"Si?" answered Liz.

Some Spanish words were spoken. Liz said "Gracias" even though she did not know what was said. Indeed, it was as she thought. The two men were waiting for her as she descended the staircase.

Jesus Hernandez was strikingly handsome, skin tanned, brown hair cut in a manner that showed his natural waves to advantage, very masculine. His friend was short in stature. His posture spoke to Liz that he was used to being seen in the shadow of his handsome friend.

Jesus reached for her hand, and kissed it. Jorge bowed deeply. Liz giggled nervously.

Both men spoke English. They said they begin showing her the town by showing her the home of a man from Key West, Julio Rockman, who was not visiting Trinidad at this time but Jesus was the caretaker. He had the key.

They walked through the Rockman dining area. There was a huge dining table with chairs set around it that Liz admired. The chairs were crudely cut wood, unfinished, with black and white animal skin stretched across the back and seat. Jesus said it was cowhide. Liz ran her hand across the skin, which felt like fur.

The men led her into the Rockman library. A massive desk dominated the room. All the walls were lined entirely with books except for one window which overlooked a central courtyard. Jesus lifted a crystal decanter and offered Liz a drink of Carta Blanca and soda, but she refused.

Jesus and Jorge drove her to see The Caves. There were many bats throughout Cuba and caves near this town attracted families of the flying mammals. This would please her editor, since she could talk about the bats she had seen there. After that they stopped at a mountaintop and open-air place for Coca-Cola. Then Jesus led her into a church.

"I wish to introduce you to my priest. He is my priest, not my brother, this one. Here he is. Father Enrique, I wish to introduce you to an American, Miss Liz…" He floundered, having forgotten her strange (non-Cuban) American name.

"Steele," she filled in.

Instead of saying 'Hello' or 'How do you do' or shaking her hand, the priest simply stood in front of her, staring at her. No, not staring. Glaring.

Liz wondered, What is this scenario? What is happening here? Why did these guys bring me to see this man? Why doesn't this priest say anything? Oh, is this a stare-off? Is he trying to see whose eyes will falter first? Aha, I can play this game. But why?

She continued the lock-eyes stance. The men said nothing. It was obvious to her she was not to drop her eyes away. She was getting bored with this game, but she knew she must hold back from laughing. She thought, What is this foolishness? This is going on forever. Will we be standing here like this until the sun goes down? Forget this. I think I've proven whatever they want. This is really stupid. I hate to quit, but what is the point of this?

Liz turned and looked at Jesus and Jorge, and shrugged her shoulders.

The men looked at the priest. He said something to them in rapid Spanish. Liz took it as some sort of approval. Apparently she had passed the test. But what? and why?

42

MORE STRANGE AND TENSE MOMENTS

Next, Jesus said he would show her one of the lovely old Cuban homes, typical of the local architecture. When they arrived at the door of a house, a man answered then Jesus said something. The man looked frightened and opened the door, allowing them to enter.

Liz said, "Jesus, I don't want to disturb this family. Let's go."

"No!", and he turned to the wife and children, huddled against a wall in the dining area. He said to Liz, "And notice the lovely murals done directly on the plaster. But let us go to the garden."

Liz was relieved to go outside of the home where she felt they were intruding. But then Jesus told her, "Stand on that high-point in the garden."

"Why?" asked Liz.

"Oh, to see the view, of course," said Jesus with a smirk.

There was a barren hillock of dirt toward the rear of the yard. She stood there for a moment and saw nothing spectacular. She started to walk back to the house, but Jesus quickly stopped her with his voice.

"Stay there!"

Once again she thought Why am I standing here? I feel like I am in front of the firing squad. What is going on? Liz kept her body in a relaxed posture with wide-eyes gaze, as if she was delighted with the view.

After a minute more, he told her to come down from the mound. She wondered Did I pass the test? W*hat do they think…that I am a spy?*

"It is time to leave here, Jesus", she told him as she continued to walk through the house and out the front door. "I am going back to my hotel now. Thank you so very much for this tour," she said sarcastically.

She continued to walk down the street, although she was not certain which was the correct direction. Jorge ran and caught up with her. He said nothing, but pointed to a corner. She turned and Jorge walked silently with her until she reached Hotel Canada.

43
WASH THAT MAN RIGHT OUTA MY HAIR

Liz decided it was the right time to wash her hair. She wished to rinse away the gray cloud of mystery from her thoughts. She sat on the balcony in one of the wooden rocking chairs. There was one other room across from her that shared the front balcony. A woman and two children were seated on the balcony when she came outside after washing her hair. She smiled at the woman, then went back inside. Returning she went over and handed the woman the bottle of her remaining hair-shampoo. The woman thanked her.

When Liz returned to her rocking chair, the woman came over and took Liz' brush. The woman brushed her hair for her until it was almost dry. The friendly exchange of the late afternoon helped Liz get over the bad feelings she had about Father Antonio's brother.

Dinnertime Liz went down and sat at her usual table, trying to decipher the menu. Then she noticed a young woman across the room who looked out of place. Strange. Then Liz realized the reason: the girl appeared to be foreign. That is, not Cuban. She looked American.

Although she had not glanced at her Spanish Phrase book in days, she had picked up a few words. She asked her waiter "Esta la senorita Americana?"

He said, "Si."

Liz went over and her English came out in Spanish phrasing. "Is it that you are an American?"

"Sure. I'm Harriet Bean from Philadelphia. Grab a seat."

Harriet told her that she was a travel agent on vacation, staying down the street at Hotel Ronda. She helped Liz chose a dinner of fried fish fillets and they chattered away like schoolgirls.

When Harriet told her that she had met several friend in Trinidad, Cuba, quickly Liz asked their names, hoping it was not Jesus and Jorge. Harriet said her friends Ramon and Geraldo were taking her to a dance at the Country Club. She asked Liz to join them. Liz agreed.

At 8:30 that evening Harriet arrived at Hotel Canada with Ramon and Geraldo, who drove them to the Country Club. Everyone was very friendly. A very tall blonde man came to their table and spoke in Spanish to Ramon, who responded by introducing Liz to Roger Baker. The evening went on until about 3:00 a.m. The hotel was locked up, but a sleepy man opened the door for Liz when she returned to the hotel.

Trinidad Cuba 5:00 a.m. I slept for two hours, but for some reason awakened. Perhaps it was the ox-cart that drove up with its wooden wheels clacking over the cobblestone street. The man is throwing logs, smooth and shiny, off his cart that is drawn by two beautiful oxen whose brown coat looks like sealskin. How indescribably lovely is the sight. The scene is silhouetted against the cobblestones from my viewpoint looking down from the balcony. The lighting is only from the front of the hotel...a golden glow.

The evening at the Country Club seemed like a typical American evening: dance, drink, laugh, talk. Roger is a good dancer. He also plays drums. He says he has a cousin who is the only white man who can authentically dance to "Ritmo Afro". Accompanying the jukebox were four or five men. They were playing on two tall drums, a set of bongos, two sticks and something else they were scraping.

Everyone was very friendly and showing off any English they knew. Roger spoke a little, Ramon and Geraldo a bit more. A Turkish man was delighted that I knew where Los Angeles, California was, because he had spent three days there once. Another man stopped us while dancing and said I danced differently from Cuban girls and it was very nice and lively and he admired it very much. (I was crushed, because I thought I was doing just like the Cuban girls.) I had a wonderful Time. But now, back to bed.

Liz slept until 10 o'clock then went for a walk. As she strolled along the dusty streets, she heard a rhythmic beat and followed her ears to an old tower of a public school. Having determined where the sound was coming from she asked a man standing outside if it would be possible for her to go up to see them playing the bells or whatever it was. This request was made in sign language: a finger pointed up and a raised eyebrow.

He said, "Si," and led her inside the building. He showed her the view from each of the four opening in the tower. She gave appreciative "ooh's", but best of all were the four men on the four bells. Later she was told the sounds they were creating was "Ritmo Afro". She wished she had been able to record the experience.

Returning to her hotel, she chose an apple and a Batido de Fruta Bomba con Leche for lunch. Luckily she remembered the words *fruta bomba* and *batido* that Juan had told her, because she had mislaid her Spanish Phrase book somewhere. She couldn't find it. No matter. The tropical fruit milkshake was delicious.

She sat in her rocking chair on her balcony overlooking the central plaza. The old men had brought their caged birds out again. The canaries were singing to the music that came from all the doorways. She had forgotten time. She wanted to stay here forever, but she must get back to Key West soon.

Earlier in the day someone had told Liz there would be a procession honoring Santa Barbara. She didn't know when or where. A man from the hotel came up and put two curled fists to his eyes, like binoculars. Then he pointed down the street. The procession was coming right past the hotel under her balcony! Many people were in the procession, having walked more than two hours. There was a small band and men carrying a statue bedecked with flowers. The woman from the adjoining balcony had watched the procession too. She said in English, "Very pretty."

44 FLYING BIRDS AND BATS

Liz continued to sit on the balcony after the parade had passed. Then there was a knock on the door. It was Harriet. The two young women went to Harriet's hotel to get her camera. She showed Liz her Cuban-bought Christmas cards. Liz thought that was a great idea and decided to buy some when she returned to Havana.

Liz and Harriet walked around the town. A band of men were playing music in front of an open bar. They had two guitars, a gourd and a strange instrument made out of a wooden box the size of two suitcases. It had four metal wires across the front. Oh, the sounds they could make! The girls when into the bar and ordered Coca-Cola so they could sit and enjoy the music.

Small brown birds kept flying onto their table, but Liz and Harriet brushed them away. It was much later that day that Harriet complimented Liz for staying calm around the cockroaches. She had feared Liz would make a scene.

"What cockroaches?"

"You know, at the bar where we had our Cokes," said Harriet.

Liz let out a scream. "Roaches! Why didn't you tell me?"

"That's why," Harriet told her. "You would have screamed."

Meanwhile, they had continued their walk. Harriet asked Liz if she would like to go sunbathing on Casilda the next day. Then, the following day, both planned to go to Santa Clara and on to Havana.

Liz returned to her hotel. She went into her bathroom, the bathroom with the high ceiling and open window. There was a bat flying around in her bathroom! She had always heard that bats get tangled in your hat, scratching to get away. She ran out and slammed the door. She went down the stairs. The desk clerk was in attendance, plus two other men. They were startled to see her advance so quickly, obviously upset.

She said to them, "There is a bat in my bathroom."

This brought no response other than blank stares.

She said, in her attempt to speak Spanish, "Come *morto* my *bato*".

This non-Spanish also did not elicit any response. She pleaded with them to "morto" her "bato", but to no avail, so she slowly went back up the staircase.

When she returned to her room, apparently the bat preferred to be elsewhere, and was gone.

Later that night Liz had a phone call from Jesus Hernandez. He asked her many questions about Harriet: if Liz knew whether or not Harriet was with the CIA. Liz said she knew nothing other than that Harriet worked as a travel agent and if he wanted some answers, he should ask Harriet directly. Liz told her about the call the next morning. Harriet laughed and shrugged off the call as crazy.

The next day the girls went by taxi to Ancon, a fishing village. Ramon Hernandez had told Harriet he would have a fishing vessel arranged to take the girls over to Casilda, but no one in Ancon seemed to know anything about that. There was a little confusion, but Harriet spoke Spanish, and finally she hired two men and their boat. The girls spent a lovely day in the sun, alone on that little island (the two fishermen stayed with their boat on the far side). It was a relaxing and refreshing day.

45
THE DANGEROUS TRAIN RIDE

The final day in Trinidad Liz paid her bill. The clerk on duty spoke some English. He advised her not to ride the train to Santa Clara. He said it was dangerously rickety. Of course Liz and Harriet ignored his advice.

There were people on the train carrying long loaves of bread, many packages, and chickens by their legs. As they traveled along the countryside the train began to slow. Harriet spoke Spanish and asked the conductor what was happening. He said there was a wild pig ahead of the train and the engineer was trying to get the hog to go into the tall rushes along the side of the tracks.

Harriet and Liz got up and went forward. They took a clear photograph through the front glass of the engineer's car of that hog. Then they were asked to return to their seats. The train was going to run behind schedule. The girls feared the hog didn't make it.

A little later, the train stopped. The conductor and a man who spoke firmly, as if with the authority of an official, told Harriet and Liz to get out of the train. Harriet became upset and refused, but the men insisted.

Liz asked Harriet what was happening. Harriet spoke with a strange, low voice, and told her the men said they wanted them to see a beautiful view.

Liz said, "Oh, swell! Let's go." Liz became aware that suddenly there was no longer the clamorous noise within the car of the train. Even the chickens had stopped squawking. Everyone was looking at the girls.

Aware there was no option, it was an order, Liz said, "We don't want to insult their good intentions, do we?"

The two men told the girls to walk ahead of the train and onto the tracks that were crossing a bridge over a deep ravine. They were told to walk out farther. The girls had to step carefully: they could see between the rails and wooden supports, down to the narrow river, far below them.

Liz looked around and smiled. She said, "Ooh" and "Ahh" and told them it was beautiful. Then the girls walked back toward the men and onto the train.

Liz noticed Harriet had not used deodorant that morning.

When they arrived in Santa Clara, Harriet said she would stay there overnight, but she would help Liz get an airplane flight to Havana. They bought Cuban-mix sandwiches and ate them in the park. A man came up to Harriet and somehow started an argument. Then a crowd gathered. It seemed to be over some stupid nothing, but Harriet kept talking with the man.

It seemed like the argument was never going to get resolved. Finally Liz told Harriet, "Let's just walk away", but Harriet said they could not.

"That would start the crowd into a riot mode. I have to talk us out of it."

What? Why? Finally Harriet talked the man down.

"What was that all about?" Liz asked.

"Never mind. Let's get you to the airport," was all Harriet would say. The girls exchanged addresses and finally went their own way.

In Havana, Liz checked into a hotel Juan had suggested. She noticed it had no bidet and took that to mean it was a budget-priced place, perhaps. She went shopping. She bought Christmas cards that were printed in Cuba and she felt they definitely did not look American. Liz thought her grandmother and Shirley and her brothers would be so impressed with her being so internationally traveled.

Next she went to the Cuban Art Center. She was intrigued with one man's work: heads chiseled out of old bricks. They were very distinctive. But as she slowly walked around the room, admiring the pieces, several men were near the front, looking at her and commenting. She didn't pay much attention but a lone man came up to her. With his back to the men, he quietly said that there might be trouble. He told her she should leave the shop as soon as possible, but not to mention he had spoken to her.

Liz chose one of the carvings and took it up front to pay for it. One of the men asked her in English why she was leaving.

She told him she had admired the works and had chosen one.

He asked Liz if 'that man' had said anything to her.

"What man?" Liz asked, looking puzzled.

The agitated man attempted to continue the questioning, but the carving was paid for. Liz smiled and left the building. She wondered, "Was that another political thing?"

Walking on the sidewalk, returning to her hotel, she noticed what appeared to be a police station or perhaps some government offices. In front was a steel turret. Sticking out the peepholes was a rifle aimed at her. A soldier stood on the sidewalk, barring her way. In English he told her, "You must walk in the street, when you pass this building."

She thought it was very rude to make a woman walk in the gutter. She was glad she was going home soon.

After dinner at the hotel, she went alone to an Argentine movie. She thought the Spanish flamenco-style dancing in the movie was wonderful. Then she returned to her hotel and addressed her Cuban Christmas cards.

The next morning, before her flight from Havana to Key West, she went to the Post Office. She bought stamps and was affixing them to the envelopes when a man in uniform told her to follow him. He led her into an impressive office. The walls were covered with awards. Behind a huge desk was an army officer.

"Why are you mailing all these letters to America from Havana? I know that you, Miss Steele, are returning home today," the officer said to Liz.

She offered the unsealed envelopes toward him. She said, "I thought it would be special to have these lovely Cuban cards with Cuban stamps received by my family."

This reasoning did not seem to impress him. Finally she said that most of them were stamp-collectors. After a bit more of stern questions, he allowed her to go back to the front desk. She sealed the cards and placed them in the mail slot.

She had sent a postcard to Juan a few days prior: "Please arrange for the entire band to meet me at the airport when I arrive at 1:30pm on Saturday. See you then."

She was ready to go home.

On the flight from Havana to Key West Liz thought about the reason she had been able to make this trip to Cuba: the editor of *The Key West Courier* expected her to write a column about her experiences. She had no qualms about that. She felt confident she had enough notes in her journal to find material for several columns.

46

KEY WEST INTERROGATION BY MR. BILL

The plane banked low over the island of Key West. She could identify Christmas Tree island with all the Norfolk pine trees, and the Navy's housing island Sigsbee Park, and the Bight where the charter fishing boats were anchored, and the beaches, and the Boulevard where Juan had kissed her.

She could see a few people waiting for the passengers, but couldn't see Juan among them. She was the last person off the plane. There were only the backs of other persons leaving the tarmac.

"Hello, Liz", said someone. Liz looked up. It was Mr. Bill.

Without hesitating, Liz asked Mr. Bill, "Where is Juan?"

"While you were out of town he received his next assignment. He was transferred to Latin America. He is in the jungles of Honduras now. He told me to tell you he was sorry he didn't have a chance to tell you good-bye and he hoped you enjoyed your trip in Cuba," said Mr. Bill.

"Honduras? For how long?"

Mr. Bill answered, "Traditionally, assignments are for a two-year term. Here comes your suitcase now," and he leaned over the turn-table and grabbed it. He smiled at Liz and walked toward his automobile in the parking lot.

Liz wordlessly followed, trying to absorb this new information. She watched as her suitcase was put in the trunk of Mr. Bill's car. He opened the passenger door and looked at Liz. She was certain he clicked his heels and gave a brief European nod. She got in.

He had only driven a short way. Turning to her Mr. Bill asked her, "Why did you tell Juan to meet you at the airport with a band? And written on a postcard?"

At first she couldn't respond. There was a lump in her throat, but she was determined not to cry. "The band, the high school band. It was a joke, you know: a big welcome home. I didn't expect Tommy Dorsey's band, just the Key West High band."

"Oh." He seemed relieved. His shoulders relaxed. Then he started to ask more questions. Things he could only know if someone had read her journal. No, if someone had been following her and making a report.

The next question was, "What do the numbers 22, 32, 59, 63 mean?"

She seemed unable to ask him why he was questioning her this way. But she answered honestly, "I had hoped to return some day to Cuba. Those were beautiful areas. I wanted to photograph them, but the bus drove past too fast to capture them."

He asked another question. "What about that girl you went with to Casilda. What does she do?"

"She's an agent," Liz said.

"An agent! What kind of agent?"

"A travel agent. What kind did you think?"

"Why did you insist on taking a photo of Rigoberto? Do you know he was killed?"

"Because I took his picture?" Liz realized this was going beyond what she could imagine.

Mr. Bill continued, Why did you stand so long on that hill in back of the house?"

Liz felt very calm now. She was being interrogated. Who did Bill work for? She answered, "What else could I have done? Should I have acted frightened? Should I have tried to run away? I had no other recourse other than to play it out. What do you think I should have done?"

Mr Bill sternly told her, "You don't ask the questions. I ask the questions."

They had arrived at her cottage. Liz told Mr. Bill, "And I don't answer any more questions." She got out and walked down the short path to her place and went inside. She locked the door. She didn't care if Mr. Bill put her suitcase outside for her or not.

She was exhausted by all the events of this day and this week.

Mrs. Pinder saw her renter walk down the pathway to the cottage. She knew the girl had been sent to Cuba by Brian Bartlett of the *Courier* because Mrs. Pinder had gone to school with Brian's wife Sara. Actually all the Conch wives on the little island of Key West kept up what some called The Conch Telegraph. Any news traveled fast, one housewife to another. Two days after Liz had gone on her trip a rainstorm had wet the mail in Liz' mailbox so Mrs. Pinder had been keeping the girl's mail in a paper bag next to the lace curtain window.

She saw Liz return and then she saw a man carry a suitcase and place it outside Liz's door, then leave. After the man had driven off Mrs. Pinder took the bag of mail and went to the cottage. She knocked on the door, explained how she had kept the mail, and asked Liz how her trip had gone.

Liz smiled, said it was a beautiful country and she would be writing articles soon. She eagerly grabbed the bag of mail, smiled, and tried to ease her landlady away so could see who had written to her. Riffling through the letters there was one from Grandma, Matt's wife, Mark, L. Olson, and a postcard from Shirley.

She turned the postcard over. It was a picture of the State of New Jersey, with a pencilled "X" on one spot. Liz turned it again and read the note. It was printed in pencil and said, "See where I live. See the X. Love, Shirley." Liz smiled. She missed her.

She picked up the letter from Canada. Mark's note was short.

I'm going to Mystic for Christmas to meet the family. Will you be there? Matthew and his wife invited us to visit with them for the holiday season.

Raven said she would spend Christmas with her parents so the Steele family can bond their spirits together as one.

Raven and I think of you often. You must know she sends her greetings to you. I hope to see you in Mystic. I have a surprise for you.

Your loving brother, Mark

Going to Mystic for Christmas? Meet the family? Was everyone going to Mystic? She reached for the letter postmarked Connecticut. Matt's wife, Marian, wrote it.

I tried to reach you at work, but they told me you are in Cuba! I don't know when you'll be back to your place in Key West, but Matt and I were hoping you might be able to join us up here for Christmas.

I know it is short notice, but we had asked Grandma Steele to come stay at our home for Thanksgiving. She had said No but she wanted a raincheck. Maybe she was kidding, but we tried again for Christmas and she wrote back she would come. We are so happy about that, and the boys are, too.

So I wrote to Mark and he will be here, too!

What about Luke? What's the story there?

Sure do hope you can make it. What a Christmas that would make!

Hugs from Marian, Matt, Joey, Max and of course Hal

She picked up the envelope from L. Olson. It was from Captain Lars.

My dear Miss Steele, there is no doubt you are an unusual and interesting young woman. Your eyes and brain and heart are processing what you see and hear, absorbing actions and revealing a picture for your readers. I am going to keep an eye on you, Miss Steele. You have my attention. I find you intriguing. Lars Olson

Liz remembered the tall Norwegian, Captain Lars Olson. His note was a surprise. She didn't know how she felt about it. But, like his final two sentences, he had <u>her</u> attention. Now it was <u>she</u> who was intrigued by him. She set his note aside.

Her thoughts went back to the family together for the holiday. Everyone was going to Matt's house for Christmas? Liz was elated, then instantly deflated. She hadn't worked at *The Courier* long enough to get a vacation. The policy was that employees could get two weeks vacation after working for the company for one year. Besides, she had just come back from Cuba, although that wasn't supposed to be a vacation. Her boss had paid for her to visit there so she could write some human-interest articles. But she was certain he would not look kindly upon a request from her for a need for vacation at this time.

She picked up the letter from her grandmother.

Matt's wife wrote to me that you are in Cuba. We are such a strange family. I didn't tell anyone when I went visiting back home to Ireland, and now it seems that no one knew you were going to Cuba. I guess you're back… you are reading this.

I look forward to a long letter telling me about it.

Matt and his wife have invited me to spend the Christmas holidays with them. At first I didn't want to barge in on their family time together, but it sounded too tempting, enjoying a Christmas with Matt and his family. I've already bought presents for their boys.

Will you be there?

With love, Grandma

Tears came to Liz' eyes. *Everyone is going to be there but me.* She felt like the cartoon character with a devil standing on one shoulder and an angel on the other. She was feeling sorry for herself, when the little angel kicked her.

It was as if the angel was telling her that she should stop feeling sorry for herself. She lived on a tropical island, she had enjoyed a fabulous experience of traveling in Cuba, her family loved her, and she was pouting because she couldn't go to Connecticut?

Liz decided the day had been too emotional. Grandma and Mark were planning to enjoy a family holiday with Matt and his wife and children. What about the mysterious happenings in Cuba that she had felt all along took her into some kind of unknown danger? All of these things had exploded inside her head today.

She was very tired. A soft tropical breeze brushed her forehead. The letters lifted up as if to blow away. Liz set a book on top of the papers and got up. She lay across her bed. In one minute she fell asleep.

Liz awakened to thoughts racing through her head: Juan was gone forever, Lars found her intriguing, Grandma and Mark were going to Matt's for Christmas.

Mr. Bartlett wanted articles written about her week in Cuba. She decided to take all her rolls of film to the drugstore for development. They were not in her suitcase. Not only was her Spanish Phrase book gone, but her films were missing, too.

A knot obstructed her throat: she was going to cry.

"No!" she said aloud. Anger chased her tears. She was angry about all the Cuban mysteries. She took a shower, washed her hair, dressed in shorts and a t-shirt. She gathered up all her laundry into a bundle, slipped on her sandals and went out of the cottage and on to her bicycle.

Tossing her bundle on the basket of her bike, she balanced it with one hand as she rode down the street toward the Laundromat. She pushed hard on the bike pedals, riding faster and faster. The wind pulled back her wet hair, sprinkling water droplets on her t-shirt.

The morning went by. Put the laundry in the washer. Put the clean clothes in the dryer. Fold the items and wrap them up again in the clean sheets. Take the laundry back home and put everything away.

47 TIME FOR A WOMAN TO WOMAN TALK

Back on her bicycle, she rode aimlessly up and down streets. She realized she was on Pigeon Lane. Heather and Fern were playing on the porch, Trish watching them. Liz slowed her bike. Trish looked up and waved.

"Hi, come on in, Liz," Trish said giving a welcoming smile.

Liz propped her bike against the fence and came up to the porch. Fern toddled over to Liz and put her arms up for a hug. Liz sat on the step and admired the dolly that the child clutched. Trish had been feeding the baby. She told Liz, "You are just in time. Heather needs burping. Want to?"

"I've never done it," said Liz

"Don't be nervous," and Trish put the baby in Liz's arms. Liz put the baby up on her shoulder, but before she could even begin a back-tap, Heather gave out a loud burp.

"Wow, you are good!" Trish told Liz

Liz kept on holding the baby, swaying her body. Heather's eyelids started to droop.

Trish said, "You're a natural". She said that Bubba was visiting his parents. He had taken a bag of Key limes from their backyard tree to share with them. Trish chattered on for a while, then asked Liz, "Watch Fern for a few minutes, will you? I see that Heather is sleeping, so I'll put her in her crib. I'll be back in a moment. Would you like a limeade?"

Liz nodded, and went over to Fern, who was engrossed in spooning invisible food into her doll's painted mouth. She asked Fern what her baby was eating, and Fern said, "nanas". Next Fern pointed a miniature baby-bottle at her doll. After a minute Liz asked Fern if she could burp her baby.

Liz held the doll on her shoulder. After a few pats, Liz gave a loud "BURP". Fern giggled and giggled. Trish returned carrying a tray with three glasses and a plate of cookies. She asked Liz what was happening.

Addressing Fern, Liz answered, "We were feeding the baby-doll, weren't we?"

Fern giggled with delight.

There was a child-size table and chairs in the corner of the porch. Trish placed a small plastic glass with milk and a cookie on the table and pulled out the chair for Fern. The child now occupied, the two young women sat nearby with their limeades.

Turning to Liz, Trish asked, "What have you been doing lately?"

Liz made a quick story about her trip to Cuba, a newspaper assignment, then faced Trish in a pathetic tone and said, "May I ask you a question?"

"Of course."

"How do you know when men are really sincere?"

Trish knew there must be a long story behind that statement, so responded, "Why do you ask?"

Liz poured out a story about a guy she had met at the beach and then seemed to pursue her. They had dated a few times. They had gone out to the Boulevard and kissed. "I know physical attraction is not the same as love, but I had a very powerful attraction that night."

Trish started to make some sort of response, but Liz stopped her.

"I thought he really cared about me. Was it just sex that he wanted?"

Trish said, "Maybe you should ask him."

"Why ask," she said bitterly. "If he cares about me, he'll say yes. But if he just wanted sex, of course a guy would answer,'I care about you'. Would they answer, 'No, I just wanted to get a little nooky'?"

Fern was feeding her doll a cookie. Since the doll did not take a bite,

Fern would take a teeny nibble, then offer it to the doll again. This game was keeping her engrossed.

"I don't have the answer, Liz. I wish I did. But you mentioned 'expectations'. It reminded me of the first argument Bubba and I had. We had been married several weeks. He came home from work and looked at the kitchen floor. He seemed embarrassed, but finally spoke up. He asked me when I was going to scrub the kitchen floor.

"I hadn't noticed it being particularly dirty, but was surprised at his question. I told him, 'Me, scrub the kitchen floor? My father always scrubbed the floor for my mother'. Bubba answered that in his house, it was his mother who always scrubbed the floor. So you see, it's always 'expectations'."

Liz laughed. "So who scrubs the floors now?"

"Me, of course," Trish answered, laughing.

"Well, I don't think I've solved anythings but you surely do make me feel better, Trish."

"Oh, it's probably just the limeade."

Riding her bicycle back to her cottage Liz thought about how many people her world had expanded to include, like her brothers and the Jackson family. She was glad she had decided her budget must include paying for telephone service to her cottage.

When Liz returned to her place she heard her phone ringing. With lightning speed she unlocked the door and jumped on the phone.

"Hello?" Liz asked, out of breath.

"Lizzie, it's me, Grandma. Sorry, were you busy?"

"No, Grandma. It's always good to hear from you. What's up?"

Her grandmother asked Liz if she had heard about Luke.

Liz said she hadn't heard from Luke.

Grandma Steele told Liz that Luke was reportedly hiding in the Bahamas where the police were looking for him. They had been watching Judy and discovered where Luke was hiding. When the police arrived they discovered Luke dead in his kitchen. He had apparently shot and killed himself, leaving a note for his girlfriend, saying he was despondent over his inability to get rich quickly and had gone on to 'Plan C': kill himself.

Liz sat down on her bedside, not saying anything, trying to assimilate that information.

Her grandmother continued, “Judy was arrested for being involved.”

The only contact Judy Pritchard knew from Luke’s family had been the phone call Liz had made from Grandma Steele’s home in New Jersey. She gave that telephone number to the police investigators. The police had contacted her, telling her the body was being held for a while but then it would be returned to Luke’s family. Liz’ grandmother mentioned cremation. She said she would bury the urn in the family plot when the time came.

Liz was impressed at the calmness of her grandmother, while she herself was trying to slow down her own heart rate. She acknowledged what her grandmother had told her. “Please tell me, Grandma, what I can do for you? I don’t know what to say.”

Grandma Steele said she was simply contacting all her grandchildren, Matt, Mark, and Liz, but she was handling everything. However, she knew each of them were willing to assist in any way, if later she needed anything. She said she loved them all and ended the call.

The next day Liz, after spending days in Cuba, found herself suffering from lethargy. Her movements were slow that morning. She got dressed, then realized there was nothing in her apartment for breakfast. Pumping the pedals on her bicycle seemed an effort. She rode to the local cafe sidewalk window, ordered Cuban bread with cheese and a cafe-con-leche. The coffee was too hot so she placed that in her bike basket, cushioning it with old t-shirt, and continued to ride her bike to work, one-handed, munching on her cheese bread as she went along.

At her desk, returning to the work regimet, she sat looking at her typewriter, gathering her thoughts about how to begin her first article, when she felt a tap on her shoulder. It was Mr. Bartlett himself who had emerged from his office to come directly to her himself.

Smiling, he asked her, “How was it?”

Liz was afraid Mr. Bartlett would be upset that she did not follow his itinerary of visiting Havana, Matanzas, Sancti Spiritus and Cienfuegos. Instead she had traveled from Havana to Matanzas, but at Sancti Spiritus she had been deflected on to Trinidad where she stayed, never visiting Cienfuegos. Instead, she returned to Havana via Santa Clara.

Nervous in the presence of the big boss, she cleared her throat and answered, "Wonderful."

"I know you'll write some interesting columns about your trip, Miss Steele. When you have finished one today, please bring it to my office. I am looking forward to reading it."

Mr. Bartlett turned and walked back to his office. While he had been talking with Liz, the only sound in the room was one phone, ringing in the distance. Suddenly there was the noise of several typewriters clacking away simultaneously as reporters returned to producing their copy for the day.

Her first submission was entitled "Visiting Cuba: Where Are the Women?"

48

SHOPPING BY SEARS CATALOG

Christmas was getting closer and Liz knew she could not get time off from work to travel to Mystic, so she went to the Sears-Roebuck catalog store and picked up her own copy of the catalog to take home and study. She decided her best bet would be to order all the gifts for the family and have them delivered to Matt's house. That is, all the gifts except Marian's After all, she felt, if Marian was going to have to wrap all her presents, at least the one to Marian herself should be a surprise. Liz had to think of something she could send from Key West to her sister-in-law.

She took the catalog out on her side porch. This was getting to be her favorite place. She would enter through her front door, lock it, and then open the sliding glass doors to her porch to view of the garden. Somedays it was a little chilly, by KeyWest standards, when it would go down to 60 degrees and she would sit out at her table wearing a sweater.

She concentrated on the Sears catalog. Not knowing what toys Max and Joey already had, Liz decided on books for each. She picked out *Swiss Family Robinson* and *The Adventures of Tom Sawyer.* Since it seemed right to get the two boys similar presents, she decided to do the same for her own two brothers. She chose a blue wool muffler for Matt and a red one for Mark. There was a page with items for pets. Liz ordered a big rubber bone for the dog Hal.

Liz looked at every page in the catalog, trying to decide what she should get for her grandmother. Not a blouse or a skirt, not an appliance, although she remembered she had wanted to buy a new refrigerator for her grandmother whenever she could get some savings together. Her goal had been to set aside ten percent of her earnings, but expenses were more than she had expected. The refrigerator would have to come later, and delivered right to grandmother's house, of course.

She finally chose her grandmother's present that was to go underneath the Christmas tree in Mystic: a Kelly green wool bathrobe and matching slippers. Liz felt good about that, and believed her grandmother would get a lot of wear out of them in New Jersey.

Her quandary was what gift she could sent to Marian? Finally, Liz made the decision to have a florist wire a flower arrangement. With that idea, she thought about Raven, in Canada, who would not be included with the Steele gathering in Mystic. She added a mental note to wire flowers to Raven, also.

She closed the Sears catalog and gazed out at the tropical flowers in the garden and the clump of bamboo, huge philodendra, ferns and palms. Liz rarely saw her landlady, except when she paid her rent on the first day of each month. She thought, I really must tell her how much pleasure I get from sitting on my porch, overlooking her garden.

Christmas shopping done, all that was left to do was to return to the Sears catalog store, place the order, and pay cash. Next would be to the florist shop to have them order Marian's and Raven's flowers. They would take a check or cash, but Liz did not have a checking account, only a savings account. More cash to the florist.

It was while she was bicycling home from the stores she decided her next article would be "Cuban Vistas". She would describe the views she remembered along the drive from Sancti Spiritus to Trinidad, plus the lush valley from the train trestle. As she thought about the conductor and the strangely insistent man, she realized that she had known, even then, that she was in danger. But why?

***

Christmas 1955, was on a Sunday. Mr. Bartlett had made an announcement that he planned to continue his usual practice of producing a newspaper on December 25th and also Monday. There would be no holiday for the staff, but they would receive overtime pay, plus an end-of-the-year bonus. Miss Geraldine, a long-time employee, would be taking her annual vacation, but otherwise the routine would be "just another day".

The letters Liz had received from home needed a response. She wrote to Mark that she was delighted to know he would be spending Christmas holidays with Grandma and their brother Matt and his family in Mystic. However, as a new employee, she would not be able to take any time off this year. Her thoughts would be with them. She sent warm regards to Raven.

To Marian Steele she thanked her for the thoughtful hospitality of inviting everyone, but repeated the story about not being able to get time off from work. Liz made sure she did not include any mention that the price of the airfare was more than she could afford at this time. She told Marian she planned to order a few items through the Sears catalog, to be delivered to Mystic.

It was as she was writing to Marian that Liz realized Christmas with two boys and guests coming to visit would be a very busy time. Instead of asking Marian to wrap five presents, she asked if she would wrap Grandma Steele's present. Liz wrote that she was asking her grandmother to wrap the other items she would forward. That way the gifts to Marian's family would be a surprise to her also.

Liz wrote a short note to Mark, explaining that she had to work over the Christmas holidays and would not be able to fly to Mystic. However, her thoughts would be with all of them and she hoped she would be able to see them some other time in the near future.

To her grandmother, Liz repeated her plan about the Sears order going directly to Matt's house. She asked Grandma Steele if she would mind wrapping the items for her two brothers and for Matt's two boys. And, oh yes, for the dog, Hal. She reassured her that she had not forgotten Marian, but something else would be coming for their hostess.

She told her grandmother she missed her very much. She wrote that she hoped everyone would take many snapshots, because it was impossible for her to get time off from work to be with them. Liz specifically requested a photograph of her grandmother, "so I can keep it in a frame on my table and see you all the time."

After having written the letters, Liz felt mentally drained. She fixed herself a quick supper, poured herself a Coca-Cola and took her supper-tray out on her porch. A Mockingbird sang, mimicking the tunes of several other birds. Two pelicans flew by overhead, drawing Liz' attention to the white cumulus clouds which were beginning to tinge with pink and orange tones as the sun began to set. As usual there was no one in the garden and its peacefulness was a healing balm.

At dusk, the mosquitoes came to life. Liz went back inside and closed the glass sliding doors. How she felt refreshed. She sealed the envelopes of the letters she had written, chuckling to herself, thinking she had certainly had done her share of writing for the day. A shower and bedtime followed and she quickly fell asleep.

The community's reaction to the articles Liz wrote about her trip to Cuba amazed Mr. Bartlett. It seemed like every sector of the town found the stories interesting. More letters in response came in to his office than anything else he had ever run. And the circulation figures increased.

After "Beautiful Vistas" she wrote about "Afro-Ritmo". She told about hearing the bells, climbing up inside the tower to watch the men beat out the rhythm. Another column was "View from the Balcony". She described the men gathering in the central park area to wait for the work truck and the old men who hung small birdcages from the trees. She wrote about the man who delivered the logs of pungent-smelling wood to the restaurant downstairs.

Mr. Bartlett could not print enough Wednesday newspapers, the day Liz' column appeared. Circulation was soaring. Mr. Bartlett was, as they say, "In Seventh Heaven."

In response to Liz's letter to her grandmother, Nellanore Steele wrote back.

You didn't even mention your trip to Cuba! Are you sure you won't be able to make it to Mystic for Christmas? Of course I'll help Marian. Wasn't it thoughtful of her to ask everyone? It will be such a nice time for Matt and Mark to get together.

I am really looking forward to this, but it is so disappointing that you won't be able to be there with us. And yes, of course, we'll take lots of pictures. Love, Grandma

49

BE JOLLY. TIS THE SEASON

Liz decided she wanted to decorate her place for the holiday season, but didn't have much money to spend. She went to Woolworth's Dime Store and bought some red paper napkins, a jar of rubber cement, two big sheets of green poster-board and one long rope of silver tinsel garland.

When she got home she cut each poster-board in a jagged triangle. She rolled each one slightly, curling them side to side, then had the two pieces meet on the edges, creating a "tree". The paste wouldn't hold until it dried, so until it stuck she fastened the edges with some of her bobby pins. She covered her small kitchen table with some of the red paper napkins and propped up her Christmas tree, pleased with the effect.

A couple of days later the mailman left a box on her doorstep. It was from Grandma. Liz set it on her table, next to the tree. The next day there were two boxes, one from Mark and the other from Matt and his family. These were piled next to her tree. Also, there was a holiday letter from Lars.

On Saturday, December 24, Liz did what any person would do who is alone and new to a town. She went somewhere that she could be with people. In Key West, it was the beach.

Between November and March there would be several "cold spells", each lasting three or four days, when the temperature would go down into the fifties. The coldest ever recorded was back in 1898, when the thermometer dropped to a low of 41 degrees. This day, however, Liz was comfortable in a bathing suit. It was a sunny 75 degrees. Not a White Christmas, but by the locals' standard the weather made it a Just Right Christmas.

Liz recognized one of the regulars: Mercedes Yates. She was wearing a Catalina bathing suit like Esther Williams wore in a recent movie. Mercedes asked Liz if she wanted to play volleyball, but Liz said she just wanted to sit in the sun. She watched the current game, bodies glistening with sweat and Coppertone.

She closed her eyes and listened to the sounds. There was the thud as the ball was hit, and the bantering comments from the players. Seagulls flying overhead were calling to each other, their cries intermingling with the sound of the waves lapping onto the shore's edge. Car motors could be heard in the distance and a mixed-up rooster was crowing at sunset.

Leaving the beach, she went to The Deli on Simonton Street to pick up something for her dinner, but it had closed early. The sign read "Merry Christmas". Everywhere seemed to have closed early. She continued to her apartment.

There was a can of vegetable soup in her cupboard. "Ah, soup *de jour*" Liz said aloud, as she poured it into a saucepan.

Someone knocked on her front door. It was her landlady, Mrs. Pinder. Her landlady had never before visited her. Mrs. Pinder didn't believe in butting into other people's private lives. However, her son had caught a large Grouper fish, and Mrs. Pinder had made a big pot of fish chowder. Neither she nor her family had ever traveled off the island of Key West. Nor did they want to.

To be alone, like this girl, was an unimaginable horror for Mrs. Pinder. She would have asked Liz to come to her home and join her family for the evening, but that was not her way. However, she wanted to reach out in some way to this girl. Mrs. Pinder stood in the doorway, extending a large bowl of her famous Grouper Chowder. A half a loaf of Cuban bread rested across the rim of the bowl.

"We had extra," Mrs. Pinder said simply.

"Thank you, Mrs. Pinder." Liz wanted to tell her how much she enjoyed the garden, but the woman had hurried back to her own home.

Mrs. Pinder was aghast at the sight of the pitiful cardboard tree and the pasted-on newspaper ornaments. She prayed that her daughters would never suffer such a hellish existence.

"Isn't this wonderful?" Liz whispered to herself. She set the bowl on the table, turned off her canned soup, and poured a glass of wine. Liz moved the candles to the edge of the sink to keep them clear of the fire-hazard paper napkins lining the table.

She ate a couple spoonfuls of the fish chowder, and then decided she would open just one present. She chose the one from Matt and Marian. It was heavy. It was a portable radio! There was a note attached. *I hear you get hurricanes down there, so you'll need to be able to get the weather reports. Matt*

"Isn't that just like a fisherman?" Liz chuckled. She ate some more chowder, sipped some wine.

Wait a minute, she thought. There'll be Christmas music on tonight. She turned on her new radio. She sat back and admired her Christmas tree, beautiful in the glow of her candlelight and the effects of the wine and the holiday music.

She couldn't resist the temptation to open another box. She vowed that she'd save one for the Christmas morning.

She spoke aloud to herself again. "I wonder what my grandmother sent?"

Inside the carton there were several items, each with a note attached.

Notes must run in the family, Liz thought. Matt had added a note, too.

The first gift she opened from her grandmother's box was a dictionary. The note said *I am enjoying your newspaper articles. Here is a book that every writer should have.*

The next item was soft-wrapped. Tearing open the wrapping paper, Liz saw a pair of crocheted slippers, the kind she used to wear to bed to keep her feet warm on cold New Jersey nights. The note explained, *I don't want you to catch cold this winter.* It was difficult for her grandmother to imagine that even the nights don't get cool in Key West.

Liz ate some more chowder and cut a hunk of bread off the half loaf. She spread it with butter, purposely delaying the delight of opening the final item in the box. At the bottom of the carton from her grandmother was a present mummy-wrapped in many layers of newspaper. She unfolded the papers, dropping them to the floor, saving them. Later she could read about news from her hometown. Finally, the gift was revealed.

It was a framed photograph of Liz and her grandmother. Liz recalled that she had posed with her grandmother in front of a picturesque stone fence, when a passer-by asked if he could snap the two women together with her camera. Grandma had kept the negatives and had an 8 x 10 glossy made for Liz.

She was teary-eyed as she read the note accompanying that gift. *We'll be taking more pictures during Christmas in Mystic. I'll send you copies. You will be there in our thoughts and conversation. I love you. Grandma*

Liz held the picture on her lap, thinking about her family, then set the photo on the table next to her Christmas tree.

Blowing out the candles, Liz turned her radio down low and left it on. She went to bed with the moonlight shining through the glass doors, illuminating the picture of her grandmother. Christmas music lulled her to sleep.

50 CHRISTMAS AT MATT AND MARIAN'S HOME

In Connecticut the airports were busy. Grandma had arrived on December 22 in an attempt to avoid some of the last-minute travel crush. Mark arrived on the 23rd, one of the last planes allowed to land before the airport was closed due to heavy snow.

Things were hectic, everyone getting to know each other, and the children in high holiday excitement. Hal was stimulated by the emotional airwaves. He went from person to person, looking up and smiling, wagging his tail vigorously.

Marian decided things needed to be calmed down a bit. She suggested everyone go for a walk to view the outdoor holiday decorations. "Just one time around the block," she urged. It took time to gather all the boots and galoshes, heavy coats and warm hats, but finally they trooped out of the house and down the sidewalk.

Halfway around the block the boys started to josh with each other, giving a little shoulder-push to get the other into deeper snow. Marian used a Mother's Diversion Technique by suggesting everyone sing Christmas carols the rest of the way home. That worked, and the six of them (Hal didn't sing, but he did wag his tail) sang gustily.

When they returned to the house Marian heated some cocoa (with marshmallows, of course). She told Joey and Max that after they finished their hot chocolate, they were to go to bed. "Otherwise Santa Claus won't be able to come."

The boys gave their mother That Look. They nursed their chocolate, making it last as long as possible but finally gave in, knowing that no presents could be opened until Christmas morning. Each gave hugs to their father and their newly met Uncle Mark and Grandma, then dutifully trudged up the stairs to their bedroom.

The four adults stayed up for many hours longer. Marian listened to the two brothers exchange stories about their childhood. Grandma Steele said little, but stared at the two men, absorbing their faces into her memory.

The next morning Marian set bowls of oatmeal at six places, and platters of sausage, bacon and scrambled eggs in the center of the table. The men entered the dining room looking scraggly, unshaven and bleary-eyed from staying up longer than everyone else. They had years of catching up to do. The boys came in, wanting to eat in a hurry, so presents could be opened.

Grandma took some candid shots of everyone enjoying breakfast. Mark took her camera and included photos of Grandma with her family. In deference to the young boys, dishes were left on the table and everyone went into the living room.

It was still dark outside, the skies overcast with winter snow. The Christmas tree lights were on, reflected doubly by the windowpane against the dark sky. Mark, still holding Grandma's camera, took a photo of the tree with packages still wrapped festively. Then the boys could not be held back any longer.

Max and Joey opened their presents, politely thanking the person who had given that gift. Although they had received a lot of things, it didn't take them long to rip open each of their presents. Next, the adults opened theirs, one at a time, the others enjoying each presentation and making comments.

The two men seemed pleased with their scarves from Liz, each insisting on wearing it in the heated house. Joey and Max said they liked their books, and Grandma bent over to put on her new slippers. This way no one could see that there were tears in her eyes. It was such a beautiful family time. How she wished Liz could have been there, too. Mark snapped more photographs. Grandma insisted the flash was making her eyes water.

All the gifts had been opened. There was nothing from Liz for Marian. The boys helped scrunch together the torn wrapping paper, stuffing it into old garbage bags. Marian was picking up the ribbons, gently pushing Hal out of the way when he helpfully got in the way. The doorbell rang.

"Mrs. Steele?" the man asked Marian. "Guess I should have delivered these yesterday, but with all the snow and all…." and he handed her a beautiful flower arrangement.

Marian closed the door, holding the arrangement.

"Who is it from, Mama." asked Joey

"It's not from me," Matt said.

Marian chuckled. "I knew that, Matt."

She set the flowers down and read the card. "Oh! It's from Liz. I haven't received a floral arrangement since I gave birth to Joey. Aren't they beautiful?" Marian asked Grandma to take a snapshot of her with her flowers, then they switched and Marian took a photo of Grandma seated at the table next to the flowers.

51
HOLIDAY TIME ON PEACON LANE, KEY WEST

In Key West, Liz woke up slowly, gradually becoming aware of Christmas music. It was coming from her very own radio! She opened her eyes, and absorbed the view of her Christmas tree and the radio, dictionary, crocheted slippers, and the photograph of Grandma and her.

"Merry Christmas", Liz said aloud. Then she wondered if talking to herself was a sign of something weird. She shrugged and said even louder, "Oh well, what the hell", daring whatever consequence that would bring about, but there was only holiday music.

She got up to get a glass of milk and saw that ants were enjoying the droplets of fish chowder that had remained in her unwashed bowl in the sink. "Merry Christmas ants." she said, addressing them directly. She didn't hear any response.

Sliding the glass door open to the porch, Liz set her milk glass on the porch table and went back inside to pick up the unopened box from her brother Mark. She sat in the wicker chair and admired the sunlight on her bare feet, her toenail polish glistening. She opened the box from Mark and found a smaller box inside the package. She wondered if there would be yet a third box inside, remembering the nested toys of her childhood.

When she opened the small box, there was a ring with a red stone. Liz sat holding the small box, her mouth agape, unable to move.

Finally, she snapped out of the trance. She looked inside the bigger box and there it was: a note from Mark:

Dear Liz, do you remember me telling you about Mr. Perry and his tales about veins of gemstones? Do you remember me telling you about aluminum and bauxite and corundum and rubies? As I suspected, the land I purchased in Canada has yielded me a few little gems. Raven and I had this ruby polished and set into a ring for you. We send it to you with our love, dear sister. Merry Christmas and a Happy New Year. Love, Mark and Raven.

Liz slipped the ruby ring onto her third finger, right hand. Perfect fit. She was speechless, for a change.

It was going to be another hot day in Key West. Liz scrubbed her dirty dishes, rinsed them and stacked them on the sideboard. She put on shorts and a blouse and was about to get on her bicycle to head for Rene's cafe for some Cuban coffee but she heard someone call her name. It was Bubba Jackson!

"Merry Christmas!" he drawled the words, in the manner of the rehabilitated Scrooge. "Merry Christmas!"

"Bubba! Merry Christmas to you. What are you doing here so early on a Christmas morn? Did you bring Trish and the girls?"

"I've come for you. Trish and I want you to spend the day with us. Come on. No arguments. Get in my car."

Trish looked around. She grabbed her crocheted slippers and put them in her drawstring bag. "Okay," she said, laughing. "Here I come."

The wooden fence was draped with greenery and there was a wreath hung on the door.

"What an interesting wreath, Trish. Did you make it?"

"Yes, it's end-branches of the Holly-Berry tree, that I twisted around. The real name is Florida Holly. It's no relative to real holly, but the berries look quite similar. Festive, don't you think? Come on in. I was afraid you wouldn't come. This will really make our day special, having you here. What did you eat for breakfast, Liz?"

"Nothing. I was just leaving to get some Cuban coffee, when Bubba strolled up my path."

Trish turned to look at Bubba. "You see. Told ya so," She looked at

Liz. "I had Bubba get three big take-out cups of cafe con leche from the little place on the corner. It's still hot. I told him you would like some, but he said he doubted you drank it. I love it when he's wrong. Unfortunately for me, he is not wrong very often," Trish said, laughing.

She led them out to the Florida Room where the girls were seated in a playpen, munching on Cuban bread. She pulled out one of the wicker chairs and said, "Here, Liz, have a seat. Help yourself to that coffee and some bread. There's some Guava jam that my mother-in-law made."

With that invitation given, Trish sat down, too, and stretched out her legs.

"I'm pooped. The girls woke up early, of course. Fern said Santa's reindeer woke her up…the hooves on the tin roof."

"Ah, yes, that would be noisy," Liz agreed.

"So the four of us have been up since some unholy hour. We opened presents and I took pictures of the mess of wrapping paper and toys scattered everywhere, including a couple of shots of Bubba, unshaven and his hair sticking up wildly. My parents will love it when I send them copies of those photos,"

Liz commented, "I see you have no glass ornaments on your tree."

"Why ask for trouble? I don't want to be fussing at the girls all the time. As it is, they really don't touch anything. I didn't put anything very tempting near the bottom. The ornaments are wooden or cardboard or things we made with construction paper and clipped on the branches with wooden clothespins."

Trish continued, "The first year I moved to Key West I thought it would be nice to string cranberries and popcorn, plus put little boxes of candy in the branches. You should have seen the ants that had a happy time with all that food! I learned my lesson. This year Fern and I cut out strips of paper and curled them onto each other, making long strands of ringed streamers, didn't we Fern?"

Fern looked up and gave a toothy grin. She threw her piece of bread at her sister. Instead of crying, Heather picked it up and sat with a piece of bread in each of her hands, looking pleased with herself.

Liz laughed and said, "They are quite a picture."

"Yes, they are our little Christmas cherubs, right girls?"

Fern nodded her head vigorously. Heather took a bite of bread.

Bubba asked, "What do you hear from your family back home?"

"I got letters from everyone last week, and some packages. My brother Matt sent me a radio and I kept it playing all night long. And look what my brother Mark sent to me." She extended her right hand.

"Wow, he must own a gold mine," said Bubba.

"No, a ruby mine," Liz said.

Bubba pretended to pout. "The only thing I have in my backyard is a Key Lime tree."

The two women sat at the table and watched Bubba play with his two daughters. He had placed Heather on the floor and she had crawled over to the pile of Christmas toys, selecting one at a time, looking at it, and tossing it aside, then picking up another.

"What are you looking for, Heather?" Bubba asked her.

Apparently she had found the desired object and was crawling toward her father with the tale of a small stuffed cat clenched in one fist. Her sister was occupied with a wooden paddle that had small chickens bobbing as she moved the paddle in circles.

"You make me feel like family, Trish. This is a wonderful way to spend Christmas", Liz said. "But Mr. Bartlett said *The Courier* would be printed today, as usual, so I plan to go in to work this afternoon. Get another column started."

Trish said, "I understand. And of course I believe we all are family. I'm so glad your sister-in-law gave you our address. She had written to me a long time ago inquiring about Josephus Fitch Packer. Besides that, Bubba is related to the Packers and Wilbur families of Connecticut, and so is your sister-in-law, Marian Packer Steele. So you see, Liz, we are family. How about we phone up to Mystic right now? That way you can wish your family a Merry Christmas."

Trish contacted 'Information' and obtained Matthew Steele's home telephone number, but they were unable to place the call. A recorded message said that all the long-distance circuits to Connecticut were busy.

"It's hard to get through on holidays," said Trish. "We'll try again later."

But they forgot to try again.

52
ONE NEVER KNOWS

Marian had arranged her living room furniture in conversational groupings. The two men had chosen to sit in the pair of wingback chairs that were angled towards each other.

The house had one bathroom currently serving six people. Grandma had deferred her showers. She asked Marian if there was anything she could help with in the kitchen. When the answer was No, Grandma asked if this was a good time for her to take a shower while the men and the boys were occupied. Marian assured her it was a good time and made certain Grandma had towels she would need.

Marian returned to the living room with the men.

Mark was saying, "Matt, I want you to know how much this visit has meant to me, meeting you and your family, and our grandmother, too. Thank you for arranging this."

"You're welcome, Mark, but this visit was suggested by my wife, because of Liz initiating all of this, remember? I'm not too good at saying sentimental things, but…" Matt looked down at the rug, then continued, "…well…you're a hellava brother."

Mark laughed and wanted to tease his brother, but understood that would only cause more embarrassment, so he changed the subject.

"Long ago I chose to move to the area where I live because of the aluminum and bauxite located in that area. I've had a dream of finding a vein of gems, and I've found it."

Marian was the first to respond. "What? A vein of gems?"

"I began to dig a little here and there, and just as I suspected, I have been able to find the corundum vein on my property. Raven and I need very little. And the gem mine is producing much more than we expected, so I wanted to tell ..." but before Mark could continue they heard a loud thud from the second floor of the house.

Everyone froze. Marian was the first to react. "Grandma? You all right?" she yelled, as she ran upstairs to investigate if the noise came from the bathroom.

Marian knew, when she saw Grandma's body had fallen halfway out of the shower, her head on the floor, blood underneath. She threw towels over Grandma and yelled to the men, "Call 911!" But she knew.

After the initial whirlwind of hasty decision-making the two brothers sat down to discuss plans. With no known will they felt burial in the family plot with Grandma Nellanore Steele's parents and husband and son Luke was the most appropriate. Date was set in three days, Wednesday.

Matt was able to reach Liz at her job at the Key West newspaper. Liz went into Mr. Bartlett's office. Crying, she told him about her brother's call.

Mr. Bartlett said, "If I had known your grandmother was ill I would have given you time off to be with her."

"She wasn't sick, not that anyone knew of," Liz said, trying to control her sobs.

"Liz, you make your arrangements right now to fly up there. Take as long as you need. Keep in touch and let me know how things are going," assured the editor.

When Liz walked out of the office she saw Bubba Jackson there.

"We just got a call from your brother, Liz," said Bubba.

Liz explained, "He reached me here. I've got to make plane reservations."

Bubba put his arm around her shoulder. "Let's go. We'll do it together." He put her bicycle in his car and they drove to his house.

Trish took over, making arrangements via telephone and told the distraught girl, "You stay here overnight with us. Bubba will take you home to drop off your bicycle and let you pack. We'll drive you to the airport for that first flight out of here tomorrow morning."

Gratefully, Liz did what she was told.

53 AN IRISH WAKE

On the day of the funeral Grandma Steele's next-door neighbor, Shirley's mother, looked across the plot at the two brothers. They had the same eyes and jaw line. At the graveside, Liz stood between Matt and Mark. A tall stranger tapped Matt on the shoulder. Matt turned, Listened to the man and nodded, moving aside.

The man put his arm around Liz' shoulder, saying nothing.

Liz assumed it was Matt, but turned to acknowledge the gesture of sharing grief.

"Lars! How did you know?"

He said nothing but continued to keep his supportive arm around her shoulder.

Prayers were said, the burial completed, and everyone returned to Nellanore Steele's house. Liz introduced Lars Olson.

Mark insisted that Grandma Steele was Irish and would want an Irish wake. "Besides," he suggested. I would rather hear good things about her than to see everyone crying."

Neighbors had brought in platters of food, and it was an Irish wake, indeed, with singing and laughter.

Time heals all wounds. The siblings promised to keep in touch planning possible reunions annually.

54

ON THE GOOD SHIP VIKING

Time does continue on and wounds begin to heal.

In old fairy tales the prince would ride up on a white horse and whisk away the beautiful princess, taking her to his castle where they would live happily ever after. According to the way Elizabeth Steele Olson would tell, her prince did not arrive via horseback, but a yacht owned by Captain Lars Olson.

Next was a whirlwind of romance and love. After a one-year courtship Captain Lars Olson and Elizabeth Steele were married. For their honeymoon trip, Liz Steele Olson's husband took his bride aboard his sailing ship '*Viking*'.

They visited the Nordic countries of Finland, Sweden, Norway and Iceland, which he had chosen, he told her, 'because, during all my travels, these are the happiest countries with the happiest people,' Lars smiled, telling his bride. "Happiness is the symbol of our love and life together."

Liz smiled at her husband, pleased he communicated his feelings of loving care into so romantic a honeymoon voyage. She reached up to her tall husband and gently pulled him closer to her. She kissed Lars and agreed with him.

And like all good fairy tales, they lived happily ever after!

55 EPILOGUE

Many years went by. Elizabeth Steele Olson eventually became a grandmother. It went like this:

Grandma Elizabeth Steele Olson and her husband Lars had two daughters:

Annabell Olson Mac and Bettina Olson Dell

Annabell Mac had a son named Yanik Mac
Bettina Dell had a son named Zaiden Dell

Story-Telling time for this grandmother was not like the long-ago campfire scene in prehistoric caves or Indian teepees. No. She brought her two grandsons Yanik and Zaiden out on the deck of the bow of their grandfather Lars' yacht *Viking.*

It was a special camping-out night. The boys arranged their sleeping bags under the stars. It was there, on the deck, she would tell her grandsons stories about adventures she had long ago, before cell phones and computers, when she had been a gypsy wanderer.

Patricia Chevrin Johnson